Hunting in Bruges

Also by E.J. Stevens

Spirit Guide
Young Adult Series
She Smells the Dead
Spirit Storm
Legend of Witchtrot Road
Brush with Death
The Pirate Curse

Ivy Granger
Urban Fantasy Series
Shadow Sight
Blood and Mistletoe
Ghost Light
Club Nexus
Burning Bright
Birthright
Hound's Bite
Blood Rite (2017)
Tales from Harborsmouth (2017)

Hunters' Guild
Urban Fantasy Series
Hunting in Bruges

Poetry Collections
From the Shadows
Shadows of Myth and Legend

Super Simple How-To Guides
Super Simple Quick Start Guide to Self-Publishing
Super Simple Quick Start Guide to Book Marketing

HUNTERS' GUILD

Hunting in Bruges

E.J. STEVENS

Published by Sacred Oaks Press
Sacred Oaks, 221 Sacred Oaks Lane, Wells, Maine 04090

First Printing (trade paperback edition), November 2014

Stevens, E.J.
Hunting in Bruges / E.J. Stevens

ISBN 978-0- 9894887-0-9 (trade pbk.)

Printed in the United States of America

PUBLISHER'S NOTE
This is a work of fiction. Names, characters, places, and
incidents either are the product of the author's imagination or
are used fictitiously, and any resemblance to actual persons,
living or dead, business establishments, events, or locales is
entirely coincidental.

CHAPTER 1

"This was Bruges-la-Morte, the dead city, entombed in its stone quays, the arteries of its canals chilled to death at the cessation of the great heartbeat of the sea."
-Georges Rodenbach, *Bruges-la-Morte*

I've been seeing ghosts for as long as I can remember. Most ghosts are simply annoying; just clueless dead people who don't realize that they've died. The weakest of these manifest as flimsy apparitions, without the ability for speech or higher thought. They're like a recording of someone's life projected not onto a screen, but onto the place where they died. Most people can walk through one of these ghosts without so much as a goosebump.

Poltergeists are more powerful, but just as single-minded. These pesky spirits are like angry toddlers. They stomp around, shaking their proverbial chains, moaning and wailing about how something (the accident, their murder, or the murder they committed) was someone else's fault, and how everyone must pay for their misfortune. Poltergeists are a nuisance; they're noisy and can throw around objects for short periods of time, but it's only the strong ones that are dangerous.

Thankfully, there aren't many ghosts out there strong enough to do more than knock a pen off your desk or cause a cold spot. From what I've discovered while training with the Hunters' Guild, ghosts get their power from two things—how long they've been haunting and strength of purpose. If someone as obsessed with killing as Jack the Ripper manifests beside you on a London street, I recommend you run. If someone as old and unhinged as Vlad the Impaler appears beside you in Târgoviste Romania, you better hope you have a Hunter at your side, or a guardian angel.

The dead get a bad rap, and for good reason, but some ghosts can be helpful. There was a woman with a kind face who used to appear when I was in foster care. Linda wasn't just a loop of psychic recording stuck on repeat; this ghost had

free will and independent thought—and thankfully, she wasn't
a sociopath consumed with bloodshed. Linda manifested in
faded jeans and dark turtleneck and smelled like home, which
was the other thing that was unusual about her. Most ghosts
are tied to one spot, the place where they lived or died. But
Linda's familiar face followed me from one foster home to
another. And it was a good thing that she did. Linda the ghost
saved my life more than once.

Foster care was an excellent training ground for self
defense, which is probably why the Hunters' Guild uses it as a
place for recruitment. Being cast adrift in the child welfare
system gave me plenty of opportunities to hone my survival
instincts. By the time the Hunters came along, I was a force to
be reckoned with, or so I thought.

The Hunters' Guild provides exceptional training and I
soon learned that my attempts at both offense and defense
were child's play when compared to our senior members. I
didn't berate myself over that fact; I was only thirteen when
the Hunters swooped in and welcomed me into their fold. But
learning my limitations did make me painfully aware of one
thing. If it hadn't been for Linda the ghost, I probably wouldn't
have survived my childhood.

The worst case of *honing my survival skills* had been at
my last foster home, just before the Hunters' Guild intervened.
I don't remember the house mother. She wasn't around much.
She was just a small figure in a cheap, polyester fast food
uniform with a stooped posture and downcast eyes. But I
remember her husband Frank.

Frank was a bully who wore white, ketchup and
mustard stained, wife-beater t-shirts. He had perpetual
French fry breath and a nasty grin. It took me a few weeks to
realize that Frank's grin was more of a leer. I'd caught his
gaze in the bathroom mirror when I was changing and his eyes
said it all; Frank was a perv.

Linda slammed the door in his face, but that didn't stop
Frank. Frank would brush up against me in the kitchen and
Linda would set the faucet spraying across the tiles...and slide
a knife into my hand. My time in that house ended when
Frank ended up in the hospital.

I'd been creeping back to the bedroom I shared with
three other kids, when I saw Frank waiting for me in the
shadows. I pulled the steak knife I kept hidden in the pocket of

my robe, but I never got a chance to use it. Now that I know a thing or two about fighting with a blade, I'm aware that Frank probably would have won that fight.

I tried to run toward the stairs, but Frank met me at the top landing. Frank reached for me while his bulk effectively blocked my escape. That was when Linda the ghost pushed him down the stairs. I remember him tumbling in slow motion, his eyes going wide and the leering grin sliding from his face.

Linda the ghost had once again saved me, but it seemed that this visit was her last. I don't know if she used up her quota of psychic power, or if she just felt like her job here was finally done. It wasn't until years later that I realized she was my mother.

I guess I should have realized sooner that I was related to the ghost who followed me around. We both have hair the same shade of shocking red. But where mine is straight and cropped into a short bob, Linda's was wavy and curled down around her shoulders. We also share a dimple in our left cheek and a propensity for protecting the weak and innocent from evil.

Linda the ghost disappeared, a wailing ambulance drove Frank to the hospital, police arrived at my foster house, and the Hunters swooped in and cleaned up the aftermath. It was from my first Guild master that I learned of my parents' fate and put two and two together about my ghostly protector.

As a kid I often wondered why Linda the ghost always wore a dark turtleneck; now I knew. Young, rogue vamps had torn out her neck and proceeded to rip my father to pieces like meat confetti. My parents were on vacation in Belize, celebrating their wedding anniversary when it happened. I'd been staying with a friend of my mother's, otherwise I'd be dead too.

I don't remember my parents, I'd only been three when I was put into the foster care system, but I do find some peace in knowing that doing my duty as a Hunter gives me the power to police and destroy rogue vamps like the ones who killed my mother and father. When I become exhausted by my work, I think of Linda's sad face and push myself to train harder. And when I find creeps who are abusive to women and children, I think of Frank.

That's how I ended up here, standing in a Brussels airport, trying to decipher the Dutch and French signs with eyes that were gritty from the twelve hour flight. It all started when my friend Ivy called to inform me that a fellow Hunter had hit our mutual friend Jinx. Ivy didn't know how that information would push all my buttons, she didn't know about Frank or my time in the foster system, but we both agreed that striking a girl was unacceptable. She was letting me, and the Hunters' Guild, deal with it, for now.

I went to master Janus, the head of the Harborsmouth Hunters' Guild, and reported Hans' transgressions. It didn't help his case that he had a reputation as a berserker in battle. The fact that he'd hit a human, the very people we were sworn to defend against the monsters, was the nail in the coffin of Hans' career.

I was assured that Hans would be shipped off to the equivalent of a desk job in Siberia. I should have left it at that, and let my superiors take care of the problem. But Jinx was my friend. Ivy's rockabilly business partner may have had bad luck and even worse taste in men, but that didn't mean she deserved to spend her life fending off the attacks of the Franks in the world.

Hans continued his Guild duties while the higher ups shuffled papers and prepared to send him away. Hans should have skipped our training sessions, but then again, he didn't know who had ratted him out—and the guy had a lot of rage to vent. I stormed onto the practice mat and saluted Hans with my sword. It wasn't long before the man started to bleed.

We were supposed to be using practice swords, but I'd *accidentally* grabbed the sharp blade I used on hunting runs. I didn't leave any lasting injuries, but the shallow cuts made a mess of his precious tattoos. I just hoped the scars were a constant reminder of what happens when you attack the innocent.

One week later, I received a plane ticket and orders to meet with one of our contacts in Belgium. I wasn't sure if this assignment was intended as a punishment or a promotion, but I was eager to prove myself to the Guild leadership. Master Janus' parting words whispered in my head, distracting me from the voice on the overhead intercom echoing throughout the cavernous airport.

"Do your duty, Jenna," he said. Master Janus placed a large, sword-calloused hand on my shoulder and looked me in the eye. I swallowed hard, but I managed to keep my hands from shaking. "Make us proud."

"I will, sir," I said.

"Good hunting."

CHAPTER 2

"It never hurts to have an exit strategy."
-Jenna Lehane, Hunter

I turned to follow a blue painted arrow and nearly ran into a scrawny guy with bad hygiene. For a split second, I wondered if this was my Belgian contact, but there was no way a Hunter's body would shake and twitch like a cat toy on a string. This guy was either on something, or jonesing for his next fix.

Definitely not a Hunter.

"You want kiss, yes?" he asked. "You give Euros, we make out, yes?"

I took one look at his jaundiced eyes and acne covered skin and shuddered. Even if the thought of kissing a total stranger wasn't completely repulsive, and potentially against Guild rules since I was technically here on business, there was no way I'd touch this guy. He had disease vector stamped all over his twitchy face.

Not that I even had any Euros. I hadn't located the currency exchange office yet. I'd only just exited baggage claim and I was still trying to decipher the signs to the train station.

My orders to leave Harborsmouth for a mission in Belgium had been unexpected. I hadn't had time to learn a new language before being assigned to this post. I'd spent the long, trans-Atlantic flight cramming French and Dutch words from a Lonely Planet phrasebook into my head, but I was pretty sure the words hadn't stuck. Thankfully, this guy seemed to know a bit of English.

"No kissing," I said, shifting the long, hard shell ski bag strapped to my back and folding my arms across my chest. I tried to look down my nose at the guy, but that wasn't easy with my five foot two frame. Even hunched in on himself, the kid had a good six inches on me. My fingers itched for the sword sheathed in bubblewrap inside the high density polyethylene plastic ski bag. "But if you show me where the

money exchange and railway ticket offices are, I'll buy you
something to eat."

"Euros? Cigarettes?" he asked.

I sighed. "If you're fast, I'll throw in some Euros," I
said. "But I'm not tipping for standing around here all day."

The guy's head twitched up and down in what I
assumed was a nod and took off. I followed my sketchy tour
guide, keeping a wary eye on his hands as he went. It wouldn't
do to be seen as a pickpocket's accomplice, especially in a
foreign country, but he kept his hands stuffed inside his hoodie.

I'd probably regret encouraging the kid, but I knew
what it was like to go hungry. Most of the foster families I
stayed with pocketed the state checks intended for groceries
and served substandard food, when they bothered to feed us at
all. I recognized the pinched skin and look of desperation in his
eyes.

If it hadn't been for the Guild, this kid could have been
me. My cheeks burned and a familiar thickness filled my
throat. I remembered the agonizing taunts from other school
kids as I walked the halls in hand-me-down clothes that didn't
fit, the pitying glances from teachers, and the apathetic routine
checks by tired social workers. Had this guy grown up in the
system? Did he have to face someone like Frank each time he
crept to the bathroom?

"So, is the train station far from here?" I asked.

My orders were to go to the train station where my
contact would give me my assignment and travel documents. I
assumed that the operative would instruct me to head into the
city, and since Brussels Airport was located on the outskirts,
the train made sense. Knowing the rendezvous location, and
not much more, I'd searched the airport website for directions
to the train station, but after two hours of shuffling through
the lines for customs and border patrol, I didn't have any
patience left for the labyrinthine building. All I knew was the
train station was somewhere in the bowels of the airport, and
the sooner I got there, the sooner I could get my assignment
and find a place to crash for a few hours.

The kid nodded.

"Food first?" he asked. "ATM?"

"Okay, fine," I said with a sigh. "Lead the way."

I used my credit card, courtesy of the Guild, to withdraw five hundred Euros. It was a lot of money, but it never hurt to have an exit strategy. Cash would help, should it come to that.

I was, of course, careful to shield the ATM's touchscreen from view, though I needn't have worried. My guide seemed engrossed in his cannibalistic efforts to remove a hangnail.

I secreted away most of the cash into two inner zip pockets inside my leather jacket and shoved some smaller bills into the back pocket of my skinny jeans. Turning from the ATM, I flashed the kid a smile and nodded toward the food court.

"Hungry?" I asked.

He wiped blood from his mangled cuticle onto filthy jeans and nodded eagerly. The realization that some of that filth was old blood smears made my stomach churn unpleasantly, but I tried to look pleased as I followed the kid as he made his way to a familiar fast food chain.

I grit my teeth, the smell of grease making my gorge rise, but I bought us two combo meals—coffee and grilled chicken salad for me and a soda, burger, fries, and an apple pie for the kid. I mechanically ate my salad, trying to ignore the kid and his trans fats. Though maintaining optimal health wasn't the only reason I avoided greasy fast food.

I shook my head. Five years, and burgers and fries still made me think of Frank. I loaded up on napkins, but I was aware of the hard, painful truth. Some things can't be fully washed away, no matter how hard we try.

I may be plagued by ghosts, but the dead aren't the only ones who haunt my waking hours, or my dreams.

CHAPTER 3

"Immortals are nothing if not patient."
-Jenna Lehane, Hunter

I stifled a yawn and handed the kid a handful of Euros. It was time to get on with my mission. I shoved a napkin with a sketch of the train station into my pocket and headed for the nearest elevator.

I followed the signs, struggling with the Dutch words, and for the hundredth time wondered why I'd been picked for this assignment. There were plenty of Dutch speakers in our organization. The Hunters' Guild had its roots in Europe and our most notorious member, Van Helsing, had been Dutch after all. So why was the girl who preferred weapons to words sent here? Was this a punishment for what I'd done to Hans, or part of my training?

The Guild was secretive, but I'd heard rumors that special assignments were used as ways to weed out the weak and advance those with the most potential. Old fears crept to the surface. *Failure. Burden. Waste of space.* During my years bouncing from one foster home to the next, I'd been greeted by those words more times than I can count. Since joining the Hunters' Guild, I worked hard and trained hard, but a shaky, childlike voice huddled in a corner of my brain and whispered that it would never be enough.

I grit my teeth and pasted on my best smile. I needed to work on my diplomacy skills; might as well start now. I was determined to succeed in this assignment, whatever it was.

I would not fail.

The area around the bank of elevators was thick with harried travelers. Ignoring the ache in my back, I leaned forward and punched the down button for good measure. The sooner I completed my mission and proved myself to the Guild's hierarchy, the sooner my return to Harborsmouth.

I may not have roots, the Guild itself was my home, but I had friends in Harborsmouth who would need me soon enough. For months now tensions had been rising between humans and the paranormal community, but it wasn't until the night before my transfer that I learned the truth.

War was coming.

Lost in thought, I'd approached Master Janus' office to receive my punishment for Hans' injuries. But even distracted, I'd hesitated before knocking on his door. Hushed voices, tight with restrained anger, argued and so I'd done what any good Hunter would—I pressed my ear to the door and listened.

Master Janus and an unknown man were already in a heated discussion over what course of action to take based on new intel. I'd missed the beginning of the conversation, but one thing was clear. The Hunters' Guild suspected that both vampire and fae leaders were amassing strength and mobilizing their supernatural armies in a deadly game of chess. Hunters were the knights and humans the pawns—and Harborsmouth was suspected to be the center of the game board.

When the voices ceased talking, I'd silently retraced my steps and reentered the corridor that lead to Janus' office with heavy footsteps, and a heavy heart. I didn't know when the game would commence. Immortals are nothing if not patient. But accepting my orders to leave Harborsmouth had been the hardest thing I've done as a Hunter.

War was brewing and, though the battle may not begin for months, years, or even decades, I swore that I would find a way to return to Harborsmouth so that I could use my sword to defend my allies, my Guild, and the innocent citizens of the city. Years ago, I promised myself that I would never let the Franks of the world win. Soon after that promise, I took an oath to become a Hunter and defend humans from rogue paranormals.

I vowed to protect the innocent from the monsters, be they human, fae, or undead, and I took my promises seriously. Sometimes that goal was all that kept me going. Life as a Hunter wasn't easy. I'd taken Guild masters for parents, my fellow Hunters for brothers and sisters, and I'd married the mission—body and soul. There was no room in my life for deep friendships or romance, which is why my actions after learning of the coming battle still managed to surprise me.

I was loyal to the Guild. They rescued me, gave me a life with purpose, and the opportunity to avenge my parents' brutal deaths at the hands of rogue vampires. But when I'd heard of the coming battle, there was someone I had to warn. Ivy Granger had proven herself to be a natural defender of the city of Harborsmouth.

Too bad she wasn't human.

Although the Guild sometimes bent the rules for exceptional paranormals, like in Jonathan's case allowing a shifter to enter our ranks, most Hunters were prejudiced against the paranormals we fought. It was easier to kill if you saw the world in black and white. But Ivy was one of those gray areas. She was half human and half fae, and she didn't follow anyone's rules.

I knew that the Guild wouldn't sanction officially bringing Ivy onboard, but someone had to warn her of the coming battle. My phone had been confiscated and it was too risky to use Jonathan's—I couldn't risk the Guild tracing the call. Good thing I had a trick or two up my sleeve.

Counting on Ivy's psychometry, the ability to read the psychic imprint left on objects, I'd stabbed my left hand and created enough pain for a strong impression and left Ivy a message. Leaving that message went against protocol, but that was only the first reckless thing I'd done. I was still kicking myself for the second.

I'd gone to Jonathan Baldwin, a friend regardless of how many times I'd turned him down or how much we got on each other's nerves, knowing that he was the one person I could trust to deliver my message to Ivy. But when he'd seen the gash on my hand, the one I'd used to invoke enough pain to create my message, something bewildering happened. Jonathan had stroked my palm, asking if I'd received the injury while training, and with his other hand he'd pulled me close and kissed me.

I don't think he had been thinking straight so close to the full moon. Perhaps, he just meant it as a simple goodbye kiss. But I'd pressed him against the wall of our tiny dorm room and kissed him with the passion of all the pain, excitement, and worry that raged inside of me.

It had been a mistake, something I'd repeated over and over until I'd stepped on that plane to Belgium. I never should have kissed Jonathan. Not because he was a werewolf, but because I didn't care for him in that way. It hadn't been right or fair of me—I'd crossed a line that never should have been crossed, and fled the country like a coward. It didn't matter that I was leaving because of my orders. It still seemed like a betrayal.

The time apart would probably be good for us both, but I would return to Harborsmouth for the coming battle. I needed to complete my mission here in Belgium and get back to the States, before it was too late.

My stomach twisted, making me regret eating that salad. The red, downward pointing triangle above the steel doors couldn't light up fast enough.

The metal doors to my right rattled open, revealing a large glass box. I melted into the crowd and slipped inside, surveying my fellow riders and the passing floors beyond the glass. At the basement level, I exited with a group of students my age. With my backpack, skinny jeans, and biker jacket I fit right in.

I quickly noted the location of potential exits as we made our way to the ticket offices. There were stairs and escalators leading down to the basement sublevel from each of the four corners of the cavernous train station. Each set of stairs was marked with a platform number and voices and the rumble of trains echoed up the stairs from the platforms below, but the station was currently empty of people except those of us disembarking the elevators.

As we approached a glass wall, a glass panel slid open with a swoosh of air and we joined the lines of people at the ticket counter. I stepped to the side, giving myself a moment to scan the crowd. Pretending to tie my boot laces, I let my gaze flit through the room and to the corridor beyond the glass walls.

Except for a man in a business suit waiting for the elevator, everyone was in line to buy their tickets. So where was my Guild contact?

I stood and stretched, shifting the backpack and ski bag strapped to my back. I turned to leave—maybe they were waiting on one of the train platforms?—when a young couple brushed past me in a hurry to catch their train.

"Pardon," the man said, jostling my shoulder.

He kept walking, but his girlfriend offered an apologetic smile.

"Sorry," she said, bending down to grab a magazine that hadn't been there a moment before. "You dropped this."

"Thanks," I said, turning the magazine over in my hands. The magazine was Hunting and Fishing, of course. These had to be my Guild contacts.

"Good hunting," she said.

I nodded and turned my attention to the train schedules on the board above the ticket counter. I waited three minutes, giving the Hunters plenty of time to leave, and then I exited the ticket office. I found the nearest bench and opened the magazine, as if I had time to kill before my train. Inside I found an envelope containing a train ticket, a Bruges city map, two knives, a length of wire with both ends wrapped in leather, a cell phone, and a dossier on the most notorious paranormals in West Flanders.

It looked like I wasn't being assigned to Brussels after all. I was heading to Bruges—and my train was leaving in twenty minutes.

I wound the wire around my wrist, careful to keep the leather against my skin as I made a bracelet out of the garrote. One knife went inside my boot and the other into a jacket pocket, along with the dossier. Pulling my backpack onto my shoulder, I grabbed my ticket and headed for the stairs to my platform.

The lights flickered as I descended and I kept my arms loose at my sides, glad that I'd taken the stairs instead of the stuttering escalator. A cool breeze chilled the air and I frowned. Waiting passengers pulled their jackets close and huddled on the platform below, probably thinking the cold air was the result of the fast moving trains.

But I knew better.

A pale woman approached the edge of the concrete platform. She paused to wipe her face with the sleeve of her jacket, then crouched down, grabbed the platform with both hands and climbed down to the tracks below.

No one tried to stop the woman. No one gasped or called out for help. They couldn't see the woman stumbling along the tracks, because she was a ghost. The other passengers' lack of reaction was one hint that the woman was already dead. The other clue was the fact that I could see the graffiti on the opposite wall of concrete through her body. The spirit had enough energy to manifest the illusion of a body, but ghosts aren't perfect.

Her body was transparent, even to my eyes, and when a phantom train came a moment later and cut her in two, she disappeared. Her mangled body was laying on the tracks, and then it was gone. At the moment of her "death" the lights flickered. I looked back at the bench where I'd first seen the woman and sure enough, there she was, already steeling herself to approach the tracks.

I sighed and looked away. Suicides are the worst. They're almost always caught in a loop, cursed to relive the moment of their death, over and over again.

Thankfully, I didn't have to wait long for my train. With a swirl of grit and hot diesel fumes, my train arrived. I quickly climbed the ladder-like steps and took a seat away from the few other passengers. I tossed my backpack onto the seat facing me, to deter anyone else from sitting with me, settled the ski bag holding my sword across my lap, and pulled the dossier from my jacket. I smoothed the pages on the small table and frowned.

My train would be arriving in Bruges before noon, but my orders were to arrive at the local Guild hall at six thirty. That gave me over seven hours to kill. Rather than cooling my heels waiting for the meeting with my liaison with the local Guild, I turned the page for details on my assignment.

It wasn't pretty.

Over twenty human bodies had been found floating in the canals of Bruges over the past two weeks. According to these documents, a culling of the large tourist population was not unheard of, but not on this scale. The average missing person rate was one or two per month, but things had escalated to nearly a dozen per week—and then there were the bodies.

If you're a paranormal who's smart enough to prey on tourists for years, maybe centuries, without getting caught, why suddenly start leaving evidence? The bodies didn't make any sense unless, perhaps, there was a new monster in town. Not that Bruges needed any more violent paranormals taking up residence.

I rubbed a hand over my face and scowled at the list of known enemies in the vicinity. There was no shortage of suspects—just my luck.

Chapter 4

"Startling a sleeping Hunter was a good way to get dead."

-Jenna Lehane, Hunter

"Wake up beautiful," an accented male voice whispered in my ear. "This is your stop, is it not?"

My body reacted before the words had a chance to sink in. Having a stranger in such close proximity while dreaming about vampires, ghouls, water hags, grindylow, and rusalki was a recipe for a broken nose, or manslaughter. Luckily for the good Samaritan, he was already stepping away or he would have received a knuckle sandwich for his troubles—and a knife in the spleen.

Startling a sleeping Hunter was a good way to get dead.

I narrowed my eyes, assessing whether the man was an enemy. I let out a breath as I realized the fact that he was here during broad daylight, which ruled out the undead. He also didn't have the storm-on-the-horizon feel of the fae. The guy appeared to be human, though a bit eccentric. His garish, puke green scarf and ridiculous feathered hat made him look the fool, but he had broad shoulders, a slender waist, and strong, capable looking hands.

He was also gaping at me like a merman out of water.

I blinked at his startled expression, adrenaline rapidly washing away the last vestiges of sleep. *Oh, right, I still had my fist in his face.* I just hoped he was too distracted by my fist to notice the knife in my other hand. I relaxed my fist and ran a hand through my hair as I hastily slid the knife into my jacket.

I looked around methodically, taking in details as cold sweat trickled down my back. The train wasn't moving, the digital time display at the front of the carriage claimed it was nearing eleven o'clock, and there was a wooden BRUGGE sign outside the window. I was in Bruges, but not for long.

I was about to miss my stop.

The guy who I'd just tried to stab was now in the aisle waving me toward the exit. I grabbed my bag from the seat, fingers fumbling with the straps as I slung it over my shoulder. The adrenaline was already wearing off, leaving my movements slow and stiff. He punched a button beside the door to the next compartment and disappeared.

I hurried down the aisle, struggling with the long ski bag that held my sword. An announcement in Dutch continued to loop as a chime sounded a warning. I lunged for the door as the train began to move forward, but my muscles were tight and my body was heavy with fatigue. I wasn't used to sitting for hours on end and the long plane ride and cat nap on the train were catching up with me.

In the adjoining carriage, holding the door open and begging me to hurry, was the guy with the hideous scarf. He looked like he wanted to help, trying to encourage me forward with an earnest look on his face. I made a decision and reached for his hand.

"Get me out of here," I said.

He froze for a moment, brown eyes going wide, then squeezed my hand and pulled me forward. We raced down the aisle, ducked into one of those dark, connecting sections of train that seemed to sway with each pounding step and then we were bursting out onto the concrete platform.

I dropped my backpack to the ground and sighed. I wasn't winded—I was used to a regiment of daily endurance training—but I felt my cheeks warm as if I'd been running all day. I cleared my throat and rubbed the back of my neck.

"Well, that sucked," I said. "But thanks, um…sorry. I didn't catch your name."

"Alistair Ashborn," he said, winking and flashing me a conspiratorial smile. "But since you've given me the most exciting morning I've had in years, you can call me Ash."

"Jenna," I said, a grin tugging at my lips.

Damn, Ash's smile was contagious.

"Welcome to Bruges, Jenna," he said, waving his hat in a flourish. "I do hope you stay awhile. I have a feeling there's never a dull moment with you around."

He could say that again.

CHAPTER 5

"In my experience, evasion was second only to lies as an admission of guilt."
-Jenna Lehane, Hunter

The moment I crossed the busy road outside the train station, entering the tranquility of Minnewater Park and passing the threshold into the old city center, bells began to ring.

"The city is rejoicing at your arrival," Ash said with a wink. "Looks like I'm not the only bloke happy that you're here."

I rolled my eyes, ignoring the way his words made my skin flush. It was a warm day. That was all.

"I'm sure you say that to all the girls who try to punch you in the face," I said.

"You'd be surprised, love," he said.

I licked my lips and looked away.

"So," I said, waving a hand at the approaching body of water. "Is that Minnewater Lake?"

Ash was playful and foolish and frivolous, but he did seem to know his way around so far, and I could use a guide. I had hours to spare before my appointment with the local Guild liaison. Maybe Ash could help provide the necessary on-the-ground intel that I needed. I could successfully complete my mission faster and more efficiently if I learned the lay of the land.

"Ah, yes, Minnewater Lake," he said. "It translates roughly to, the Lake of Love."

Okay, maybe that wasn't so helpful, though the name might explain the large number of ghosts in the vicinity. The tree lined banks of the lake shimmered with spectral activity. I shivered and focused on the footpath, ignoring the flickering image of a man jumping off a nearby bridge.

The gravel path was split into two sections, marked clearly for bicycle and foot traffic. As we walked, a group of men and women rode toward us, filling the bike path to our

left. The person in front of the tour group was talking so loudly
that I nearly missed the sound of a bike approaching us from
behind.

I spun as the bike clipped Ash, not even slowing down
as it did so.

"Watch it!" I yelled, shaking my fist at the cyclist. I
turned to Ash, who was bent over, a scowl on his face. "Are you
alright? God, that asshole practically drove straight through
you. How could he not see us?"

"Bad luck is all, love," he said.

Yes, if it hadn't been for the tour group taking up the
bike path, the cyclist may never have veered onto the footpath.
Speaking of which, every damn tourist was now ogling us like
we were some kind of sideshow attraction.

"What are you all looking at?" I asked, hands on my
hips.

"Are...are you alright, lady?" an overweight man asked.

"Me?" I snorted. "I'm fine, but my friend is pretty
banged up no thanks to you."

The man's chubby face paled. He stammered something
under his breath, shook his head, and the wide-eyed tour group
pedaled away like I was a crazy bitch. Whatever, maybe they'd
think twice before hogging the bike trail again.

"Bloody tour groups," Ash muttered.

He retrieved his hat, brushing off dirt and pine spills.
The fabric held the distinctive imprint of a bike tread. Maybe
now he'd lose the fedora. That ridiculous hat had seen better
days.

"Looks like it's time for a new hat," I said.

"A new hat?" he asked. With a flick of his wrist, he
knocked out the worst of the dents, fluffed the purple and lime
green feathers, and set the dusty hat on his head at a jaunty
angle. "What's wrong with this one?"

"The feathers for starters," I said. "Are there even birds
with feathers that color?"

"A bird, no," he said cryptically.

I grit my teeth. In my experience, evasion was second
only to lies as an admission of guilt. Some girls might find
mystery seductive, but I just saw it as a puzzle to crack,
possibly with my fists.

Of course, even if it turned out he was wearing an
endangered species on his head, I'd get in trouble if I killed the

guy over what kind of feathers he had stuffed in his hat. And there'd be paperwork. I hated paperwork.

"So what's the story behind that hat anyway?" I asked.

"I'm making a fashion statement," he said with a shrug and a cocky smile.

If that statement was, 'I'm colorblind' he was doing a bang up job. Not only did the lime green and bright purple of the feathers clash, but it actually hurt my eyes when combined with the puke green scarf he wore around his neck.

"And why does it look like someone went after it with scissors?" I asked, gesturing at a series of jagged cuts along the brim and a hole big enough to put my thumb through.

When it was clear he wasn't going to elaborate, or get rid of that hat, I sighed and started walking again. I was beginning to regret my decision to let Ash tag along, but I had to consider my mission. There was a monster taking the lives of innocent men and women in this city. If Ash could help me get my bearings, and fill in some of the local history, putting up with his annoying personality was a sacrifice I was willing to make.

"Come on," I said. "I have to be at the Schuttersgilde Sint-Sebastiaan by seven. If we hurry, you can show me around the city."

Ash tilted his head and paused, leaning forward. He eyed me from head to toe, lingering on the ski bag strapped to my back.

"You're an archer then?" he asked.

"Why do you ask that?" I asked, narrowing my eyes at him. He dressed like a fool, but looks can be deceiving.

"Because the Schuttersgilde Sint-Sebastiaan is Dutch for the Archers' Guild of Saint Sebastian," he said. "People either go there for archery or for tours of the building. I assumed since you're carrying something the length of a bow, and you're going there so late in the evening, that you must be the former. Unless they're throwing some kind of party. If that's the case, I want an invite."

Leave it to the Guild not to translate that important tidbit, but once I mulled it over, it made sense. I could see the benefits of using an archers' guild for our local headquarters. Hunters could walk around the property in plain sight, armed with bows, and no one would suspect a thing.

It also gave me a great cover story.

"There's no party," I said. "I'm there for a tournament."

"So you are an archer then," he said, a smile twitching his lips.

"I'm not bad with a bow," I said.

"I thought so," he said with a nod. "You look like the competitive type. I bet you win every tournament."

"Something like that," I said, noncommittally.

Ash wasn't the only one with secrets. He had the origins of his mysterious hat, and I belonged to a secret society that hunted and terminated rogue paranormals. Okay, my secret was much bigger, but I was telling the truth about being good with a bow. There were plenty of monsters back home who could have vouched for that fact, if they'd lived to tell about it.

"Come on then, love," he said. "We better hurry if I'm to show you Bruges in one day, though I wager this won't be our only time together while you're here."

"I doubt that, Ash," I said, shaking my head. "This isn't a pleasure trip. I'm here on business. I don't have time for hanging out."

I was a Hunter. I didn't have time for a social life, and this sure as hell wasn't a vacation, but I had a nagging suspicion that Ash was right. I wasn't getting rid of him that easy.

CHAPTER 6

"Vampires may turn to dust when killed, but one thing remains behind—their fangs."
-Jenna Lehane, Hunter

I ignored the *clop, clop* of horse hooves on cobblestones and the rattle of carriages. It wasn't the first time I'd heard or seen things from another era, but I had to admit that the ghostly sounds fit this medieval city.

Bruges was a city frozen in time. From the cobblestone streets to the building façades and stone bridges that arched across a network of canals, walking in Bruges was like stepping into the past. No wonder the monsters liked it here.

Immortals dislike change. Human tourists may come here for the novelty, but I wouldn't be surprised if this place was a hot spot for ancient fae and centuries old vampires. For the long-lived, Bruges would feel like home—if home included some very large waterfowl.

"What's with all the swans?" I asked.

There were dozens of swans swimming in the canal and lounging on the grass verge to our left. I imagine the scene probably seemed idyllic to most of the city's visitors, but I let out a heavy sigh. The feathers of at least half of the swans shimmered.

Bruges was home to a flock of swan maidens.

Swan maidens, both male and female, were shapeshifting fae. Like the selkie, their saltwater cousins, the swan maidens' ability to change shape is tied to their skins. I scanned the banks of the canal, spying a cluster of feathers at the base of a tree.

At least one swan maiden walked amongst us.

I chided myself for not reapplying faerie ointment once I'd landed in Belgium. The ointment I'd put on in Harborsmouth had worn off, leaving me blind to faerie glamour, but TSA rules restricted liquids on board the plane. I'd packed my ointment with my sword, not thinking I'd need it so soon.

I was wrong.

My fingers itched to tear into the ski bag strapped across my back, but I left it for now. There was no easy way to get into the container without risking someone seeing my sword. I'd gather what information I could from Ash until I could find a private place to retrieve the faerie ointment.

At least swan maidens are relatively harmless. They give off pheromones that fill humans with feelings of love and contentment, but as far as mind control goes, that's nothing. Some Hunters speculate that it's a defensive mechanism and I'd have to agree. The love not war vibe they were pumping out was pretty damn strong.

I blinked and focused on Ash's words.

"In a revolt against Maximilian of Austria, the people of Bruges captured Maximilian and his advisor, Pieter Lanchals," he said. The feathers in Ash's hat fluttered with his broad hand gestures. "The townspeople made Maximilian watch as they tortured Lanchals for two days."

Ash was animated, but he didn't seem affected by the swan maidens' pheromones. At least he wasn't staring at me with goo goo eyes. Probably because the pheromones just amplified the fact that he was in love with himself. He certainly liked the sound of his own voice.

"Does this really have anything to do with swans?" I asked.

"I'm getting to that," he said. "Right, so Lanchals was tortured for days until finally, he was beheaded."

He pulled a finger across his throat, eyes rolling back as he flopped his head to the side, but sadly his hat defied gravity, staying on his head.

I frowned, wishing the man could just convey the facts without flamboyant theatrics. I rolled my hand for him to get on with it.

"Lanchals' head was put on a pike out on the Gentpoort, one of the city gates, for all to see," he said. "It would have been a bloody mess and when Maximilian got free and regained power, he didn't arse about. He threatened the entire city with a curse."

I leaned forward. Now that sounded interesting, even if Ash had seemed to forget we were supposed to be discussing waterfowl.

"A curse?" I asked.

Ash nodded excitedly.

"The name Lanchals means long neck and the man's family crest was a swan," he said. "So Maximilian threatened that the city must keep swans in the canals of Bruges for all eternity, or face the consequences of the curse."

"What consequences?" I asked.

Ash shrugged.

"Don't think anyone ever wanted to find out," he said, gesturing to the gaggle of swans.

Sounded like Pieter Lanchals was a swan maiden, and Maximilian had found a way to protect Lanchals' flock from the superstitious townsfolk. I cast the birds a wary eye, not liking the numbers, but at least the swans weren't all fae.

Not all of the birds shimmered or moved with unearthly grace. A swan with plain, white feathers waddled across the grass and hopped inelegantly into the canal. Ripples spread out from the swan, bringing my attention to the dark waters.

The canal was wide here where it connected to Minnewater Lake, separated only by the lock gate. I stared at the murky water, imagining bloated human bodies choking the surface. How many more innocents would have to die before the killer was caught?

I grimaced, turning away from the canal, and starting to walk down the cobblestone street. If the killer was undead, we might see more bodies tonight. Now that was a cheery thought.

My hand went to the necklace I wore beneath my dress. *Chicago, Milwaukee, Harborsmouth, Harborsmouth…* I mentally listed off the locations of sanctioned vamp kills, each one corresponding to a pair of fangs on my necklace.

Vampires may turn to dust when killed, but one thing remains behind—their fangs. *Ashes to ashes, dust to dust, all except for the fangs.* Not only do vamps leave their fangs behind, but as their bodies deteriorate to dust the fangs retract and shrink.

No one knows why, but I had to thank Fate. The necklace I'd strung gave me something to hold onto, a constant reminder of what I'd lost and what I was willing to do in return. I had no patience for rogue vampires. If I discovered that they were behind the recent killings, I'd show them no mercy.

I could always use a new addition to my necklace.

I rubbed each fang, like a macabre parody of a rosary. *Click, click, click.* A grim smile tugged at my lips. The vampires of Bruges better say their prayers.

"Jenna, look out!" Ash yelled.

I jerked my head up, mouth falling open even as my body responded to the threat. I spun and somersaulted onto the grass verge to my left, narrowly missing being run down by a horse drawn carriage.

"You have got to be kidding me," I muttered, spitting out a piece of grass.

I'd been so mired in my thoughts of revenge that I'd mistaken the horses and their carriages for ghosts. But there was nothing spectral about the two thousand pounds of muscle, bone, wood, and metal that had come barreling down the narrow street.

"Sodding hell, you alright?" Ash asked. "You look a right mess."

I clenched my fists, knowing one "long neck" I'd like to strangle. Of course I was a mess. I'd nearly been run over.

"I'm fine," I said, trying not to bare my teeth at the man. "Guess it's just not our lucky day."

"Think I'd rather take my chances with the bloke on the bicycle," he said, shaking his head.

He had a point.

"For once, I agree with you," I said.

"Well, while you're in an agreeable mood, let's grab you a pint," he said. "There's a pub there on the corner."

"I don't drink," I said.

Alcohol was a quick way to lose your edge in battle. Plus, I didn't need another impairment. Seeing ghosts was proving to be plenty dangerous.

"Not worried about your age are you?" he asked. "You're not in the States anymore, love. Legal drinking age is sixteen in Belgium. You look young, but I daresay you're older than that."

"I'm twenty," I said, meeting his eyes and daring him to argue. "I just don't like to drink."

I did look younger, which was something I often used to my advantage while hunting. It was often beneficial to be underestimated by your opponent. Plus, there were plenty of monsters that preferred their prey young. That came in handy when I needed to play the role of bait.

But with Ash's eyes on me now, I suddenly wished for the curves that no amount of training would add to my body. I shook my head and frowned. Why did I care what Ash thought?

Damn swan maidens.

"Lunch then," he said.

My traitorous stomach growled, but that didn't mean I'd go wherever Ash wanted. I wasn't being led to some den of iniquity that happened to serve up food.

"Fine, but not a pub," I said, crossing my arms over my chest.

"I know just the place," he said.

CHAPTER 7

"Fighting and killing weren't the only skills the Hunters' Guild taught its initiates."
-Jenna Lehane, Hunter

"You can't visit Belgium without trying the frites," Ash said with a wink. "There's a law."

We were standing in the market square, aptly named Markt on my map, which was located in the very center of the city. Ash had led me to one of two food trucks parked in the shadow of a stone behemoth, but I didn't have a chance to ponder the beauty of the bell tower. I was too busy wishing I'd settled for eating at a pub.

"Frites are fries?" I asked, nose wrinkling at the smell of hot oil.

"Not going to start in on how your body is a temple, are you?" he asked.

"I'm in training," I said, narrowing my eyes at him.

It wasn't a lie. If he thought I meant training for an archery tournament, rather than keeping fit to chase down monsters, that was his mistake.

"No reason not to indulge now and again," he said with a wink.

"Let me guess, you're one of those people who can eat anything you want and never gain weight," I said.

"Naturally," he said.

"Well, I'm not," I said through clenched teeth.

"You could stand to gain a stone, love," he said. "There isn't a gram of fat on you."

"That's the idea," I said, shooting him a nasty glare. The bastard thought I was too skinny? He was lucky I hadn't gone for my sword.

"Come on, live a little," he said.

I never wanted to stake a human so badly in my life, but Ash had a point. I couldn't let my past rule my life, and being more casual with my eating habits would help me blend in while working undercover.

I swallowed hard, stomach twisting, but I refused to let the memory of Frank make we weak. I lifted my chin, meeting the man behind the counter's smile.

"Okay, I'll have an order of frites," I said.

"With mayonnaise," Ash said. "Trust me, it's good."

"And there's that law," I said, rolling my eyes.

"Exactly," he said.

The guy behind the counter raised an eyebrow, but I just shook my head.

"Fine, frites with mayo," I said, giving my order.

At least Frank never ate his fries with mayonnaise. An image of his ketchup stained t-shirt filled my head and I shivered.

"You cold?" Ash asked. "Come on. The Burg will be less windy."

I handed over a few Euros, grabbed my frites, and followed Ash across the street. This time I looked both ways, careful not to get run down by one of the many horse drawn carriages. I rubbed my neck as I waited for my turn to cross. I still couldn't believe how stupid I'd been.

Wind howling at our backs, we left the market square. Ash turned up a narrow side street, filled with pedestrians and lined with chocolate shops. I might have caved in and visited one of the heavenly shops, adopting Ash's live a little outlook, if I wasn't immediately hit by a wall of stench.

"Oh, god, what is that?" I asked with a groan.

"What?" Ash asked, slowing his steps. "Are you alright?"

He moved closer, eyes darting to shadowed doorways.

"Are you kidding?" I asked. "You can't smell that?"

"Oh, you mean the sewers," he said, visibly relaxing.

"How can you stand it?" I asked.

The street smelled worse than rotting ghoul guts.

"Sorry," he said with a shrug. He waved a hand at his face and grinned. "No sense of smell."

I grimaced. Some guys have all the luck.

"Well, I guess that comes in handy in a canal city," I said, realizing the high water table must be contributing to the sewage overflow.

"I guess," he said, a wistful smile flitting across his face. "But I do miss the smell of chocolate."

We passed the chocolate shops and found a bench facing into another cobbled square. The Burg was smaller than Markt and ringed on three sides by tall buildings that blocked the wind. The buildings had elaborately carved façades, but I was too intrigued by Ash's comment to pay them much attention.

"So, you weren't born without a sense of smell?" I asked.

He fidgeted with his scarf and I dipped a fry in mayonnaise, wondering if I shouldn't have pressed him for answers. This wasn't an interrogation.

"No, I lost it...in an accident," he said, looking away.

I wanted to press further, but he shoved his hands in his pockets, focusing on a small dog that was barking across the square. There were three carriages lined up, waiting for tourists, and the dog was jumping back and forth, teasing one of the horses. We watched the dog in silence while I ate my frites.

"So, why are you in Bruges?" I asked, finally breaking the silence. "I take it you're not a local."

"Why do you say that?" he asked.

"Because," I said, pointing a fry at him. "You sound more like Sherlock Holmes than Van Damme."

Ash laughed. That typical carefree, devil-may-care look was back on his face.

"Yes, but I'm not as stuffy," he said.

I raised an eyebrow. No, he wasn't stuffy at all, but he was just as eccentric as the fictional detective.

He may sound like Sherlock Holmes, but I had to wonder if Ash had Romani blood. Dark, shoulder length hair and thick brows framed even darker eyes and full lips. Compared to the close-cropped, utilitarian, military style haircuts of most of my guild brothers, Ash's hair was practically sinful.

Sitting askew atop those glossy locks was his tattered hat. His neck was wrapped in that garish scarf, and he wore a short, tailored, pinstripe vest over a charcoal gray dress shirt. The shirt was tucked into a pair of black pants that were in turn tucked into a pair of supple leather boots. Sprouting from his vest pocket was a hairy thing that may have been a fur hanky, or a dead rat, and a chain that was quite possibly attached to an honest to god monocle.

"Stuffy is one adjective I wouldn't use to describe you, though I can think of a few," I said.

"Dashing, handsome, adventurous….," he said.

I shook my head. *Not even close, buddy.*

"So if you're not a local, why are you here?" I asked.

"I was going to University here," he said.

"Was?" I asked.

I wasn't all that surprised that Ash was a drop out. He didn't really seem like the kind of guy who sat through long, boring lectures. Plus, they probably wouldn't allow him to wear his hat.

"Yes, things…didn't work out," he said, a frown flittering across his face so fast, I could have imagined it.

I understood all about life throwing curveballs, but most people had a home to go back to, a family to fall back on when things didn't work out. The fact that Ash was here in Belgium made me curious.

"Are your parents mad about it?" I asked.

He looked so sad, I was sorry that I'd asked.

"I don't know," he said. He swallowed hard, eyes downcast. "I haven't had a chance to see them. I was trying to go home—that's why I was on the train—but I found that I couldn't leave the city. I had to return to Bruges. It was as if there was something I still needed to do here before moving on."

"Well," I said. "I'm glad for my sake you were on that return train. I would have missed my stop, for sure."

"I'm glad too," he said, lifting his head. His eyes traced my lips, and I cursed inwardly. Did I have mayonnaise on my face? I blushed, feeling the fool, but he smiled. "If I hadn't been on that train, I never would have met you."

I fidgeted with my napkin, finally crumpling it into a ball and tossing it into the empty frite bag. I wasn't good with compliments, and I was even worse when it came to relationships with guys my age. My friend Jonathan was the exception, and we'd gone through hell before finally settling into a comfortable pattern that didn't trigger his werewolf hormones or send me flying at him with fists and blades.

Flirting put me on the defensive. I'd grown up believing that I wasn't worthy of love. It was easier to wall my heart away from the hurt and loss that came from caring about anyone other than myself. I'd been doing it for so long that when Jonathan—dear, sweet, handsome Jonathan—had professed his love, I threatened him with decapitation if he spoke of it again. Then, when he was finally treating me like a friend, I'd kissed him for no reason.

By Athena, I was broken.

But there was something about Ash in that moment that made me wish there was superglue for damaged souls and broken hearts.

I pulled one leg up onto the bench and rested my head on my knee, the fabric of my jeans cool against my cheek. I snuck a glance at Ash, wondering what it was that made him so special. None of the other women walking by gave him a second glance.

I shook my head. There had to be a logical explanation for a stone cold Hunter acting like such a fool. Maybe it was the lingering effects of being in a city swarming with swan maidens. Like I needed another reason to hurry up and complete my mission and get transferred out of this city.

I pulled my eyes from Ash and scanned the square. Tourists loitered taking pictures of the buildings that rose from the dark gray cobblestones like elaborately frosted wedding cakes.

"So, what are these buildings?" I asked, waving a hand. "Are they famous, or something?"

"Aye, those buildings to the left are the Brugse Vrije, the Liberty of Bruges, and the Civil Registry," he said. He pointed to an archway that was part of a squat, white, renaissance building bedecked with golden statues and red and gilt trim. "That archway leads into Blinde Ezelstraat, or Blind Donkey Alley. They say that back in the days when a mill stood there, the townspeople put a blindfold on the donkey to save it from the tedium of walking in circles day after day."

I frowned, thinking that I'd rather be aware of my surroundings, no matter how tedious, than be blinded from the truth. *Poor donkey.*

"And the taller building?" I asked.

The adjacent building had a pointed roof and turrets that reached to the heavens. The pale gray stone of the façade was broken by tall, arched, Gothic windows and dozens of somber statues.

"That's the Stadhuis, one of the oldest town halls in Europe," he said. "It's still used as a city hall, though it's open

to the public most days. The building doubles as a museum for
the tourists."

"What's inside?" I asked.

If it contained an old armory, that might be useful.
Fighting and killing weren't the only skills the Hunters' Guild
taught its initiates. I knew a thing or two about requisitioning
weapons in a pinch.

"Some old documents and the hall itself," he said. I
wrinkled my nose. *Maybe not so useful.* "Hey, don't knock it.
The hall is bloody gorgeous."

I shrugged.

"I'll take your word for it," I said, already scanning the
Burg for something that might aid in a hunt.

My breath hitched, body going still. Crouching in a
dark corner of the square was a building made of dark stone
that seemed to swallow the light and embrace the shadows.
Now that seemed interesting. Two towers rose above the
building and as I stood to toss my trash in the bin, and brush
away frite crumbs from my lap, the bells cradled in those
towers began to toll.

"And the dark building in the corner?" I asked, my boots
already carrying me across the cobblestone square.

"That is Basiliek van het Heilig Bloed, the Basilica of
the Holy Blood," he said in a soft, almost reverent voice.

I grinned, my right hand reaching up to stroke the
necklace of fangs beneath my dress. Finally, something useful.

CHAPTER 8

"The living impaired were rarely sentient, often just an imprint of emotion left behind like an unsightly blood smear."
-Jenna Lehane, Hunter

"So tell me more about this blood," I whispered.

We hadn't yet entered the basilica, but there was something about standing within its shadow that demanded respect. We spoke in hushed voices, ignoring the tourists who cast us peculiar looks. I could only assume that the furtive looks were due to Ash's unusual fashion sense.

"The basilica has in its safekeeping a phial containing a cloth with drops of blood from Christ Himself," he said.

I shook my head.

"How could Christ's blood end up here in Belgium?" I asked. "That doesn't make sense."

"There are holy relics throughout Europe, many with fascinating histories, and the story of the blood is no exception," he said. "Some say that Joseph of Arimathea collected the blood from Christ's body on the cross. Later the Sangreal, Holy Blood, was placed in a rock crystal phial and sealed with wax."

"Okay, but that still doesn't explain how this phial of blood ended up in Bruges," I said.

"I'd explain that, love, if someone would stop interrupting," he said, eyes squinting in amusement.

I folded my arms and sighed.

"Fine, I won't interrupt," I said, rolling my hand for Ash to get on with it.

"During the 4th crusade, Constantinople was sacked and the phial and other holy relics were taken by Baldwin I," he said.

"Wait," I said. "Who's Baldwin I? European history isn't my strong suit."

The only details I recalled from European history were those I'd learned during Hunters' training. But we'd been schooled on the events that were pivotal to the supernatural world, not much else. Mundane history never interested me all that much.

"Baldwin I was the first emperor of Constantinople," he said. He smirked like I should have known that, and I bit the inside of my cheek. "Prior to becoming emperor, Baldwin had been Count of Flanders and so when the Holy Blood came into his possession, he enlisted the Knights Templar to carry the phial back to his home in Bruges. The basilica here became the repository for the Holy Blood. To this day the relic is venerated daily, with many people making long pilgrimages to touch the blood. There's even an annual procession in which the phial is paraded throughout the city and events from the city's history are reenacted."

"People *touch* the Holy Blood?" I asked.

I wasn't squeamish. I'd spilled plenty of blood since becoming a Hunter. But I had a hard time believing that the church would allow tourists to handle a precious relic.

"The touching is mostly symbolic," he said. "It's more like touching the aura of the blood by placing your hand on the other side of a glass barrier, but it's no less powerful."

I had my doubts about the authenticity of this supposedly holy relic, but I'd seen enough magic to know better than to discount it completely. Whether by design or belief, some objects held great power.

"When do they allow tourists to touch the blood?" I asked.

"You're in luck," he said. "That's what those bells were for, calling the faithful for the veneration of the blood. Shall we go in?"

"Since I'm here, I might as well," I said.

I shrugged and fixed my face into a bland expression to hide my interest, and followed him into the church. Once inside, I slowly climbed a spiraling stone staircase, allowing my eyes to adjust to the dim light. If there was magic at work here, I'd need to be on my guard.

At the top of the stairs, we stepped into a large, open chamber with high ceilings that echoed every wail and moan of the tormented ghosts that fluttered through the rafters. I stiffened, body going still. Places of religious worship were often peaceful, a sanctuary from the spirits who walked the earth.

Not here.

I couldn't be sure if it was a geographical anomaly, or a situation unique to the basilica. Either way, it was clear that something was terribly wrong with the spirits of this place. I took a deep, steadying breath and forced myself away from the stairs, and the exit.

I tried to discreetly catch the attention of passing specters, but they drifted past without a word. They seemed only capable of unearthly wailing, their faces frozen in perpetual torment.

I shook my head, and proceeded to ignore the room full of ghosts. If they wouldn't, or couldn't, talk to me, it was best to ignore their tortured cries. They were probably completely unaware of my presence anyway. The living impaired were rarely sentient, often just an imprint of emotion left behind like an unsightly blood smear.

Having tried to communicate with the ghosts, I turned my attention to the basilica itself. A large, stone basin stood to my right, filled with water.

I went to the stoup, dipped my hands in the holy water, and made the sign of the cross. I hadn't grown up with much exposure to religion, but the Hunters' Guild was an offshoot of a militant religious order and, though the Templars hadn't existed for centuries, our Guild traditions were intertwined with ritual.

I wondered idly if the Guild's illustrious forebears really had carried Christ's blood from the Holy Land. If so, why had they brought such a powerful relic to Belgium? Was it due only to the emperor's influence, or was there more to the story? I could think of more than one monster that might want to control, or destroy, the phial and its contents.

Holy Blood—I didn't even want to consider what vampires would do with such a treasure. Thankfully, unlike the dead flickering around the room, the undead cannot enter holy ground.

They also have a severe allergy to holy water.

I reached inside my jacket and twisted the cap off a metal flask. With the restrictions against bringing fluids onboard aircraft, I'd had to leave Harborsmouth without my usual supply of holy water. Never one to miss an opportunity, I proceeded to fill my flask and an empty sports bottle from my backpack.

"Got something against vampires?" Ash asked.

Damn, he was quiet—when he wasn't talking. My hand shook, spilling some of the water.

"Why do you say that?" I asked.

"Is there some other reason for stealing holy water?" he asked.

"I'm not stealing it," I ground out between clenched teeth.

"My mistake," he said. "So why then are you *borrowing* holy water?"

"Because it's holy," I said. *Asshole*, I mentally added. I would have said it out loud, but I didn't fancy being struck by lightning, or stabbed with a knitting needle. I gave the old ladies on a nearby pew a wary glance, slipped the bottle of holy water into my bag, and took a step away from the font.

"Right, then," he said. "And vampires?"

"What about them?" I growled.

"Are you a fan?" he asked.

Candlelight flickered, making the shadows dance around us, and a chill ran up my spine. Something glinted in Ash's eyes, but whether it was mirth, curiosity, or deadly seriousness, I couldn't tell.

"No," I said. "Not. A. Fan."

"Funny," he said, leaning back to admire the ceiling. "I thought all American girls liked vampires. Think they're glittery and all that rot."

Rot, was right. Beneath all that glittery, swoon-inducing glamour lays the decaying body of a hungry, long-dead predator.

"I'm not your typical American tourist," I said.

"No, love, you're certainly not that," he said.

I shook my head and strode down the center aisle of the church, putting distance between me and Ash's teasing voice. I hurriedly took a seat in an empty chair, the caning squeaking in protest. I needed a moment to think, to process what I now knew of the situation here in Bruges, away from Ash's incessant, inane chatter.

Damn, I missed the meditative quiet of my training sessions. Back in Harborsmouth, I slew monsters, but that didn't mean my life was chaos. I had a routine; run, spar, weight train, practice my kata, clean and check my weapons, and go hunting.

So long as I didn't deviate from the routine, things ran smoothly. But here I was in Belgium, floundering like the wailing ghosts overhead, unable to find peace, even in a church.

Ash came and took the seat beside me, hands folded in his lap.

"So, love, are you going to touch it?" he asked.

A smile twitched his lips, and I narrowed my eyes at him.

"You better be talking about the blood, or I'll be spilling some of yours, church or not," I said.

He lowered his voice and leaned forward, "I'd like to see you try."

I wasn't sure if he meant try to touch him, or try to attack him. Not that it mattered. Ash licked his lips and smiled, but I just rolled my eyes. Damn him for being such a pain in the ass.

If I wasn't going to get any peace, I might as well go touch the Holy Blood and get it over with. I went back up the row, passed the group of old ladies who were all scowling at me as if I were here to tangle their knitting, and went into the side chapel to my left. There was a short wait and I fidgeted with the strap of my ski bag, reading the Latin inscription on the wall.

Sanguis Christi, inebria nos. Blood of Christ, inebriate me.

I swallowed hard, wishing I could draw my sword. This city gave me the creeps.

There was one creature that became intoxicated from drinking blood, and I didn't want to think about what would happen if a vampire drank from this particular relic. Would a vampire become more powerful? Would they transform into a new breed of monster? Or would a vampire spontaneously combust from imbibing such a holy draught?

I held onto that last scenario. One could hope.

When the red velvet rope was lowered, I climbed the steps and bowed my head. I dropped a few Euro coins into the collection box and placed my hand against the thick, bulletproof glass that encased the Holy Blood. The glass was cool against my palm, but warmth filled my chest.

Images flashed through my head at lightning speed, taking my breath away. Frank's leer, the smile of my mother's

ghost, the victims of rogue vampire attacks their bodies
drained and broken all played through my mind at breakneck
speed.

I gasped, taking a step back. This was no fake. The
Holy Blood was real.

But even with such a powerful relic in its possession,
the humans of this city were dying. It's hard to fight what you
don't understand. The local authorities were woefully
unequipped to fight monsters, but someone needed to put a
stop to the killing.

The monsters couldn't be allowed to win.

I wiped hot tears from my cheeks, and renewed my
promise to myself and to my Guild. I was here for one purpose.

Protect the innocent.

Chapter 9

"Hunters don't break their promises."
-Jenna Lehane, Hunter

I lit a candle and surreptitiously wiped my tears.

"What did you wish for?" Ash asked.

"It's a prayer, not a wish," I said, blinking away the last of the tears.

"Same thing," he said with a shrug. "Did you lose someone? Is that why you're crying?"

"I'm not crying," I said, pushing past him. "I got smoke in my eye."

"Ah, right," he said. "Bloody cheap candles."

"They're not cheap," I said. "Just...just leave it be."

"Shhh!" someone hissed.

I looked up to see a row of old ladies giving me the stink eye. I guess that's what I get for defending the church's candles. I just can't win.

Ash strolled past as I rummaged in my jacket pockets for a tissue. The mischievous look on his face told me it was time to leave. I didn't feel like being thrown out of the basilica.

I sighed and started forward, but I was too late.

"You have got to be kidding me," I muttered.

Ash stopped in front of the old ladies and started to do the chicken dance.

"What are you DOING?" I asked, running up and grabbing his arm.

"Shhh!" the ladies hissed.

Son of a boggle, he was going to get us kicked out.

"I'm dancing," Ash said with an impish grin. "Always wanted to do that in a church. What should I try next? The Macarena?"

"Are you CRAZY?" I asked.

One of the ladies let out a strangled growl, grabbed her cane, and started to stand. Her hissing friends weren't far behind.

"Sorry," I said, eyes wide.

No way was I getting into a pissing contest with a bunch
of church ladies. I pulled Ash toward the door, struggling not
to laugh...or commit murder inside a church. We took the
stairs two at a time and burst out onto the Burg square.

"Bloody hell, that was fun," Ash said.

"Fun?" I asked. "Fun? Are you insane?"

"You should have seen your face," he said.

I pictured me, bug eyed and gaping as Ash danced like
an epileptic chicken. A smile tugged at my lips, and I let out a
snort.

"They must think we're evil," I said.

Ash shrugged.

"So what now, fellow hooligan?" he asked.

I was wound up from our brief flight to safety, and our
close call with geriatric fisticuffs. I needed to burn off the
excess adrenaline. Plus, it would be smart to leave the Burg in
case those women called the police. I didn't feel like explaining
to foreign authorities why we'd disturbed the peace. I was
pretty sure that "always wanted to do that" wouldn't hold up in
court.

I scanned the area and spied the bell tower looming over
the buildings to our left. I started walking down Breidelstraat
toward the market square. I needed to burn off some unspent
adrenaline, and I knew just the place.

Ash lit up a cigarette as we walked through the sewer
stench and dodged pedestrians, making our way back onto the
market square. I frowned and narrowed my eyes at Ash. I
wasn't sure what was more vile, the putrescence of rotting feces
or the acrid smoke.

"Come on," I said, waving Ash toward the bell tower.

The food trucks were dead ahead.

"Hungry again, love?" he asked.

"No," I said. "I want to climb the tower."

I'd felt off balance all day, and part of the reason for
that was the break in my routine. I was used to rigorous
training. I may not have access to the guild training grounds
yet, but a run up the tower was a start.

"It's three hundred and sixty six steps to the top, love,"
he said, grinding out his cigarette.

I grimaced, giving a nearby ashtray a significant glance.
He sighed and picked up the stub, tossing it in the ashtray.

"Happy?" he asked.

"I will be," I said, a slow grin sliding onto my face. I was about to make him regret that smoke break. "Race you to the top."

"Right, then," he said, tugging on his hat. "Fancy a wager? Say, loser buys lunch tomorrow?"

"You're on," I said.

I turned and ran for the building, Ash close on my heels. It wasn't until we reached the top that I realized what he'd done. I hadn't planned on seeing Ash again after today, but I'd accepted his wager.

Now I had to see him again tomorrow. It was a matter of honor. Hunters don't break their promises. Ash looked over at me and winked.

Sneaky bastard.

CHAPTER 10

"Hunters train daily. When the option is train or die,
the choice is simple."
-Jenna Lehane, Hunter

I scowled at the door and pressed the bell, again. It was
unlike the Guild to be late, but I'd tried the bell three times
since my arrival, and no one had come to answer the door. I
was considering calling the emergency contact number in my
file, when I heard the distinct sounds of boot treads and the
clink of weapons.

Whoever it was, they were taking their sweet time.

"We're closed," a man said, opening the door, and then
rudely shutting it in my face.

From the brief glimpse I'd had of the man, he wasn't
much older than me, early twenties, but unlike me he was tall
and blond. Judging from the way his t-shirt stretched tight
across his chest and biceps, he was physically fit. He also wore
a sword over his cargo pants, belted at his hip. I had a bad
feeling that this was my Guild liaison—just my luck.

I clenched my teeth and rapped my knuckles on the
door.

"What?" he barked, whipping the door open.

"I have an appointment," I said, keeping my voice low
and steady. Yelling wouldn't do me any good. I didn't need to
get in trouble for insubordination. "My name is Jenna
Lehane."

"You have got to be kidding me," he said. His lip curled
in disgust as his eyes traveled along my body. "They sent a
little girl?"

"Hey buddy, size doesn't always matter," I said.

"If you believe that, then you haven't been with a real
man," he sneered.

I held myself rigid, calming myself with a methodical
analysis of his weaknesses, and how I could exploit them with
my weapons. He leaned across the doorway, arm outstretched
to block my way. He probably thought it made him look cool.

Think again. *Foot sweep, elbow to the throat, a dagger to the kidneys*...there that was better.

My breathing slowed and I lifted my chin, meeting his gaze.

"If I meet one, I'll let you know," I said.

He jerked his head back, nostrils flaring, and I ducked under his arm and pushed my way past his bulk. Being tiny did have its advantages, regardless of what this narrow-minded prick thought.

"We don't need any more women in this Guild," he said, slamming the door shut behind us. "Bitches should be at home where you belong."

My hands closed into fists and I bit the inside of my cheek to keep from giving the chauvinistic creep a piece of my mind. I was used to macho bullshit, but this asshole was out of line. I'd flown halfway around the world to run a mission here. A little common courtesy from a Guild brother shouldn't be too much to ask for.

"Since you don't make Guild recruitment policies, how about we skip the chitchat and you show me to Master Peeters' office," I said.

"Master Peeters is in Brussels," he said, eyes glinting. "So are most of the senior staff."

"And my handler?" I asked. "There must be a senior Hunter for me to report to."

"That, sweetheart, would be me," he said.

Oh shit.

*****

As I'd expected from our initial meeting, Simon "Chad" Chadwick was a nasty piece of work. His behavior didn't improve as he gave me a brief tour of the Guild's parade grounds and training facilities. I kept my weapons close at hand, fully aware that we hadn't met a single soul—which was unusual for a guildhall. Hunters train daily. When the option is train or die, the choice is simple. That just made the empty sparring mats and unoccupied weight rooms seem all the more alien to me.

Chad hadn't exaggerated about most of the Hunters being called away. The Bruges Guild was running on a skeleton staff. Master Peeters was attending the supernatural community's version of a UN summit in Brussels, and the

Guild master had taken his best Hunters with him. With the
possibility of war on the horizon, something the European
branches of the Hunters' Guild seemed well aware of, Peeters
had gone prepared for the possibility of battle.

Unfortunately, that meant that he'd left his least
valuable Hunters behind to keep things running here. From
Chad's account, that left him in charge of the rejects. I'm not
sure what that was supposed to make me, and I didn't want to
know. Being sent away from the Harborsmouth Guild had
been tough enough. I didn't need to take another blow to my
self esteem, though I'm sure that's what Chad intended.

That guy had a definite hard on for his ideal of a men's
only, human only Guild. His hatred of women was matched
only by his loathing for supernaturals. I suppose that made
him a good Hunter in the field. He could use that anger and
self righteous belief to fuel him in the fight against the
monsters, but there was a flaw in that line of thinking.

Not all supernaturals are monsters.

That was a lesson I was continuing to learn. Before
being assigned a werewolf roommate, I too had reservations
about trusting supes. Jonathan had been a wake up call for
me. Our friendship helped open my eyes to the possibility that
supernaturals were not all villains waiting to sink in their
fangs. Ivy Granger, a half human faerie princess, and Kaye
O'Shaye, a powerful witch, had further helped to banish my
prejudices when they risked their own lives for the human
inhabitants of Harborsmouth.

I might have pitied Chad's blind ignorance, if he hadn't
been such a dictatorial prick. Master Peeters had given Chad
power over the few Hunters left in residence here, and he
didn't miss a chance to abuse his superior position.

When I didn't cow from his ongoing demeaning
monologue, Chad upped the ante by showing me the
dormitories and introducing me to Celeste Dubois. If I thought
Chad treated me bad, it was nothing compared to how he
behaved around Celeste.

Celeste was female, and a witch. That made her less
than garbage in Chad's eyes, and he made a point of letting her
know how he felt, repeatedly.

"I'm done wasting my time with you, Lehane," he said.
Chad smirked on his way out of Celeste's room, the twist of his
mouth as ugly as his soul—if he had one. "She's yours, witch.

I'll leave you two to gossip, or whatever it is your kind is good at."

He swatted a basket of herbs from a shelf on his way out, knocking them to scatter on the ground.

"Clumsy, witch," he said. "Clean up your mess."

Celeste dropped to her hands and knees, hastily sweeping the herbs into the fallen basket.

"Sorry," she muttered.

"On your knees, eh," he said. "Good, that's about all your good for."

With that repulsive comment, he walked out the door of her room, his laughter trailing his movements down the hall. I reached down to help the woman up and she staggered to her feet.

"Is he always like that?" I asked.

"Chad?" she asked. She shrugged and went to sit on the edge of her bed, eyes glazed. "I guess so." She scrunched up her face as if trying to concentrate. "He's been worse since Peeters left, I think."

"Why would Master Peeters leave someone like Simon Chadwick in charge in the first place?" I asked.

Even if the sudden usurping of power was what had made Chadwick a tyrant, he obviously had some deep seated issues. At a guess, I'd say he was probably a bully, with or without his newfound position as interim leader. I frowned. Placing Chadwick in charge had been a foolhardy decision. Most Guild masters wouldn't make that kind of mistake.

"Simon's father hunted with Peeters until an ogre ripped out his spine," she said. She turned vacant eyes on me, and whispered as if forgetting I was there, "How long must we remain indebted to our fallen?"

"So," I coughed, giving Celeste a moment to pull herself together. We were all haunted by the memories of those we've lost—some more than others. I didn't want to intrude on her grief, but understanding the local politics was important. "Chadwick is in charge while the others are away in Brussels, because Master Peeters feels he owes a debt to the Chadwick family?"

Celeste attempted to shrug, but lost her balance and fell back against a pile of cushions.

"Are you okay?" I asked.

Had she hit her head? She'd dropped to the ground pretty fast when Chadwick had knocked her herbs all over the floor. I leaned in to see if she was alright.

"Oh, I'm fine," she said, smiling wide.

It was creepy. She shouldn't have been smiling like that. There was nothing to be that happy about, ever, and Chad had just treated her like a discarded toy he enjoyed stomping on from time to time.

As far as appearances went, Celeste and I were opposites. Where I was pale, she had an olive complexion. Unlike my dark blue eyes, her eyes were a light golden hue, like honey, and almond shaped. She was also tall, curvaceous and looked sexy as hell in her tight fitting mini dress—not like me at all.

There was one more thing that set us apart and it wasn't her witch powers. It was the sickly sweet scent of Mandragora smoke on her breath. Mandrake root, and the drug made from it, is highly poisonous to humans. Witches, though otherwise human, have an extra set of chromosomes from which their magic was thought to come. That genetic difference was also notable in their reaction to mandrake. Not only did they not die from ingesting it, but witches had also found a recreational use for the plant—a drug they called Mandragora.

The drug caused hallucinations, euphoria, and was highly addictive. When taken regularly, it could cause attention deficit disorder and memory dysfunction. That made Mandragora a highly dangerous drug. The last thing you wanted in a witch was ADD and memory loss. Mental focus and the ability to recall incantations were integral to spellcasting.

If Celeste continued smoking Mandragora, she'd lose the ability to use magic, and in the meantime she'd become a menace to other Hunters. I wasn't going to sit back and let that happen.

Celeste lay back against a pile of pillows, humming happily to herself, and I took a slow, methodical tour of her room. The shelves of herbs and other spell components weren't unusual, but the long stemmed pipe and bag of resin coated mandrake root certainly was.

I reached for the pipe, but jerked to a halt at Celeste's screech.

"Don't touch that!" she yelled.

She held a pointed finger out toward me, her hair floating around her head. Her lips were pulled back, baring her teeth, and the whites of her eyes showed around large, dilated pupils.

She probably couldn't reliably cast a spell while under the influence of Mandragora, but I couldn't take that chance. I wouldn't be able to save too many humans from the monsters if Celeste turned me into a frog.

I backed away, hands raised palms out.

"Easy," I said. "It's alright, Celeste."

Once my steps took me to the door, her face broke into that hideous smile. Her hair fell limply to her shoulders, and she lay back on the cushions of the bed, singing softly to herself. Celeste thought that the threat to her stash of drugs was over.

She was wrong.

CHAPTER 11

"It's never a good idea to startle a man with a scalpel."
-Jenna Lehane, Hunter

I slipped out of Celeste's room and hurried down the hall, winding through the dormitory, and taking the stairs down to the lower levels. If this building was designed anything like the guildhalls back home, an infirmary should be located down in the basement.

There it was, right next to the morgue—just like back home.

I always thought that having the morgue at such close proximity to the infirmary was depressing, but the Hunters' Guild was nothing if not pragmatic. Patients don't always survive their injuries. Having the morgue and infirmary side by side kept things efficient. I could get behind that idea, if it wasn't for the ghosts.

The ghosts of dead Hunters wandered in and out of the morgue. At some point the location of the doorway must have been moved, because more than half of the ghosts passed through the wall a few yards to the left of the actual opening. That wouldn't have been unusual in your garden variety ghost, but Hunters tend to follow the rules, even after they've reached their expiration date.

I pushed up my sleeves and strode to the infirmary, pointedly ignoring the hungry looks from the men and women staring at me from the morgue. I've never understood why, but some ghosts get trapped in a place where their body spent time. Morgues, hospitals, battlefields, and graveyards were the worst. They attracted the dead like blowflies to a corpse.

"Hello?" I called out, stepping into the infirmary.

It isn't smart to walk into a Hunter's territory unannounced, and our doctors were no different. Most got their training as combat medics, which meant they spent time on the front lines like the rest of us. Plus, it's never a good idea to startle a man with a scalpel.

"In here," a man said from the back room.

I pushed past a white curtain, senses heightened as I took in the unfamiliar rows of cots. There were privacy curtains between each cot and I checked the area behind each before continuing on.

"In the supply closet," the man said.

My eyes cut to movement in a dark room at the far back of the infirmary, in the same direction as the muffled voice. A white, medical coat fluttered past the open doorway so quickly he resembled a ghost.

"Sorry about that," he said, carrying out an armful of supplies.

I followed him past the empty beds to a desk at the front of the infirmary. It gave me a chance to study him. The man was older, maybe late twenties or early thirties. He wore a bright white lab coat over scrubs, but that's where the good hygiene ended. He hadn't shaved, he smelled like I'd interrupted his dinner, and he was covered in dust.

He slapped at his clothes, ran fingers through greasy hair, and held out his hand.

"You must be the new girl," he said. "Sorry about the mess. I was doing inventory while things were slow."

I shook his hand quickly, and resisted the urge to wipe my hand down the front of my jeans. He may be a bit ragged around the edges, but he seemed nice and I appreciated having at least one of the Hunters greet me with a smile that wasn't drug induced.

"Jenna Lehane," I said. "I'm looking for the doctor."

"That would be me, Benjamin Martens" he said. "Here, have a seat."

He moved a pile of gauze pads from a chair and nodded. Rather than take the offered seat, I blinked at him owlishly.

"You're Doc Martens?" I asked. "Like the British TV show?"

"Like the steel-toe boots," he said, casting a significant look at his feet.

He was wearing combat boots with the telltale yellow stitching around the sole.

"Isn't that kind of lame to be wearing your namesake?" I asked.

"You want a boot in the ass, girl?" he asked.

I snorted and shook my head, taking the offered seat across from his desk.

"No thanks," I said.

"What can I help you with?" he asked. "Feeling sick from traveling? Peeters said you'd be flying in from the States."

"I'm fine," I said. I sat down and leaned forward, putting my hands on the desk. "I'm here about Celeste."

"Dubois?" he asked. "What's wrong with her?"

I raised an eyebrow, wondering just how a doctor could miss the signs of her addiction.

"She's using Mandragora," I said.

He waved his hand and leaned back in an old, wheeled office chair that was practically upholstered in duct tape.

"Madrake isn't poisonous to witches," he said. "If she wants to smoke the witch drug on her own time, I don't see the problem."

My lip curled, baring my teeth. It was an expression I'd picked up from Jonathan. Spend enough time living with a werewolf and some things were bound to rub off.

"It's a problem," I said, biting off the words.

Celeste needed help with her addiction before she lost her powers, or got someone killed. Letting her use recreational drugs was beyond irresponsible. If we didn't do anything to stop her, we might as well hand her a sword and tell her to kill herself, and take out a few of our brothers while she was at it.

"What do you want me to do about it?" he asked with a sigh.

"Call her down here, drug her if you have to, and keep her here until every trace of Mandragora is out of her system," I said.

"And how am I supposed to get her down here?" he asked. "In case you haven't noticed, we're a bit short staffed. I'm just one doctor, and she's a powerful witch."

"She's a young woman who's stoned out of her mind, and you're a goddamn combat trained doctor with the resources of the Guild at your disposal," I said. "You'll think of something."

I would have offered to help, but I was pretty sure that tossing a stranger into the mix would only make the situation worse. Plus, regardless of the fact this post was working on a skeleton staff, there were other Hunters available to help out. Hunters that Celeste might feel more at ease with.

"And what am I supposed to do with her once she's down here?" he asked.

"You have everything you need right here to keep her calm and comfortable," I said, nodding my head at the row of beds.

He threw his hands in the air in an "I give up" gesture and I sat back in my chair.

"Fine," he said. "I'll see what I can do."

"Good," I said. I licked my lips and glanced at a metal door along one wall. "Now that's settled, how about you show me the morgue."

"Why?" he said. "There's nothing in there, nothing but empty metal drawers."

"Isn't that where you keep the bodies?" I said. "I'm working the serial murder case. Examining the bodies could go a long way in determining what kind of threat we're facing."

"The bodies aren't there," he said, shaking his head. "They've all been incinerated."

I narrowed my eyes at him, but he just shrugged.

"I was following policy," he said. "You don't like it? Take it up with Master Peeters when he gets back from Brussels."

I ground my teeth, but nodded curtly. Nothing I could do about it now. Railing at Martens wouldn't bring the bodies back, and I'd already pushed my luck with the good doctor. If I wanted his cooperation, I had to know when to back down.

There was no question that I'd need his continued cooperation. He'd be in charge of autopsying the body of every victim we fished out of the canals. And make no mistake, there'd be more bodies. No one would be safe until this monster was caught.

I just wished I had a lead on what kind of creature we were up against. I sighed and reached out my hand.

"Without bodies, I'll need to look over your autopsy reports," I said.

He shook his head.

"Everything was in the case file we sent you," he said.

"That's it?" I said. "That file was pretty slim."

"You know as much as I do," he said. "If another body comes in, I'll give you a call."

"You do that," I said, letting my hand drop to my side. I gave him a hard look and headed for the door. "Later, Doc."

I knew that busting his balls wouldn't further my mission, so I forced my breathing to remain steady and strode out the door. No sense wearing myself out in a pissing battle with Martens.

I'd save my energy for the monsters.

CHAPTER 12

"Knowing your adversary can mean the difference between living and dying."
-Jenna Lehane, Hunter

There was one more place where I might find answers. The Hunters' Guild groomed its members to be skilled fighters, but it also valued knowledge. The Guild had archives that rivaled the Vatican, filled with secret histories and encyclopedic catalogues of the supernatural.

While there were large central archives for the most delicate documents, each guildhall had its own small library. After a few wrong turns, I found the door I was looking for. The door was engraved with the image of a Hunter fighting a horde of monsters, a scroll in one hand and a book-shaped shield in the other. It symbolized how knowledge could be used as a weapon against our enemies, and how it could also shield us from danger.

I preferred weapons to dusty old books, but even I had to admit the importance of good intel. Knowing your adversary can mean the difference between living and dying, hence my visit to the archives.

I raised a fist to knock on the heavy, ironclad door, but it swung open, nearly knocking me off my feet.

"Celeste, girl, that you?"

A behemoth of a man stood filling the doorway. He stood over six feet and wore camouflage pants and a tight tank top that showed off his chocolate brown skin and rippling muscles. In other circumstances I might have found his size intimidating, but he was smiling wide, showing perfect white teeth. It was a nice smile.

I raised an eyebrow and crossed my arms across my chest, a wry grin on my lips.

"Do I look like Celeste?" I asked.

"I wouldn't know," he said, waving a hand in front of his face. "You might be as ugly as a yeti, for all I know. Though, from what I can tell, you're not nearly tall or smelly enough."

I winced, taking in the pink scar tissue on his face and his damaged eyes.

He was blind.

"Sorry," I said, glad he couldn't see my burning cheeks. "I didn't know. I'm Jenna Lehane."

Out of habit, I started to reach out to offer him my hand, but thought better of it and, after a moment's awkwardness, shoved it back in my jacket pocket.

"Ah, right, the visiting Hunter," he said. "I'm Darryl Lambert, archive librarian. What can I do for you?"

A blind librarian? I tilted my head, examining the man. He would have been a formidable Hunter before whatever accident robbed him of his sight. But I wasn't so sure about his skills in the archive.

"I was hoping for some information on local supes," I said. "The nastier the better. I'm working a serial murder case, but the case file I received isn't all that helpful. Neither is Simon Chadwick, my liaison while I'm here."

"Chadwick's a Grade A asshole—if you'll pardon my French," Darryl said. "Come on in. Let's talk."

Darryl led me, with slow, measured steps, inside the archives, a labyrinth of bookshelves and wooden file cabinets. His lips moved as he walked, as if counting off our position. I suppose it was a bit like pacing off the distance to a target while in the field.

"So, is this a new gig for you?" I asked. I looked around the archives, trying to think of something positive to say. "Looks like a nice place to work."

Darryl stopped walking. He turned to face me, brow furrowed.

"You're not feeling sorry for me, are you girl?" he asked. His voice dropped low. "'Cause I don't need your pity."

"Um, no," I said, swallowing hard. "Just curious, I guess."

"Can't fault you for that, I suppose," he said. "Girl after my own heart." He started forward again and waved a hand toward the rising stacks. "Archives are a good a place as any for the curious."

"Isn't it hard though," I asked, frowning. "I mean, librarians have to be able to read and locate information. It must be tough. Seems kind of shitty of the Guild to stick you down here."

"Where else you think they gonna stick me?" he asked. "You want me operating on you? Providing cover fire? No, I asked for this post. Always liked the archives, and everything I need to do my job is up here."

He tapped his head.

"Good, then let's get to work," I said.

CHAPTER 13

"Hunting after a transatlantic flight probably wasn't the wisest of choices."
-Jenna Lehane, Hunter

It was late when I finally called it a night and left the archives. I'd doubted Darryl when he said that everything he needed was in his head, but the man hadn't been bragging. The librarian may have been blind, but he'd spent a lot of time down in the archives before his accident and he had a photographic memory.

Not only did he know where every document was located in those archives, but he could also recite passages from every book he'd ever read. Add to that the high tech gadgets he'd acquired for accessing the Guild's central database and he did just fine.

Darryl was damned handy.

Too bad I still had no idea who, or what, was killing humans and dumping their bodies in the picturesque canals of Bruges. Too many monsters roamed Europe, with more than a dozen predators claiming territory in West Flanders. If I was going to narrow the scope of my investigation, and find the killer, I'd need to go out in the field.

Not that searching the city streets and waterways would be a problem. Thankfully, that's where I did my best work.

I stifled a yawn and went upstairs to gear up for a night on the town, Hunter style. With so many Hunters attending the peace talks, there was no shortage of available rooms. I took one on the same floor as Celeste. I considered stopping by her room to see if Martens had managed to get the witch to the infirmary, but shook my head and continued down the hall. Celeste wasn't my problem. For someone who'd been here less than twenty-four hours, I'd already meddled enough.

Once in my dorm room, I changed into a black body suit and strapped on a skirt made from strips of black cloth and reinforced leather that would protect some of my arteries

without hindering movement. I added the garrote cuff
bracelet, leather boots, and a black underbust corset. The
corset's boning was coated in iron and silver, but most
importantly it provided support and protection to my lower
back and internal organs.

It also had the added benefit of selling the impression
that I was just a young, petite, Goth girl out for a night on the
town. With that disguise in place, I could add the final element
to my costume—my very sharp, very real katana. I wore the
sword at my hip, in plain sight. In a city that promoted its
connection to the past, I was willing to bet that walking around
like I was a tourist ready for a Renaissance fair wouldn't
attract too much attention.

I slid knives into each boot and strapped an assortment
of stakes, crosses, iron nails and other weapons into the lining
of my skirt. I smeared a thick layer of faerie ointment onto my
eyelids, blinking until the stinging subsided. Once my vision
cleared, I went to the one dark window in the room and met my
reflection with a feral smile of my own.

It was time to go hunting.

*****

At this time of night the city streets outside the central
market square were mostly empty. I was alone except for my
shadow trailing along behind me, and the specters that
haunted the streets and buildings that pressed in from both
sides.

The dead stared out from nearly every window, their
eyes like gaping holes in their pale faces. I kept my eyes on the
street, ignoring the human-shaped specters and the tendrils of
mist-like ectoplasm twining around my boots, climbing my legs,
and whispering in my ear. The sibilant hiss and moan, like a
radio channel out of tune, set my teeth on edge.

The walk from the guildhall to the canal took less than
five minutes, but it felt like I'd been running that gauntlet of
the dead for days. I slid from shadow to shadow as I made my
way down Carmersstraat, Blekersstraat, and finally St-
Annarei.

I sagged against the wall of a lace shop when the
buildings on my left and right receded to reveal a wide canal
running north and south. Two narrower canals joined here,
heading to the west and southwest.

Since taking this case, it was obvious that someone had been slacking on their paperwork. There was surprisingly little information about the victim's bodies and the dump sites. I needed details, and that meant going back to the source. It was too early to tell where the actual murders took place, but the locations where the bodies had been found were a good starting point.

More than one body had been fished out of the water here. Whether that was a result of the geography of the canals or indicated the hunting grounds of a supernatural predator remained to be seen.

I inhaled deeply, ignoring the stench of mildew and decay. I needed to stay focused, keeping my attention on potential threats, but the presence of so many ghosts was taking its toll. I mistakenly thought that I'd built up a tolerance to the dead during my time in Harborsmouth, but my old home had nothing on Bruges. This medieval city was swarming with angry spirits, and it was giving me a headache.

I rubbed my temples, took another deep breath, and felt the pressure in my skull ease enough to regain my focus. Fatigue wasn't helping. Hunting after a transatlantic flight probably wasn't the wisest of choices, but every night that this monster, or monsters, remained on the loose, meant the potential for more dead bodies.

Those dead bodies would be on my head.

I lifted my chin and pushed away from the wall. No, I wasn't going to let the people of this city, or the Guild, down. I had a job to do and, by Athena, I was going to do it right.

I swung over a metal railing and landed silently on a steep embankment. Keeping to the shadows, I crept down to the murky water of the canal.

The bodies had been found where they'd caught on the pylons beneath the nearby stone bridge that spanned the canal. I needed a better look, but I didn't have access to a boat. Having to find an alternative route along the canal complicated things, but I had a feeling that asking Chadwick's help in requisitioning a boat through the normal channels would cause even greater complications. I'm sure he'd like nothing better than to dangle a carrot in front of my face.

I'd just do things the hard way.

This looked like the best access point, but it wouldn't be easy. The footing was precarious at best. If I wasn't careful,

I'd end up in the canal—the same canal that was home to all sorts of potentially deadly predators. I needed to make my way along the canal and into the inky blackness beneath the nearby bridge, but there was only a slimy, narrow stone sill that ran here along the water's edge, the foundations of buildings forming a moss covered wall that rose several feet above my head to the street level.

I maneuvered onto the sill, standing on tiptoe and digging my fingers into tiny crevices where mortar had eroded over the years. Using the handholds for balance, I inched my way along the canal. Something dropped onto my head and I flinched, my foot slipping off the ledge.

I held my breath, my boot dangling an inch above the water, as a large, hairy spider scuttled across my face. I didn't dare blink until the eight legged critter made its way down my neck and onto my left shirtsleeve. No sense pissing it off on exposed skin.

I had no idea if it was poisonous, and I didn't want to find out.

Now that the spider was crawling down my sleeve, I let out the breath I'd been holding. Using the fingers of my right hand, I shifted my handhold and regained my balance. As soon as I had both feet back on the ledge, I shifted my weight to the left, holding myself steady with my left hand. I inhaled deeply, and as I exhaled I grabbed the spider with my right hand, and smashed it against the wall.

I wrinkled my nose and continued along the ledge until I neared a low, stone bridge that crossed the canal. The bridge reared up high over my head and I blinked into its dark, gaping maw, trying to make out the dim shapes ahead.

Using my feet to feel my way, I tiptoed over to a partially submerged stone platform. Water lapped against my boots and I closed my eyes, listening for potential threats. The arched cave-like space beneath the bridge seemed to warp sound, twisting the *slap slap* of water and skitter of tiny feet into strange sighs and echoes.

Muscles tightening in readiness, I drew a Maglite from a thigh holster, aimed it into the darkness, and set it on a shelf-like projection of stone at shoulder level. In one quick movement, I switched on the flashlight, strafed to my right, and drew my sword.

All I managed to do was startle a nest of river rats.

I sighed, slid the sword back into its sheath, and retrieved the flashlight. I scanned the arched ceiling, aimed the light at the damp floor, and began walking slowly, searching for clues in a grid pattern.

Maybe I'd be lucky and find something the other Hunters had missed. From all accounts, the local Guild was stretched so thin, they didn't have the manpower to do a proper search of each dump site.

But after a thorough search all I'd found were a few small bones that may have been from rats for all I knew, and a large grate that, judging from the smell, covered a discharge pipe from the sewers. I wrinkled my nose and tried to open the grate, but it was locked with a massive, iron padlock. I wasn't getting inside that sewer tunnel, not tonight, not without heavy duty bolt cutters.

I wiped my hands on my pants and frowned. They weren't coming clean. I held my fingers beneath the flashlight and gasped. The grate wasn't wet with water and algae.

It was covered in blood.

The dark red liquid hadn't been noticeable on the black iron of the grate, but against the contrasting paleness of my skin the telltale color of blood was obvious. I licked my lips and smiled. Someone, or something, had been using the sewer tunnels to access the canals where they'd dumped the bodies of their victims.

Eyes on the padlock, I let the tension in my body ease and I rolled my shoulders in a satisfied, catlike stretch. It would take more than a locked grate to keep me from putting an end to this killer. I'd be back.

I turned off the flashlight and returned to the ledge once my eyes adjusted to the dim light of the moon. I passed the splattered spider, its legs and mandibles still twitching. Doing a grid search beneath the bridge hadn't taken me long. I still had time to check out one more dump site, if I was quick about it.

I climbed the embankment quickly, a black shadow breaking away from the murky canal and rising to the street, determined to find the monsters in this city—and make them pay.

CHAPTER 14

"The dead were annoying, but sometimes they remembered just enough to help find the creature that murdered them."

-Jenna Lehane, Hunter

I leaned against a tree and scanned the small park that ran along Rozenhoedkaai and the southern bank of a narrow canal. I stifled a yawn, fatigue making me wish I'd gone straight back to the Guild and my bed. I was tempted to rush my search, but there was something about this place that made me cautious.

I didn't like it, not one bit.

I took my time, examining the spaces between the trees, the park benches, and the surface of the canal. The only movement was a pale form sitting on one of the benches facing the water. A little boy sat there, tiny legs swinging back and forth, staring vacantly at the canal.

Yeah, that wasn't creepy or anything.

I pushed myself away from the tree, and walked over to the bench. The boy didn't look up—he didn't even blink—but that wasn't surprising.

He was dead.

The front of his shirt was missing, along with most of his internal organs. My chest tightened at the sight of all that damage. I looked up from his wounds and forced a smile on my face.

"Mind if I sit here?" I asked.

I normally make a policy of avoiding the dead. Acknowledging lost spirits was often all the encouragement they needed to follow you around wailing and moaning until they got bored or found some other poor sap. But I made exceptions while working a case. The dead were annoying, but sometimes they remembered just enough to help find the creature that murdered them.

This child though was a mere static image, a shard of trauma, nothing more. He didn't respond, his only movement the swinging of his legs and the flicker of his transparent body as he wavered in and out of focus.

I took a seat on the bench anyway, examining the small child. He had been five or six when he died—when a monster had scooped out his guts like his internal organs were candy. I frowned, shaking my head. That part had been left out of the autopsy report.

The reason I'd been curious about this dump site was the difference in age of the victim. The other bodies that the Guild had dragged from the canals in the past few weeks had belonged to adults. The fact that a child's body had been found dead either meant the killer was changing his MO or that we were dealing with more than one monster.

I was glad the kid's ghost wasn't experiencing the pain and horror of his injuries, but it was too bad that he wasn't sentient enough to give me answers. The unfortunate fact was that there were way too many monsters out there with the ability to do that kind of damage to a child's body.

Murder, especially the murder of a child, went against our laws, but I was all too aware that superaturals didn't always follow the rules. It's why I became a Hunter, to put down rogue paranormals who broke our truce and murdered innocent humans.

I sighed and turned my attention away from the ghost child, watching the canal where he continued to stare unblinking. The water rippled and I reached for my sword, jumping to my feet. A head resembling a large frog broke the surface of the water, its face breaking into a Cheshire cat grin.

The grindylow's smile showed off a wide mouth filled with sharp, needle-like teeth that glinted in the moonlight. Of course, most people wouldn't see those teeth—not until they were buried in their vital organs. Thankfully, I'd applied a generous amount of faerie ointment to my eyes before heading out on this hunting excursion.

"Come, child," he said. "Fancy a swim?"

My lips drew back in a silent snarl. He wasn't talking to the child on the bench. The grindylow was talking to me. That was a mistake, and if I found out he was the monster who'd killed this little boy, it wouldn't be his first.

I held my sword in front of me and glared.

"No thanks, Grindy" I said. "I'd rather swim with a barracuda."

He tilted his head, the smile never leaving his slick, mottled green face.

"Come now, let's be reasonable," he said, spreading his hands wide. "There's no need for that shiny toy here. We have much better things to play with down below—treasure and playthings beyond your wildest dreams."

He had long, spindly, webbed fingers, thin arms, and a frail body that didn't look large enough or strong enough to support the considerable bulk of his head. But I wasn't fooled. Grindylow moved awkwardly when on land, but I knew that so long as he remained in the water this guy was fast as a shark and just as bloodthirsty.

"Treasure?" I asked, taking a step forward.

The grindylow's long, gray tongue snaked out and proceeded to prod at his eyeball, slathering it with mucous. I swallowed hard, momentarily regretting applying faerie ointment to my eyes. Without the magic infused ointment, I'd be seeing the creature's glamour, the illusion of a young, handsome prince. The story of a frog being turned into a prince came from this illusion, though knowing that didn't make the grindylow any more charming.

His body trembled with anticipation as he stared at my booted foot. I shifted my weight, the slight movement crunching gravel beneath my feet and holding his attention. Just a few inches closer and he could snatch me into the water.

"Yes, youngling," he said, flexing his hands. "Come closer and I will show you treasure and toys, and we can play such fun games together."

"Games?" I asked. I slapped my best "oh goody" look on my face, tossed my sword on the grass behind me, and dropped into a low crouch. "Let's play."

Before the grindy could snatch my leg and drag me into a watery grave, I drove a dagger down through his hand, nailing him to the ground. I rolled to the side, kicking out as I spun, smashing him in the face with one boot as I used the other to propel myself to my feet, just out of his reach.

The grindylow shrieked in pain, a ring of spiked cartilage flaring out from his neck. A second, larger fin sprung from his back while spines lifted along his arms. I shook my head and laughed at his attempts to look more threatening.

"I'm not interested in your games," I said. "I know all about your false treasure. And in case you hadn't already noticed, I'm no kid."

I raised an eyebrow at the grindylow, hands on my hips, sword back in its sheath. Not only had the creature underestimated me, but I'd taken advantage of its weakness for children. Grindylow preferred young flesh, and considered human children a delicacy. They could survive by eating fish, river rats, maybe even a few swans, if the swan maidens let down their guard, but he wouldn't be the first grindylow to go native and start hunting innocent children. And what better location than a secluded spot in a public park for luring little kids into the water?

The grindylow's eyes bulged, making him appear even more froglike. He jerked his head back and struggled to pull his hand free of the embankment.

"Let me go!" he yelled.

"I might set you free," I said, giving him a hard look. "So long as you answer my questions honestly."

He nodded rapidly.

"Yes, yes, I'll tell you what you want to know," he said. "Set me free!"

I drew a knife from a thigh sheath and he blanched, his slick skin turning a sickly gray.

"You know about the human bodies that have been turning up in the canals lately, right?" I asked.

I started to clean under my fingernails, using the tip of my knife. He nodded his head.

"Yes, I've heard, b-b-but it wasn't me," he said, voice shrill. "It wasn't me!"

I raised an eyebrow and shook my head.

"I know how much you like to eat human flesh," I said. "Why shouldn't I suspect you?"

"B-b-because we grindylow don't eat tough, old flesh," he said. "Everyone knows that!"

"So what you're saying is, you only kill children," I said, eyes narrowing.

"No!" he yelled. "No, that's not true. I eat fish, lots of fish."

I gave the grindylow a hard look, rolling my knife along my knuckles.

"Well then, if you want to convince me of that, then maybe you can point me in the direction of the killer," I said.

I wasn't convinced that this grindylow hadn't murdered the child, but I had no proof that he was a human killer other than his attempts to get me to go for a swim. If I could get him to work as an informant, I might let him live—for now.

But I'd sure as hell be keeping an eye on him.

The grindylow licked his lips, and his gaze darted back and forth. He knew he was up shit's canal and I was either going to carve him to pieces, or back off. The crux of that decision was whether or not he made himself useful.

He better hope he got a paddle and not a sword.

"Talk to the Rusalka," he said. He squirmed, mouth pulling into a frown. "That bitch Natasha knows everything that goes on in these canals."

I stared at the grindylow a few minutes longer, and then drew a syringe from the folds of my skirt. I popped the cap, knelt, and pressed the plunger as I jammed the needle into the grindylow's arm.

"What was that for?" he asked, baring his teeth. "I gave you the information you wanted."

"It's a tracking device," I said. "I'm letting you go, that was the deal, but that doesn't mean I won't be checking up on you. And if you've lied to me, I'll skin you alive and make boots out of your hide."

"Fine, then set me free!" he yelled.

I set my jaw and stared him in the eye.

"Fine," I said, shifting my weight. I could grab the knife and spin backward before the grindy had a chance to attempt revenge. I wasn't stupid. I didn't trust the little toad.

I bared my teeth, leaving the grindylow with a few parting words.

"I'll remove the knife, but you even think about eating any children while I'm here and I'll take you apart piece by piece."

If he valued his life, he'd take those words to heart. It was that or a slow, painful death. The choice was up to him.

Chapter 15

"It's funny how well you can sleep after stabbing someone."
-Jenna Lehane, Hunter

I slept late, finally catching up on much needed sleep. It's funny how well you can sleep after stabbing someone, especially when that person might be a homicidal killer. I pulled out my phone and checked the grindylow's location. He was still near Rozenhoedkaai. A grin touched my lips, but it didn't reach my eyes.

I would have liked to have done more than stab the grindylow, but I had no proof that he was our killer. The fae can't tell outright lies, but they were damned good at twisting the truth to their own purposes. My gut was telling me that he was guilty of something, and I swore that before I left town I'd discover what mischief the grindy had been up to. But right now, I needed to do some more digging into the serial murder case.

I strode to the window and looked out onto the training grounds below. There were archery targets along one of the stone walls that encircled the courtyard and Simon Chadwick was there practicing with a crossbow. I smiled and hurried as I rummaged through my things, tossing on jeans, a lightweight sweater, boots, and my leather jacket. I added the necessary accessories—knives, stakes, garrote bracelet, silver cross necklace—and headed for the door.

I looked back once and sighed. It was bright and sunny outside and I didn't want to attract attention carrying the ski bag that contained my sword, so I was leaving it behind. I cast one last longing glance at my favorite blade and closed the door.

There was just one more thing I needed from the armory. I took the stairs two at a time, the sound of my boots echoing throughout the empty stairwell. The guildhall was like a ghost town except for the fact that there weren't any actual ghosts here. The Guild must have special wards in place to keep the dead out. If I ever got on Celeste's good side, I'd have to ask her about it. That would be a handy spell to know.

I hurried into the armory, making a beeline for the tool counter. The focus of the room was weapons and armor, but the Guild also stocked other handy items. I reached for a pair of bolt cutters, but I went rigid at the scuff of shoe leather on stone.

Chadwick was outside, and Celeste should be down in the infirmary with Martens, so who was in the room with me? I spun around to see a muscular man grinning from the other side of the room and juggling two grenades. He was wearing cargo pants and a tank top which made the fact he only had one arm all the more noticeable. The other arm ended in a metal hook shaped prosthetic.

The Guild had plenty of crazy, thrill seeking types, but there was something about this guy's smile that was contagious. I returned the smile, raising an eyebrow.

"You do realize those aren't toys," I said, gesturing to the grenades he continued to juggle.

He nodded.

"And you realize breaking and entering is a crime in Belgium, yes?" he asked, in a thick Russian or Eastern European accent.

"Don't worry, I'm not going on a crime spree," I said, holding up the bolt cutters. "Just crashing a party."

"You need to blow your way in?" he asked. "Don't let the arm fool you, I'm the best demolitions guy in the city."

"I'm guessing you're also the only demolition's guy in the city," I said.

"Shhh, don't let my secret out," he said, holding his hook to his lips. "Don't tell the others. You'll ruin my reputation."

"You're secret is safe with me," I said.

"Well now, since we're keeping each other's secrets, don't you think it's time you told me your name?" he asked.

"Jenna, Jenna Lehane," I said.

"Aleksey Zharkov," he said.

He lifted his hook and it took me a minute to realize he wanted to bump knuckles. I laughed and stuck out my fist. He now held the grenades in his good hand and in the crook of his arm.

"So, we blowing shit up or what?" he asked, eyes sparkling.

I shook my head.

"Not this time," I said. "This is just a scouting run. I want to know what's behind door number one, but if door number two has more than a padlock, you'll be the first to know."

"You know where to find me," he said. "Good hunting."

I grunted my thanks and left the armory, managing to make my way out of the guildhall without running into anyone else. There'd been a close call when Chadwick had come in off the training field, but I ducked in behind a suit of armor until I no longer heard the stomping of his boots on the stairs. Chadwick might be my assigned contact here at the local Guild, but he was also a prick. I'd get more done and save more lives if I just avoided his inflated ego and sense of self entitlement.

Once on the street, I strode toward the canal. This part of the city looked different during the day, but one thing hadn't changed. The buildings on either side of the street were filled with ghosts. I avoided their staring eyes and walked faster.

I made it to the canal in less than five minutes. Once there, I looked up and down the street. Satisfied that I had no living witnesses, I jumped over the safety railing and hurried down the embankment, keeping my body low to the ground.

I came out of my crouch where the embankment ended at the narrow stone ledge. It was still covered in slimy algae and moss, but the slick stone was easier to navigate in daylight. Humming a song I'd heard in the airport yesterday, I shimmied across the ledge without incident, dropping into the darkness beneath the bridge in seconds.

I was making good time. If I was quick about it, I could explore the tunnels beyond the locked gate I'd discovered last night and be back in time for a quick shower and lunch with Ash.

I clicked on my flashlight and pulled the bolt cutters from where I'd tucked them into the back of my jeans, hidden beneath my jacket. Someone had shortened the handles, making them easier to carry, like a sawed off shotgun, but it also made them more difficult to use.

It took me a few tries before cutting completely through the padlock, but it finally dropped to the stone platform with a thud. The sound echoed down the tunnel, and I flashed my light into the darkness.

I cocked my head to the side and listened for the telltale sound of footsteps, but the only sounds were the squeak of rats and the dripping of water. Satisfied that I was alone, I wrenched the metal grid away from the opening, revealing a tunnel that was large enough for two adult humans to walk upright side-by-side.

I left the bolt cutters under the bridge and drew one of my knives. Leading with the flashlight in my left hand, I held my knife in a hammer grip, elbows at my sides. Sidestepping a pool of foul smelling liquid, I strode into the tunnel.

I gasped, nearly losing my footing as my boot hit a slick surface as slippery as ice. Damn, that was close. I did not want to end up on my ass in a sewer pipe. I grimaced, shining the light at my feet and along the walls. The tunnel was coated in thick slime.

I frowned and continued forward, gingerly stepping through the filth. In some places it looked like something had been dragged through the sludge. If it had been one of our victims, I just hoped they were already dead at the time. That liquid smelled like the ass end of an ogre.

I grit my teeth and tried to hold my breath until I started to see stars. Grimacing, I inhaled shallowly, but the sparks of light didn't go away.

"What the hell?" I muttered.

I'd come to a metal door set into the tunnel. The bottom of the door had narrow openings for allowing the flow of sewage, but the rest of the door was solid metal. I couldn't see into the tunnel beyond, but I had a feeling that the monster behind the killings had spent time here. There were bones strewn all around the door.

I lifted what may have been a femur from the floor and probed at the sparkling air in front of the door. The bone kicked out of my hand and I was flung down the tunnel, my boots sliding in the muck. I shook my head and glared at the shifting light.

Son of a bitch.

The door was sealed by magic, warded against being opened from this side. I straightened and returned to examine the area around the door more closely. There, engraved into the stone on either side of the door were a series of strange symbols.

I sighed and traced the design with my eyes. Maybe I could convince Celeste to come down here and take a look at it—if she was still talking to me. That was one bridge I probably shouldn't have burned. Funny how I managed to alienate myself from the local Guild members in less time than it takes to make a pot of coffee.

I shook my head and scowled at the magically sealed door. For now, there was nothing else I could do. I wasn't making it through that door without the help of a witch.

A skull leered at me from the pile of bones at my feet and I frowned. I'd hoped this lead would pan out, but I wasn't getting any answers from these tunnels today.

It was a dead end.

Chapter 16

"Dead bodies carry a unique smell of rot and decay that's hard to forget."
-Jenna Lehane, Hunter

A few of the restaurant patrons gave me funny looks, and I felt heat rising to my face. Did I still smell like the sewers? I had a feeling that my hasty shower hadn't been as effective as I'd hoped. It was a good thing that Ash had no sense of smell.

Then again, maybe they were just appalled at the way his scarf clashed with his hat and vest. Today he was wearing a lime green patterned scarf that looked paisley, but on closer inspection was a riot of white and red zombie unicorns. He also had on his tattered fedora with the purple and green feathers, and an orange and black pinstriped vest that made him look like some kind of Halloween mob boss.

The overall effect added to the headache, that I suspected was from my close proximity to a group of giggling ghosts who were tittering at us from behind lace hankies. I massaged my temples and ordered a black coffee and the Flemish stew.

"Will that be all?" the waiter asked.

I shrugged and waved a hand at Ash sitting across the café table.

"I don't know, ask him," I said.

The waiter looked over at Ash, who waved him off. The waiter fumbled his order pad and hastily backed away, muttering something about crazy Americans. He seemed all too happy to make his escape. Maybe I looked as grumpy as I felt.

I leaned back in my chair and let out a groan.

"Long night?" Ash asked.

"You have no idea," I said.

"I find that oddly reassuring," he said.

"How's that?" I asked.

A kid in an apron brought me my coffee, and I took a sip. It was strong and black and came with a sprinkling of chocolate. I let out a deep, gratified sigh. By Athena, that was good.

"It means, love, I'm glad you're not as stodgy as you look," he said with a wink.

"Stodgy?" I asked.

"Aye, priggish," he said.

I rolled my eyes.

"If you're going to insult me, at least speak English," I muttered into my coffee cup.

Ash smiled and leaned forward.

"So, tell me all the gory details," he said.

"About what?" I asked.

"Your night on the town," he said. "What do you think of Bruges?"

I tilted my head, considering my night. I'd been attacked by a canal spider, rummaged through some old bones, hung out with a disemboweled child, and stabbed a grindylow. But I was pretty sure those weren't the kind of gory details Ash was after.

"I almost fell in the canal," I said, a grin tugging at my lips.

His eyes gleamed, and one of his eyebrows became lost beneath the brim of his hat.

"And?" he asked.

"And now I have a headache," I said.

He let out a pleased laugh.

"You'll have to let me show you a night on the town before you scamper," he said.

I shook my head.

"I don't think you could handle a night with me," I said.

"Is that an invitation?" he asked.

I let out a strangled *ngh*.

"You are the most..." I started, at a loss for words.

"Handsome, charming, witty," he said.

"I was thinking more like arrogant and irritating," I said, stabbing at my food.

The dish had appeared seconds before, delivered by a wide-eyed bus boy who obviously didn't want to get caught in our argument. I scowled and chewed the chunks of meat and vegetables. Why did every conversation with Ash have to turn into an argument?

More importantly, what was I doing still hanging out with the guy?

"Hey," I said, narrowing my eyes at Ash. "I thought the whole point of this lunch was me paying off my debt. Aren't you going to eat something? It's on my dime."

Yes, he'd won our race to the top of the bell tower. I had no idea how that was possible. The way the guy smoked, he should have been winded after the first hundred steps or so.

"No, love," he said. "You can pay me back with a walk along Minnewater Lake."

The Lake of Love? He had to be kidding. But that had been where I'd seen a gathering of swan maidens yesterday. Now that I was wearing faerie ointment, there was a good chance I'd be able to see what the fae were up to. With Ash at my side, we'd look like just another young couple hell-bent on a romantic walk.

"Fine," I said, letting out a sigh. "But that's it. I told you before. I'm not on vacation."

"I know, I know," he said, waving his hand dismissively. "But all work and no play make Jenna a stodgy girl."

I scraped my bowl clean and eyed my coffee cup longingly, but I didn't have all day to sit around on my ass. I needed to figure out what was going on in this city's supernatural community before another body turned up in the canals.

At least I wouldn't have to listen to those tittering ghosts anymore. I stood and dropped a few Euro notes on the table, and muttered, "so what's so goddamned funny?" as I passed their table. That just made the ghosts laugh harder. A couple at the next table over looked apoplectic, but they kept their eyes studiously averted.

I shook my head. Damn ghosts. They had a habit of making me look like a crazy person.

I hurried away from the café, following Ash down a familiar street. We were heading back in the direction we'd come yesterday on our walk from the train station. I smiled, noting a few recognizable landmarks. I was finally starting to get the hang of this place.

But when we turned the corner, near a fountain with carved horse heads, the stretch of green along the canal was empty. I hurried to a nearby railing, leaning as far as I could to get a look at the water below. There was nothing here but a handful of ducks and a mundane pair of swans.

The swan maidens were gone.

"What's the matter, love?" Ash asked, leaning against the railing.

He looked like he was posing for a fashion magazine, though I doubted even runway models would be caught dead wearing that outfit.

"Where are the swans?" I asked, hurrying along the railing for a better look.

Ash sighed, but followed.

"They're right there," he said, pointing at the two white birds swimming below.

It was my turn to sigh. I grit my teeth and tried not to snap at him. It wasn't completely his fault. It's not like I could tell him that the birds I was looking for were really shapeshifting faeries.

"But, there were a lot more of them yesterday," I said.

Something had the swan maidens spooked.

"You have a point," he said, scanning the shore for signs of the elusive water fowl. The skin around his eyes tightened and he frowned, but when he turned around again the look was gone.

"Oh well," I said with a shrug. "I guess I should have taken a better look at them yesterday."

"Bit difficult to admire the beauty of the city's heraldic bird when you're throwing yourself in front of a moving carriage," he said with a smirk.

"Damn it, Ash," I said, shaking my head. "That was an accident."

"Well then, we'll have to be careful on our walk," he said, holding out his arm. "We don't want any more accidents."

I pushed past, ignoring his arm, and walked down toward the lake. But as we stepped onto the bridge that sat just above the lock gate, where the canal met Minnewater Lake, I was hit with a vile stench and this time it had nothing to do with the sewers.

The smell of death was unmistakable. Dead bodies carry a unique smell of rot and decay that's hard to forget. Unfortunately, I'd been around my fair share of dead people.

There had been another murder. I was sure of it.

Chapter 17

"You never can be too careful with a supernatural predator on the loose."
-Jenna Lehane, Hunter

I had to wait until later that evening to investigate the lock gate. During the daytime Minnewater Park was filled with tourists. But now the place was still as the grave.

I shivered, pulling up the neck of my leather jacket. Night had fallen and lanterns cast the mouths of doorways and alleys into ink black shadow.

Standing in a secluded spot beside the back wall of the Beguinage, I watched for any sign of movement. You never can be too careful with a supernatural predator on the loose—I wasn't the only hunter who stalked the city at night.

Mist rolled in off the lake, swallowing the landscape. It took patience, but I studied the shifting fog until I was certain of my surroundings.

The swan maidens were gone. Wherever they'd flown off to, they weren't yet ready to come out of hiding. If what I'd smelled earlier was any indication, I couldn't blame them. Swan maidens thrive on the happy energy that humans give off when they're in love or lust, but someone had left a nasty little gift in their love nest.

There's nothing like a dead body to ruin the mood.

Satisfied that there were no obvious threats, I slipped through the shadows toward the lock gate. Instead of walking out onto the stone bridge, I slung a leg over the metal railing designed to keep tourists from disturbing the swans. Once I was past the railing, I crouched and moved down to the water's edge.

Looking back the way I'd come, I checked the street one more time before turning on my flashlight. I directed the beam of light under the bridge to the lock gate itself. There was an assortment of floating detritus; grass clippings, leaves, a Styrofoam cup—and a dead body.

I shook my head and swore. I'd hoped that it would be the body of a river rat, or maybe even a dead swan, but the victim was human. Our killer had taken another life.

I turned off the flashlight and dialed the one person who could help me retrieve a body and transport it back to the Guild's morgue.

"Hello?" Benjamin Martens' sleepy voice answered.

"What's up, Doc?" I asked.

"A boot up your ass is what's up," he said. "Do you have any idea what time it is?"

I heard the sound of fabric against vinyl as he sat up. Martens must have fallen asleep on the cheap couch in the infirmary's waiting room.

"Yes, it's time you got your grouchy old ass down to the lock gate at Minnewater Lake," I said.

"And why the hell would I do that?" he asked.

"Because we have ourselves another dead body," I said.

Martens swore and hung up. I guess the guy wasn't a morning person. Or, maybe he just didn't like me very much. I'd given him a hard time about the lack of information in his autopsy reports and then tossed him the responsibility of getting Celeste sober. I probably wasn't his favorite person right now.

While I waited for the doctor, I snapped off pictures of the crime scene with my cell phone and poked around the embankment. When Martens pulled up with the Guild's hearse, I'd already pulled a branch down from a nearby tree and used it to steer the body to shore.

"You better not be wasting my time with someone's dead cat," Martens said, stumbling down the embankment.

"I know what a dead body looks like, Doc," I said. I tapped my foot, fidgeting with the branch in my hand. "Can I bring *the body* on shore?"

I'd waited for the doctor out of respect for his position within the Guild, but now I wondered why I even bothered. His shirt buttons were done up wrong, and he smelled like cheap beer. He nodded an affirmative and swayed on his feet.

I shook my head and grabbed hold of the corpse, dragging it onto shore. At another nod from Martens, I flipped the body over. Martens let out a heavy sigh.

"Come on," he said. "Help me get this up to the hearse. We need better light than this if I'm going to determine cause of death."

From the look of the body, I'd say we needed a garden hose. The dead man, or woman, was covered in mud, matted leaves, and darker stains that were probably blood. I'd hoped to learn more about our killer as soon as we pulled the victim from the canal, but Martens was right. We needed to get the body back to the morgue.

I nodded and we proceeded to do the grisly job of hoisting the waterlogged corpse into a body bag, onto a portable stretcher, and carrying it up the embankment. Once we had it safely stored inside the hearse, with none of the citizens of Bruges the wiser, I smiled.

"Good thing you had a hearse," I said. "I'd hate to try getting a body into most of the compact cars you guys drive here."

"It's the Guild's," he said. "Comes in handy for situations like these."

I started to walk toward the passenger door, but Martens shook his head.

"You're going to have to ride in the far back," he said.

"With the corpse?" I asked, incredulous.

"Sorry, no room up here," he said.

It was then that I noticed the sleeping bag in the back seat along with a basket of clothes and empty food wrappers.

"You living in here, Doc?" I asked.

There were also kid's things in the front seat, a discarded doll and some books. Was he living here with his kid? I shook my head and walked to the back of the hearse. With a frustrated growl, I climbed in, pulled the door shut, and slid in next to the body.

I tried breathing in through my mouth, ignoring the swampy, fishy smell of the canal and the putrid stench of death.

"Things have been tough since my wife died," Martens said, pulling away from the curb.

His words were a welcome distraction and I tried to ignore my seat mate.

"Sorry," I said.

"Don't be," he said. "She was a Hunter, she knew the risks."

Silence descended on the hearse, but I had no idea what to say to lighten the mood. I was much better at killing monsters than dealing with people.

At the Guild, Martens pulled the hearse into an underground garage with a bay door that led directly into the morgue. When he turned the motor off, I hopped out and helped him with the body. I was anxious to find out if this victim could give us some answers, but Martens paused before going further into the building.

"Look, you seem like a good kid," he said. "I know you want to make a name for yourself while you're here. It's as a plain as day that you have something to prove. But keep in mind that you're a long way from home, and Master Peeters isn't here to roll out the welcome wagon. So let me give you a word of advice; stay off Chad's radar."

"Are you telling me not to do my job?" I asked, folding my arms across my chest.

"I'm telling you to keep your head down," he said. "Chad's a zealot who hates women in the guild almost as much as he hates supernaturals."

"Like witches," I said.

What he said about Chadwick tracked. I'd seen how the guy treated Celeste. I wouldn't be surprised if he was partly responsible for her Mandragora addiction.

"Precisely," he said, nodding. "He says that women and supernaturals dilute the purity of the Guild. He won't stand by and watch as some girl steals his limelight."

I grimaced and shook my head.

"This isn't a game I can throw," I said. "These are people's lives at stake. I'm not backing down because some prick has a problem with women."

"Well, do your best to stay away from him while you're here," he said. "He's trouble and I don't trust him."

"I'm a big girl," I said with more confidence than I was feeling. "I've dealt with macho assholes before, but thanks for the heads-up."

He nodded and we got back to work. Once we had the corpse on the autopsy table, Martens unzipped the body bag. I took a step back, wrinkling my nose at the stench.

Martens pulled down a hose and started rinsing off the body, making notes into a recording device as he worked. When he came to the victim's neck, he paused.

"What?" I asked, leaning forward. "Did you find something?"

"Hold on, let me get a better look," he said. He examined the neck with a handheld magnifier and sighed. "Here, take a look."

Martens stepped out of the way and offered me the magnifier, but I didn't need it. I'd seen plenty of bite marks that matched the puncture wounds on the victim's neck. It looked like our serial murders were the work of vampires.

Vampires, of course it was vampires.

CHAPTER 18

"Faeries love to bargain, and that desire can become their downfall."
-Jenna Lehane, Hunter

Now that I knew vamps were to blame, their involvement seemed obvious. I should have figured it out sooner. The clues were dotted here and there like blood splatters.

I wanted to grab the Guild's witch and run out and bust through that magic ward in the sewers, but Martens reminded me that Celeste was still recovering from the withdrawal symptoms, that were a result of my meddling. He insisted I give the young woman one more night to recover. I'd grumbled, but the doctor didn't back down.

That's what I got for trying to be helpful. With a heavy sigh, I geared up and headed out to have a little chat with the local supernatural gossip. If I couldn't stake some vamps, then at least I could arm myself with knowledge about the local supernatural hierarchy.

A quick call to Darryl Lambert, the Guild archivist, confirmed that the rusalka Natasha could usually be found down near the boat docks. So now here I was, overlooking the docks, crouching in the shadow of the Blinde-Ezelstraat bridge.

At the bottom of a flight of wooden steps, bathed in the glow of a streetlight, sat a beautiful woman with pale skin and emerald green hair. She dipped her feet into the canal and her skin sprouted iridescent green and blue fish scales wherever the water touched. The rhythmic shifting of color as she splashed her feet was hypnotic, and I shook my head.

Rusalki were not overly powerful faeries, but that didn't mean the water nymph wasn't deadly. Like mermaids, rusalki use their beauty and the magic of their voices to lure their victims into a watery grave.

Natasha was sitting combing her hair, and she appeared to be alone. I wasn't afraid of one rusalka, but I wasn't so confident of my odds if her sisters showed up to the party. I better keep this brief.

I pasted on a smile, checked the draw of my iron dagger, and strode out of the shadows onto Huidenvettersplein. At the top of the stairs, I paused, waiting for the rusalka to acknowledge my presence.

"Hail, Natasha," I said. "I've come to bargain for information."

The comb in Natasha's hand froze mid-stroke, and she turned to face me. She licked her lips and beckoned me forward. Faeries love to bargain, and that desire can become their downfall. I could tell that I already had this water fae's attention—hook, line, and sinker.

The woman was beautiful, but there was no warmth in her smile. Her eyes were glowing chips of ice, and her lips were the color of frozen blood.

"What answers do you seek Hunter?" she asked.

Her voice was like beautiful music burbling from her lips and I had to dig my fingernails into the palm of my hand to stay focused. By Athena, she wasn't even singing.

"I want to know about the bodies in the canals," I said.

"And what will you give me in return?" she asked.

She wet her lips and languidly stretched and crossed her legs, showing off her body to perfection. Luckily for me, I wasn't into women, or trading sex for secrets. That was a downward spiral that, in this case, would lead me to the bottom of the canal.

"How about I promise not to kill you," I said.

Her eyes blazed with green light, and she hissed.

"You dare threaten me on the threshold of my home?" she asked.

"Think of it as buying an insurance policy," I said.

Of course, if I found out that Natasha was killing innocent humans, I'd make sure she ended up dead. By the terms of the bargain, her death couldn't be by my hand. That didn't mean I couldn't enlist another Hunter to do the job.

She tilted her head, considering the offer. Finally, she laughed and nodded.

"Very well," she said. "You promise not to harm me, or my sisters, and I will give you information about the killings."

Crap, I hadn't planned on giving her sisters a free pass, but there it was. It was nearly impossible to out bargain a faerie.

"Done," I said.

"The undead are draining humans and dumping the bodies in the canals," she said.

"Vampires," I said, spitting out the word.

"Yes," she said.

"Some vampires are dumping bodies while some of the ghoul servants are being more careful," she said.

"More careful?" I asked.

"Yes," she said, the cadence of her voice was like the hypnotic rise and fall of waves. "The ghouls dump only the bones they've stripped bare of flesh."

So, the ghouls were better at cleaning up the table scraps? Good for them. Ghouls were just the vampire's servants. I wanted the ones doing the killings.

I paced the dock, keeping a wary eye on the rusalka.

"Where can I find these vampires?" I asked. "Are they down in the sewers?"

"There are vampires in the sewers, yes," she said. "The undead prefer the lightless tunnels to the city streets."

I knew it! I pounded my fist into my other hand. Damned leeches. The bastards must be using that magically sealed sewer tunnel for dumping the bodies into the canals. I needed to get Celeste to help me take down that ward tomorrow. We couldn't allow another night of killings.

I blinked, realizing that I still had no idea why the local vamps had changed their feeding habits.

"Any idea why the vampires are on a killing spree?" I asked.

Natasha leaned forward, a slow smile building on her lips.

"Perhaps a better question is, why one of your Hunters is helping them?" she said.

There was a traitor in our midst.

"No," I gasped.

She threw her head back and laughed. I turned away, hurrying back to the Guild, the rusalka's laughter hounding my footsteps.

CHAPTER 19

"Faeries cannot tell an outright lie, but they sure as shit know how to manipulate."

-Jenna Lehane, Hunter

I took a deep breath and bent down, hands on my knees. *Come on, Jenna, calm the hell down.* Running blindly through the streets wasn't going to do anyone any good. Neither was bursting into the Guild and pointing fingers.

I couldn't let Natasha's words make me sloppy. Faeries cannot tell an outright lie, but they sure as shit know how to manipulate.

"I am nobody's pawn," I muttered.

But my mind was already racing, analyzing every member of the local Guild. Who was doing the vampire's dirty work? Benjamin Martens' autopsy reports had lacked crucial details, and he was living out of the company hearse, so he obviously could use the money. That made him a suspect, though he wasn't the only one.

Was Celeste's Mandragora addiction a means of stifling the pain of guilt? Or, perhaps she owed her drug supplier more money than she made hunting monsters. It was hard to say.

It was even harder to see how Darryl Lambert could be our traitor, though in his service to the Guild he'd lost something irreplaceable. Perhaps behind that friendly smile lay an angry man with a vendetta.

Then there was Chad. Simon Chadwick was an asshole, and Martens didn't trust him. For that matter, neither did I. But would someone like Chadwick set his ideals, twisted as they may be, aside to betray the Guild?

Maybe the demolitions expert was a more logical choice for traitor. Aleksey Zharkov was obviously a thrill seeker, and, from what I'd seen, the Guild hadn't provided him with the best prosthetic money could buy. It wasn't too much of a stretch to see Zharkov playing the double agent.

I shook my head. I'd heard about paying an arm and a leg, but these theories were getting outrageous. I rubbed my face. I'm sure this would all make more sense after a good night's sleep.

"Help!"

A woman's scream pierced the night and all thoughts of sleep fled as adrenaline pumped through my body. I sprinted down the street in the direction of the woman's cry, scanning the sidewalks and alleyways, and listening for any sign of trouble.

"Please, somebody help me!"

The voice was weaker now, but I nodded to myself, suddenly sure of where the attack was taking place. I put on more speed, vaulted over a metal railing, and raced down the embankment toward the canal. The woman's scream had come from beneath the bridge—the same bridge that hid the mouth of the sewer tunnel with the bloody grate and magically warded door.

I palmed a silver combat knife and a wooden stake as I ran, a fierce snarl curling my lips. I was not going to allow another vampire kill. Not on my watch.

Heart pounding, I eyed the narrow ledge leading into the dancing shadows beneath the bridge. There was no way I could make my way across that expanse of moss slick stone without discarding my weapons.

"Damn," I muttered.

I shoved the wooden stake into a loop in my battle skirt and bit down on the silver knife, holding it between my teeth. I'd need both hands free to make the climb to the bridge. If I was dealing with vamps, I'd rather lead with the stake, but there was a chance that this was a mugging or rape. Vampires weren't the only monsters that preyed on the weak.

It would be foolish to bring a stake to a knife fight. Everyone knows that.

Shoulders tight, I shimmied across the ledge. I was exposed, vulnerable, but the whimpering sound ahead of me kept me going. As my foot hit the wet platform with a splash, a clawed hand grabbed my leg in an iron grip.

My attacker wasn't human.

I slashed out with the silver knife and the hand retreated, leaving behind a searing pain in my calf where the creature's talons had punctured flesh. Working fast, I retrieved the wooden stake, and with a flick of the wrist, turned on my flashlight and tossed it into the shadows. The flashlight spun, illuminating a crumpled heap near the iron grate and three vampires: one to my left, one to my right, and one scuttling along the ceiling like a cockroach.

It was a goddamned ambush.

I didn't know if the woman crumpled on the ground was still alive or not. Her cries had ceased, but there was nothing I could do for her at the moment. I was too busy trying to stay alive.

I spun to the left, slashing upward with the silver knife. The vamp on the ceiling hissed and scuttled to the right, giving me some breathing room. I shivered, my subconscious mind reeling in horror. These vamps weren't even bothering to maintain a glamour. Instead of being drop dead gorgeous, these guys were just dead—as in mummified.

Skin the color and texture of dried parchment was stretched tightly over skeletal bodies that moved with an insectile, alien grace, but their grinning faces were the worst. I've seen a lot of monsters during my time as a Hunter, but there's something about the fanged, rictus grin of a vampire that gives a girl chills—and not the romantic kind.

As soon as a vampire dies its first death, their body begins to dehydrate. It's part of what makes them appear so monstrous in their true form. There's just something nauseating about seeing such a grotesque caricature of a human moving around animated with life.

These vamps with their empty eye sockets and gaping sinus cavities were a prime example. As a vampire's body deteriorates, the soft tissue is the first to go, which makes for some butt ugly vampires. Drinking blood helps, but nothing can fully restore life, not even necromancy. Vamps are nothing more than dried up, walking corpses.

Too bad their desiccated bodies don't slow them down.

If I was going to survive this, I'd have to out think my opponents. I feigned a minor stumble, and the vamp on my left didn't hesitate. The monster lunged in, fangs bared, the hollow pits of his eyes intent on my jugular. *One, two, three...*

He closed the distance and I thrust the wooden stake up beneath his ribcage and into his chest cavity. The vamp froze, completely paralyzed, and I knew I'd staked him through the heart. It wouldn't kill him, but it would keep him out of the fight until I had the time to finish him off—and add his fangs to my necklace.

I grinned, showing my own small, white teeth.

"Okay, boys," I said. "Who's next?"

I drew my sword, now glad I'd worn my hunting gear to my visit with the rusalka. I'd had a feeling I might need my favorite blade. I guess I was right.

Lightning fast, the vamp struck. One second he was circling to my right trying to flank me, and the next he was tearing away a chunk of my flesh. The iron and silver coated steel boning of my corset deflected the worst of the attack, but one of his talons managed to slash through the space between.

I heard the sizzle of his claws, knowing the silver was eating away at the tips of the talons that scored across my abdomen and flank. I let out a satisfied grunt, but the zing of pleasure was premature.

Hot blood leaked from my side and the two vampires shrieked in hunger. *Shit.* The blood was stirring them into a feeding frenzy. I had to end this now, or I'd be the body they'd find in the canal tomorrow.

I drove my sword through the air, separating the vampire's head from his body. The creature continued to cling to the ceiling for a moment, but when the head hit the cement with a meaty thud, both pieces of the beast burst into ash.

The sound of the vamp's falling head still echoed throughout the chamber beneath the bridge as ash fell like grisly snow. The remaining vamp and I warily circled each other, searching for a weakness. Vampires like to play with their food, but I didn't kid myself. Saliva was dripping from his elongated fangs and a leathery tongue darted out to lick dry, papery lips.

If I gave this one the opportunity, he'd go straight for the kill.

I struggled to keep my sword up and shifted my weight to allow for the wounds in my leg and side. I swallowed hard and grit my teeth. Every move tugged at the edges of the gash in my side, making it burn and bleed.

My knuckles whitened as I increased the grip on my sword, readying for the kill.

"Jenna!" a familiar voice cried out. "Behind you!"

I dropped to the ground and rolled, never hesitating. As I came to my feet, I faced not one vamp, but two. A female, judging from the sagging breasts, had joined the party. I flicked my eyes to the ground where the "victim" had been curled up just moments before.

The woman was gone.

"You smell delicious, ma chérie," said the female vampire.

Oh yeah, this had been a trap from the very beginning. I let out a low growl, but it was cut short by movement over the vamp's shoulder. Ash was running down the embankment, reaching into his guitar case as he rushed toward us.

No! The fool, what was he going to do, bash them over the head with his guitar? But I lost sight of Ash as the male vamp lunged from the side, barreling into me like a freight train. My head hit the stone wall with a sickening crack and the chamber fell out of focus.

"Jenna!" Ash cried.

I blinked rapidly, clearing my vision. The vamp was tearing at my leather jacket, trying to get to my neck, but he was slowed by the silver mesh I'd sewn into the collar's lining. I pulled a stake from my belt, turned it in my fist, and shoved it up through his gut for all I was worth.

Once the vamp was paralyzed, I used my sword to take his head. A rancid death rattle passed his lips before he exploded in a cloud of ash. Duh, duh, duh, another one bites the dust. The old rock song ran in the background, my addled brain giving the moment a ridiculous soundtrack. I snorted and shook my head.

Big mistake.

I dropped my sword with a gasp. The bridge above my head started spinning, and I bit the inside of my cheek to make it stop. Either I'd suffered a minor concussion, or I'd lost more blood than I thought. Either way it was time to get up and save Ash's ass before the idiot became the female vamp's dinner date.

Knees wobbly, I grabbed hold of the damp, stone wall and pulled myself upright. I blinked, staring open mouthed at the scene before me. The female vamp was immobile, staked to the ground, and Ash faced off against three more vamps who were pouring out of the tunnel like sewer rats.

I grabbed my sword and rushed forward as the first vamp went down beneath Ash's blade. He hadn't been carrying a musical instrument in his guitar case. He'd been carrying a sword. We fought alongside each other, slipping into the easy rhythm of practiced movements.

It was a good thing I went through my kata daily. After that blow to the head, I was letting muscle memory lead my sword through each block and stab.

As the last vamp exploded in a cloud of ash and dust, I turned to study the man at my side. He wiped his sword on the pants of one of the two staked vampires, who were still staring blindly from the ground where we'd left them, and he flashed a rueful grin from beneath his ridiculous hat. We were close in age, with Ash being just a few years older, and he moved with a strength and grace I hadn't noticed until now.

I shook my head. There was no mistaking it.

Ash was a Hunter.

"Son of a bitch."

CHAPTER 20

"Interrogations don't go so well when the person asking the questions is hunched over in pain."
-Jenna Lehane, Hunter

"You and I are going to talk," I said, narrowing my eyes at Ash.

He sighed and moved away from where I stood, keeping his eyes on the vampires we'd left staked on the ground. There was nothing left of the other vampires, nothing but dust and ash.

"Right, then," Ash said, nudging the female vamp with the toe of his boot. "What should we do with these two?"

I crouched down beside the vamps and shone the flashlight along their bodies. Now that the only thing they had left to plead with was their eyes, they'd grabbed hold of their glamour, making them look like young fashion models. I guess trying to plead with empty eye sockets was less effective.

But even with the vamps staked into immobility, I was careful not to hold their gaze. The last thing we needed was to become mesmerized into setting them free. That would not end well.

I slipped on a pair of gloves and, wrinkling my nose in disgust, proceeded to run my hands through their hair, down their bodies, and inside the pockets of their clothes. All I found was a strange ridge of scar tissue on the small of their backs.

"Help me roll them over," I said.

I flipped the female vamp face down and dragged one of my arms across my forehead to wipe sweat from my eyes.

"What the blue blazes is that?" Ash asked, pointing at the male vampire's lower back.

There, like a tramp stamp, on the back of both vampires, was a strange symbol like a fleur-de-lis.

"They've been marked," I said. Ash raised an eyebrow, and I continued on. "Some vampire masters mark their people."

"Like branding cattle," he said.

"Yes, except a cattle brand would set a fanghead on fire," I said. "Not a smart thing to do to one's property. So instead, they use silver."

"Bloody hell, they carve their mark into the vamp's flesh and pack silver under the skin?" he asked.

"Yes," I said, snapping off a picture of the markings with my phone. The pictures might help us identify which vampire master we were dealing with.

Ash dragged over the last vamp, one of the ones to pour out of the tunnel. I'd nearly forgotten about the vamp, since he was nearly real dead. His head dangled oddly, partly severed from his body. I grimaced, but at least there wasn't much blood. This vampire hadn't fed recently.

Ash unceremoniously rolled him over, face first into a puddle, and pulled up the man's shirt. My eyes widened as I leaned down for a closer look.

"That's interesting," I said, shining the flashlight on the vampire's back.

"Is that a lion?" Ash asked, tilting his head to the side.

That was a good question. Better yet, why was this marking different from the others?

"I wonder what the different markings mean," I said, taking a picture of the lion shaped symbol.

"Maybe different ranks within the nest?" he asked.

I brought my sword down across the vamp's neck, finishing him off, and went over to do the same to the other two.

"Maybe," I said with a shrug.

I sheathed my sword and began sifting through the ash.

"What are you looking for now?" he asked. "I thought you already searched the bodies."

"Fangs," I said, voice tight.

"What bloody for?" he asked.

I looked up and held his gaze. His brow wrinkled, but my emotions were too raw, too confused by the night's events for that kind of sharing. Some things are best left unsaid.

Eyes never leaving his, I lifted the necklace of fangs from inside my shirt and let it hang out for him to see plainly. I shrugged with one shoulder and looked away.

"We all have our secrets," I said.

He winced.

"Aye, that we do, love," he said, wearily. "That we do."

*****

After retrieving the fangs, and kicking the piles of ash into the canal, we began the slow trek up the embankment. I was moving stiffly, the wounds in my leg and side bothering me more than I'd like to admit.

"Those vamps knew who and what you were, and they knew your weakness," Ash said.

"My weakness?" I asked, frowning.

"Aye, love, that idiot drive you have that has you rushing headlong into danger at the slightest hint an innocent human might be in harm's way," he said.

I grunted, cheeks warming. Oh, that weakness.

"If I had a weakness, which I'm not admitting I do," I said, scowling at Ash. "How could they know that? I only just arrived in the city. Even I didn't know I was coming here until a few days ago. It's not like my being here is public knowledge. And someone would have had to meet me, or have eyes on me, to know whether or not that ruse of theirs would work."

That left an informant.

"Well someone told them about you," he said.

It had to be one of my fellow Guild brethren or the one supernatural gossip who knew that a new Hunter was in town.

"Damn, Natasha," I swore, shaking my head. "Looks like I need to have a chat with a certain rusalka."

"That can wait," he said. "Let's go get you cleaned up."

I snarled and he backed away, hands in the air.

"Fine, your bloody funeral," he said.

I stomped down toward the docks, forcing myself to stand up straight as I walked. Interrogations don't go so well when the person asking the questions is hunched over in pain. I lifted my chin, palming one of my knives. I wanted answers and the rusalka was going to give them to me.

Chapter 21

"Last I checked decapitating vampires wasn't part of college curriculum."
-Jenna Lehane, Hunter

The talk with the rusalka didn't turn up much. She was dead. Something was going on here, but I didn't have enough pieces of the puzzle. Not yet.

I was bone tired, and the gash in my side was starting to throb. I needed to sterilize it before infection set in. It's not like I'd been crawling around the cleanest places this evening.

But first, Ash and I were going to have a little talk. As we passed through the Burg, I led us to the bench where I'd eaten frites my first day in Bruges. Ash sat, but I stayed on my feet.

"Talk," I said, narrowing my eyes and sliding into a fighting stance.

The rusalka was dead, but that didn't mean there wouldn't be any interrogations tonight. Ash wasn't leaving that bench until I got some answers.

"So, you've caught me out, eh?" he asked.

He sat fidgeting with his hat and I nodded.

"You're a Hunter," I said.

"Good, it's better you know," he said. "I'm a dreadful liar, especially when a pretty girl is involved."

I ignored the compliment, recognizing it for the distraction he intended. Ash wasn't getting off that easy.

"You said you were a university student," I said. "But last I checked decapitating vampires wasn't part of college curriculum."

"You noticed that then?" he said, wry grin on his lips.

"Yes, I also couldn't help but notice the blade you used to do it with," I said. "And I'm pretty sure most students don't carry swords in their guitar case."

Ash sighed and ran a hand through his hair.

"Look, I used to be a Hunter," he said. He looked down at the dew damp cobbles and sighed. "That's where I learned to use a sword...and how I know about supes."

"You left the Guild?" I asked, eyes wide.

He winced and rubbed the back of his neck.

"I know I owe you an explanation, but can we do this tomorrow?" he asked.

"Fine, but you have some explaining to do, buster," I said. "I want answers, not fiction."

"Understood," he said. He pulled himself to his feet and put the rumpled fedora back on his head. One of the feathers was bent at a funny angle as a result of our battle with the vampires, and suddenly all of the cuts, holes, and tears on that silly hat made sense. "But let's get you back to the Guild before someone notices you're bleeding."

I was wearing black, and we hadn't met any humans walking around on the streets this late at night, but Ash was right. It would be foolish to stay out here with a wound I couldn't explain. If the local authorities got involved, they'd probably also notice that my sword wasn't some cheap replica, and that Ash and I were both packing deadly weapons. The Guild had the kind of clout that could get us free eventually, but I didn't fancy the idea of a night in jail.

I grunted and hurried toward Genthof which eventually became Carmersstraat, the street the guildhall was on. We walked in silence, both of us deep in our own thoughts. When we reached the Guild, I turned to Ash and cleared my throat.

"Are you coming in?" I asked.

"No," he said, shoving his hands into his pockets.

"No you won't, or no you can't?" I asked.

I wanted to know more about his break with the Guild. The Guild was my family, my life. I couldn't imagine just up and leaving it.

"I'm no longer an active member of the Guild, Jenna," he said. "I...I'm not welcome here. And the Guild is good at keeping out those it doesn't want inside its halls."

I sighed. That was true. The Guild was built on rules. If Ash was no longer a member, he wouldn't be allowed beyond the threshold. I could just imagine what a prick someone like Chadwick would be if we just strolled inside.

"Okay," I said. I shrugged, but winced, the motion tugging the ragged gash on my side. "See you around."

"Good hunting, Jenna," he said.

"Good hunting, Ash," I said.

I walked into the guildhall, for once feeling more alone inside its walls than the first day the Guild had shown up and rescued me from another five years in the child welfare system. Somewhere in this building was a traitor, perhaps the same person who'd sold me out and given the vampires the information they needed to set up that ambush.

The door snapped closed, cutting off the light from the street and the last glimpse of Ash, the man who'd just saved my life—a man who had once been a Hunter. I shook my head and limped toward the infirmary. I was too damned worn out to figure out what it all meant.

Chapter 22

"It's amazing how fast you can run with enough adrenaline coursing through your veins."
-Jenna Lehane, Hunter

Simon Chadwick, my local Guild liaison and downright pain in the ass, stepped out from behind a marble column and halted my shuffling walk across the lobby. I tried to straighten, but hissed at the pain in my side.

"Where have you been?" he asked. "Do you have any idea what time it is?"

"It's late, Chad," I said. "Give it a rest."

I wobbled on my feet, the room beginning to spin. I limped over to the stairs. That way I'd have something to grab onto if I passed out.

"What's that?" he asked. "Are you injured?"

He scowled and pointed at the blood dripping from the gash in my side. I may have survived the ambush, and won the fight, but the vampires had left me a parting gift.

"It's nothing," I lied.

"Foolish woman, you're bleeding all over the floor," he said. "Don't you realize you're wounded? Come on. We better get you cleaned up."

I sighed, but I didn't have the energy to argue. I was pretty sure that I needed stitches and the ones I'd get in the infirmary would be better than what I could accomplish with a first aid kit up in my room.

"Fine," I said.

I grit my teeth as Chad led me down to the infirmary. He lectured me the entire way, and by the time we made it inside, I was ready to strangle the prick.

"Take a seat over there," he said, indicating a bed draped with a white sheet.

"I'm sure Martens doesn't want blood..." I said.

"Shut up and sit down," he said, cutting me off.

I frowned, but managed to limp over to the infirmary bed. Chadwick disappeared into the back room, and I waited for Doc Martens.

A chill breeze shifted the white curtains that hung between the bed, making them wave and dance. I shivered, seeing a dead man walk past the infirmary door. It was strange, but until now I hadn't noticed that the only ghosts in this building were down in the lower level. The morgue always attracted the dead, but it seemed odd that I'd never seen any ghosts in the dormitories.

I was jolted out of my thoughts by the clatter of metal instruments as a metal pan was tossed onto a rolling tray beside the bed. Chadwick stood over me, rolling up his sleeves, a strange glint in his eyes.

"Come on," he said. "Let's have a look."

I frowned, trying to make sense of his words. He shook his head and gave a quick, disgusted snort.

"Why, Lord, do you test me like this?" he asked, turning his gaze to the ceiling. "Women are so...so stupid." He turned his attention back to me and sneered. "I need to take a look at your wounds. Lift. Your. Shirt."

"Wait...where's Martens?" I asked.

"He's down in the garage, passed out drunk in the hearse, the freak," he said. He shook his head, a hard smile on his lips. "I don't know how he can sleep in that thing. The man's not right in the head."

If Chadwick thought he was going to get to play doctor, he wasn't right in the head either. I winced and put a hand on my side, feigning a twinge of pain. It wasn't hard. My entire side was on fire.

Chadwick's lips parted and I swear he started panting as his eyes slid down from my face. I was pretty sure my pain turned him on. While Chadwick's eyes strayed to my chest, I palmed a knife in one hand and managed to grip a wooden stake in the other.

I shifted my weight, ready to bolt, and bit the inside of my cheek, determined not to pass out. I had a feeling Chad would just love having a vulnerable woman fall into his lap. I shuddered and lifted my chin.

"Get fanged, Chad," I said. "If Martens isn't here, I'm heading to my room. He can take care of the cuts in the morning."

"You're not going anywhere," he said, nostrils flaring.

"Get out of my way, Chad, or I'll scream," I said.

"Go ahead and scream," he said, a smirk on his mottled face. "We're all the way down in the basement. No one will hear you."

He leaned in aggressively and I could smell garlic on his breath. Maybe if he brushed his teeth, he might have more luck with women. He reached for my boob and I growled. No, probably not.

I slashed at his reaching hand and drove the blunt end of the stake into his manly bits. He dropped, collapsing into a ball on the floor. I knocked the rolling tray of medical instruments over onto his head and ran, my boots squeaking on the recently polished floors.

I ran, gripping my knife and stake in white knuckled fists, the pain from my wounds forgotten. It's amazing how fast you can run with enough adrenaline coursing through your veins.

I could hear Chad's guttural roar of rage coming from the infirmary as I made my way across the lobby. Hands shaking, I reached for the door to the outside. I blinked, only now realizing that I had to put away one of my weapons in order to turn the knob.

Shaking my head, I hastily shoved the stake into my belt, twisted the doorknob, and burst out of the guildhall—and into Ash's waiting arms.

Chapter 23

"Never mess with a Hunter, not unless you sleep with one eye open and both hands on your weapons."
-Jenna Lehane, Hunter

I pushed away from Ash's chest and raised my knife, holding the blade out between us.

"What are you doing here?" I asked.

"Jenna, are you okay?" he asked.

"What are you doing here, Ash?" I asked, voice going shrill.

"I never left," he said, hands wide. "I just...had a lot to think about."

It was still dark out and I realized that less than thirty minutes had passed since saying goodnight to Ash. I'd asked him about his relationship with the Guild, and he'd said it was complicated, a story to share at a later time when we weren't exhausted and I wasn't bleeding on the front steps. He'd been out here battling his own demons, unaware of what was happening to me inside.

I faltered, the knife in my hand wavering.

"I..." I said, choking on the words.

"Jenna, did something happen?" he asked, his tone uncertain.

I looked away, blinking away traitorous tears. I swore I wouldn't shed another tear for the Franks of the world, and here I was blubbering. I took a deep breath and tried again.

"Chadwick he...he," I said. I bit my lip, cheeks burning.

"Bloody hell," Ash said.

He pulled me into his arms, mindless of the blade in my hand. I tensed, but when all he did was hold me, I closed my eyes. He held me like that until I lifted my head and pushed slowly away.

"We need to get out of here," I said. "He'll look outside eventually."

Chadwick was probably tearing through my room right now. I shuddered and turned away, heading down the empty street.

"That's a bunch of bollocks," Ash said. "He's the dodgy bastard. He's the one who should be out on his ear. You don't have to leave."

The muscles in Ash's neck were corded, and he held his guitar case in both hands. The message was clear; he was willing to draw his sword to defend my honor and my right to stay. It was kind of sweet, especially coming from Ash, but I shook my head.

"Please, Ash," I said. "I don't have the energy for a fight. Just help me find someplace safe where I can crash for a few nights, preferably something cheap without a curfew."

"I know just the place," he said. "But Jenna? Chad will get what's coming to him. You have my word on it."

Never mess with a Hunter, not unless you sleep with one eye open and both hands on your weapons.

"Yes," I said. "Yes he will."

CHAPTER 24

"You never know when the monsters will come, and when they do a good Hunter is always prepared."
-Jenna Lehane, Hunter

At Ash's recommendation, I got a room at the Vandenberghe Inn. It was a small bed and breakfast run by a married couple in their forties. Their English was good and the price of the room was even better.

When I was done, I went outside where Ash still waited. I needed to thank him for walking me here and suggesting this place. I smiled, pocketing my new room key. Sofia and her husband Nicolas were good people. Their rates were fair and they didn't complain when I came in trying to get a room in the middle of the night.

I stepped out onto the sidewalk, eyes going to the lightening sky. Hell, it was practically morning.

"The Vandenberghe's get you settled?" he asked.

"Yes," I said. "They only just returned from holiday, so I'm their only guest at the moment."

"Sofia will have plenty of opportunities to spoil you then," he said.

I frowned. I didn't need spoiling. I wasn't some kid.

"Look, thanks for helping me find this place, but it's late," I said.

"Saying goodnight already?" he asked. "Aren't you going to invite me up? I can help you with those cuts. Wounds from vampire claws are a bugger."

"I know," I said. "I've got it covered."

"You'll need stitches, love," he said.

"I can take care of it," I said.

"You sure?" he asked.

"Yeah, you go on," I said, waving him away.

He looked like he wanted to say more, but after a moment he took a step back and shrugged.

"Alright, but let me come with you tomorrow night," he said.

I let out a heavy sigh. I preferred to work alone, but my injuries would slow me down, and Ash had proven himself useful with a sword. If I encountered more vampires, he'd be a valuable asset.

I nodded and made my way back into the inn and up the stairs to my room. The room was small, but it had its own bathroom. After tonight, I didn't think I could stomach walking down a dark hallway to a shared bathroom.

I shrugged out of my leather jacket, wincing as the motion sent a jolt of pure agony through my side. I tossed the jacket over the one chair in the room and added my sword and battle skirt to the pile. I kicked off my boots and added my knives to the growing pile on the chair. I'd have to wipe down my gear before crawling into bed, but first I needed to treat my wounds.

I went into the tiny bathroom and clicked on the light. Untying the corset was a bitch, but I finally undid the knots and tossed it in the sink. I ran cold water and added some of the complimentary shampoo and left it to soak. I sighed, fatigue making my movements slow. I'd need to sew the torn cloth panel—just another job to complete before bed.

A Hunter never sleeps until her gear is in good working order. It was a rule that I was starting to resent. But rules are there for a reason. You never know when the monsters will come, and when they do, a good Hunter is always prepared.

Though at the rate I was going, I wouldn't get to sleep until next week. I rubbed a hand over my face, wishing I'd taken Ash up on his offer after all. I chided myself.

Chin up, Jenna, you haven't even gotten to the tough stuff.

I grit my teeth as I peeled off my body suit, tossing it with a wet splat into the bathtub. I had to sit on the toilet to remove my socks and leggings. It was that or fall over and crack my head, and I didn't need to do that more than once in one night. My skull wasn't that thick, no matter what some of my foster parents used to think.

Standing under the shower, I lathered up with hotel soap. I was getting used to the burning pain of the water against my side and leg, but the tears came anyway. There just wasn't enough soap in the world to wash away Chad and Frank and all the ugliness in this world.

When the tears finally stopped, I grabbed my bloody body suit. I scrubbed at it until the water ran clear. I wrung the garment out, hanging it on the towel bar, and stared at the pink water circling the drain at my feet.

Blood in the bathtub? I shrugged. No big deal. That was just another night for a Hunter.

I padded out to retrieve my first aid kit, and began the unpleasant job of stitching myself back together. It was surprising how bad I was at it, considering all the practice I had. Standing there naked, I surveyed my work. The ragged gash at my side was now a mess of puckered skin and black thread. It would leave another scar to join the dozens of others on my legs, arms, and torso. I flicked off the light and squeezed my eyes shut.

It could have been worse.

The corset had kept constant pressure on the wound, minimizing the bleeding and keeping it from tearing open wider as I fought the vampires, and later Chad. I opened my eyes and pulled on the terrycloth robe that lay folded beside a box of tissues. I'd have to wash the blood out of the robe later, but it was better than standing here shivering in the dark.

Why did there have to be so many monsters in the world?

Feeling the threat of new tears, I grabbed the needle and thread I'd been using to stitch myself back together and returned to the bedroom. Breath quickening, I went to my jacket and retrieved a small, cloth wrapped bundle. The cloth held fourteen fangs that sparkled in the lamplight as I perched on the edge of the chair and began sorting them into pairs. I pulled my necklace over my head and began stringing and knotting the fangs into place.

A grim smile touched my lips as I worked, bits of ash and dust sifting through my fingers. Tomorrow I would rid this city of rogue vampires, and after that I'd take care of Simon Chadwick. I'd made a vow not to let the monsters victimize me or anyone else ever again.

I kept my promises.

CHAPTER 25

"No sense leaving your weapons behind when you can find a way to hide them in plain sight."
-Jenna Lehane, Hunter

I looked out the window at the gathering clouds and smiled. The sky was threatening rain, which gave me an idea. I hurried down the stairs to the inn's reception desk, careful not to pull my stitches in my haste. Nicolas Vandenberghe was behind the counter, a ready smile on his face.

"Hi, um, I was wondering...do you have an umbrella I can borrow?" I asked. "I don't mind paying for it."

"Ja, een minuut," he said. He left the room and came back a moment later with a long, black umbrella.

"Thank you, um, dank u!" I said.

I took the stairs two at a time, setting my punctured calf on fire. Back in my room, I went to the desk and opened the umbrella. Holding it upside down, I unscrewed the handle from the top of the umbrella. Next, I lifted my sheathed sword and pointed it into the space left by the missing handle. With a few quick alterations, including using my black thread to stitch the fabric to my sword's sheath, I had what would pass on the streets for an umbrella. No sense leaving your weapons behind when you can find a way to hide them in plain sight.

Ever see one of those umbrella's with a sword handle? Well, that's exactly what this looked like. Except instead of an umbrella trying to look like a sword, it was a sword that looked like an umbrella. I grinned, admiring my handiwork. I'd purchase a new umbrella for the Vandenberghes while I was out today and no one would be the wiser.

Armed and ready to face the day, I raced back downstairs. Sofia was just coming through the door to the Vandenberghe's apartment in the rear of the building, and she carried something that smelled heavenly. My mouth watered, and my stomach growled out loud.

Sofia giggled and handed me a small loaf of bread, fresh from the oven.

"You need to eat more," she said with a warm smile. "Now go. Have fun!"

Once on the street, I tore into the fragrant bread, cramming pieces the size of my fist into my mouth. I couldn't remember the last time I ate. If I could find a trough of coffee, this day would be off to a perfect start.

I turned a corner and nearly choked as I ran headlong into a man's chest. I backed up, eyes wide as I recognized the outrageous scarf and tattered hat. Ash raised an eyebrow at my puffed up chipmunk cheeks, and I felt my face warm. I swallowed the mouthful of bread and frowned.

"What are you doing here?" I asked.

"Walking to the café," he said. "I had a late night rescuing a damsel in distress and now I'm gasping for a cup of tea."

I frowned and put my fists on my hips, which wasn't easy with a chunk of bread in one hand and a sword umbrella in the other.

"I am not a damsel, and I was not in distress," I said.

Ash sighed.

"If we are going to argue, can we at least do so with copious amount of caffeine at our disposal?" he asked.

"Fine," I said. "I was heading out for coffee anyway."

I hastily finished the last of Sofia's bread and followed Ash as he led the way to a bakery with a few booths and tables. Once we settled into a booth by the front window, I fixed Ash with a glare.

"Come on, spill," I said. "You owe me details, and now is as good a time as any."

Ash grimaced, but nodded. He turned his attention to the sugar dispenser, flipping the little metal flap at the top up and down. The noise was like nails on a chalkboard, and I sighed with relief when the waitress brought over the coffee and tea I'd ordered. She gave me a funny look, and I wondered if I was supposed to tip her now, like a bartender.

I dug out a few Euros and handed them to her with a polite, "keep the change." She nodded and backed off, hurrying to help her other customers. When she turned away, Ash took a sip of his tea and cleared his throat.

"As you've guessed, I wasn't here in Bruges for university," Ash said. "I was here for a different kind of training."

"You carry a sword around in your guitar case," I said, nodding toward the case propped on the booth beside him. "You're a Hunter."

I knew it had to be true. Ash hadn't run in fear when faced with the supernatural. He hadn't hesitated when the vampires attacked. Even so, if he'd drawn a gun or fought hand to hand, I could have kid myself that he was someone with police or military training. But he had deftly used a sword with the grace and skill reserved for few in this world.

Ash was a Hunter.

"Yes," he said. "As for the guitar case, it's a prop I use and a handy way to carry my weapons. Sometimes I even carry a guitar. Busking is a jolly good way to hide in plain sight."

It was true. People didn't question why beggars and street performers lingered. They were a part of the city and therefore the perfect cover for surveillance. But his hunting methods weren't what I wanted to talk about.

"Why didn't you tell me sooner?" I asked.

People were sneaking glances at us as they passed and whispering behind the guide maps they held between us like flimsy shields. Hadn't they ever seen two people talking before? Maybe it was Ash's scarf. Today it was a putrid shade of yellow that made my eyeballs hurt.

"Well, the thing is, love," he said, rubbing the back of his neck. "I wasn't kidding when I said things didn't work out for me here."

"You left the guild?" I asked, mouth gaping open.

Last night I'd managed to convince myself that I'd misheard him or misunderstood what he was trying to tell me. There had been a lot going on, after all. Because what he was saying was unheard of. He took an oath. How could he leave his guild brothers and sisters? How could he abandon the mission?

"It's not what you think," he said. "I am not dishonorable. I believe in the mission."

"If you believe in protecting humans from the evil that lurks in the shadows, then why...oh," I said, leaning away from the table.

I took in his off kilter smile and strange taste in fashion. I'd brushed his eccentricities off as the quirks of a music student, but now that I knew he was a former Hunter, I had to wonder. We see a lot in our line of work, most of it not easy for the human brain to process. Was Ash crazy? Just yesterday he'd worn a puke green scarf covered in frolicking zombie unicorns, after all.

I'd seen a lot of bizarre things as a Hunter, but zombie unicorns? That was just plain nuts. There's no such thing as a creature that eats brains and farts rainbows. I should know.

"Bloody hell, you think I'm a raving nutter," he said.

"Well, are you?" I asked.

That probably wasn't a wise thing to ask a crazy person, but aside from dealing with a werewolf's moods during the full moon, I had no experience with this sort of thing. It's not like I had a lot of friends.

I waited for his reply, but he just stared cross-eyed at a patch of sun dappled tabletop.

"Um, is that a yes?" I asked.

"Sorry, love," he said, pulling a face. "I was waiting to hear what the voices in my head had to say on the subject."

I snorted and shook my head.

"God you're immature," I said.

"You should have seen your face," he said. "You were right ready to take a runner."

"Was not," I said.

"Was too," he said.

"I was not afraid of you," I said. "I fought *each uisge* last summer. You, Alistair Ashborn, do not scare me."

"Good," he said with a wink. "Then let me walk you around the city. I know all the best hunting spots."

I was following before I realized that he'd done it again. I sighed and shook my head. Ash never did tell me why he left the Hunters' Guild.

Chapter 26

"Drug users make the perfect victims for vamps."
-Jenna Lehane, Hunter

One of the places Ash showed me earlier on our tour of Bruges hunting spots was Van Haecke's Maleficium. It hadn't looked like much in the light of day, but now there was something sinister in the way the shadows caressed the narrow entry.

There was also something unnatural in the way the building seemed to stand untouched by time. The Maleficium backed onto a canal, but where the constant damp had taken its toll on the nightclub's neighbors, this building remained intact. Vines aggressively dug in their roots, pulling down the other buildings stone by stone, gradually reclaiming the land along the canal.

What was so special about the Maleficium? Was the building protected by magic?

I fidgeted with my sword, glad at least to have it back on my hip instead of in its false umbrella sheath. That was one benefit of hunting in a place like this where the average clientele wore everything from Victorian mourning costumes to full suits of armor. The dress code seemed to dictate that so long as you were wearing black, anything goes. My sword and black hunting clothes didn't even garner an eye blink from the club's patrons as they sauntered past.

Ash and I had agreed to meet here after nightfall, and so I paced the street outside the club waiting for him. I'd give him five more minutes, and then I was going inside on my own. I may have a few injuries, but that never stopped me from hunting alone in the past.

Then again, most of my favorite hunting grounds didn't make my skin crawl as if I was pacing in front of a tank of cockroaches. That probably had something to do with the place's disturbing history.

Van Haecke's Maleficium was a club for rich vamp wannabes, romantic Goths, and—if Ash was to be believed—

Satanists. According to Ash, the club was originally founded by
the infamous Satanist Louis Van Haecke. Van Haecke was
rumored to be the man who author Joris-Karl Huysmans based
his despicable character the canon Docre from the novel La-
Bas, The Damned. Whether that was true or not was a matter
of historical debate, but I had to admit that there was a lot of
evidence of Van Haecke's nefarious hobbies.

It all seemed to begin with the arrival of a French
woman, Berthe Courrière. Some claim that she was sent to
Bruges to corrupt Van Haecke, who was chaplain of the
Basilica of the Holy Blood here in Bruges. If that was her goal,
it seemed to have worked. After their first meeting, Van
Haecke made several trips to Paris where he was accused of
celebrating black masses.

Although the accusations of Van Haecke's evil deeds
were never proven during his lifetime, I still could not fathom
how the man remained in such a position of power within the
local church. As chaplain of the Basilica of the Holy Blood, he
would have had at least limited access to the holy relic. It was
a good thing that the Brotherhood of the Holy Blood kept such
tight security, or this vile man might have done something
truly evil.

A hand landed on my shoulder and I spun, blade at the
ready.

"Whoa, it's just me, love," Ash said, holding up his
hands. "I called your name, but you seemed lost in thought."

My cheeks flushed hot and I put my knife away.

"You're just lucky I didn't gut you," I said. "This place
gives me the creeps."

I expected a witty comeback, but instead Ash stared at
Van Haecke's Maleficium with an uncharacteristic serious look
on his face.

"That's because you have good instincts," he said. "This
place is owned by vampires."

I gasped and shook my head.

"And you want to go in there?" I asked.

"It's as good a place as any to hunt vampires," he said.
"They hide in plain sight, so why can't we do the same thing."

It was true that with their glamour, vampires had the
perfect pale beauty to fit in with this crowd. They would be
right at home in a club that encouraged its fashionable patrons

to wear top hats and bustle skirts. I wasn't so confident of a pair of Hunters strolling through the door unnoticed.

"Are you sure they're going to let Hunters stroll right through their front door?" I asked.

"I happen to know that one of the local Hunters spends a good deal of time here," he said with a frown. "Everyone has vices."

And the Maleficium catered to vices, of that I had no doubt.

"Okay," I said. I sighed and ran a hand through my hair, for once glad of its shocking red color. It seemed to be a popular color for many of the women entering the building, though mine was probably the only natural hair in the lot. "This is your old turf. How do you want to do this?"

I twirled one of my blades, rolling it over my knuckles as I watched the building.

"Whoa, we're not going in there with blades flashing, that's for bloody sure," he said. "We'll watch for vamps stalking their prey, and follow any who lead their victims out of the building."

I nodded and slipped my knife away, still within easy reach. We crossed the street and waited our turn in line. Ash walked past the bouncer without so much as a head nod, but as I tried to follow, the large bearded man held an arm across the entrance.

"ID," he said. I stiffened, but showed him my passport. He squinted at my picture as if not believing I was old enough to enter, but finally passed it back and held out his hand. "Ten Euros."

"It's not like he asked Ash for money, or an ID," I muttered, stepping into the smoky club.

"It pays to be a trendsetter like myself," Ash said, a wide smile on his face.

I raised an eyebrow at his ridiculous hat and scarf and shook my head.

"Come on," I said, walking deeper into the lion's den. "Let's find us some fangheads to stake."

*****

I stepped into a smoky back room and grimaced. The smell of hashish and Mandragora was strong, permeating the fabric of the velvet couches and the walls draped in dark red cloth. Drug users make the perfect victims for vamps. If we were going to catch a bloodsucker in the act, it would be here.

I started to slide into a low booth when my gaze fell on a familiar, scantily clad witch.

"Shit," I muttered. "Can't Martens do anything right?"

I changed directions, grabbed Ash by the arm, and stomped over to where Celeste Dubois reclined languidly on a velvet fainting couch.

"Ah, Jen, come join me," she said. "You're in luck. I was just about to order something special off the menu. Maybe you can help me make up my mind. They're both so beautiful, it's hard to decide."

She let out a sultry laugh that probably made other people's toes curl. It just made me queasy. Celeste was a Hunter and yet she was here buying sex and drugs in a vamp owned nightclub.

"The name is Jenna," I muttered. I gave the half-naked waiter and waitress a hard look and nodded toward the door. "Beat it. Celeste and I have business to discuss."

They both moved on to the customers waiting at a nearby booth. I swallowed hard, my stomach twisting. I guess I knew now why the booths had curtains.

Celeste pouted.

"If you're going to be such a spoil sport, then at least introduce me to..." she said. Her eyes widened, and her dilated pupils shrank to normal size as she stared at Ash. She blinked at my hand on his arm then focused again on his face. "You! What...how...?"

"It's a long story," he said with a shrug.

"B-b-but..." she stuttered.

"You two know each other?" I asked, looking back and forth between them.

"Yes, we used to hunt together, back before I left the Guild," Ash said, giving Celeste a significant look. There was obviously more to the story, and I made a mental note to ask him more about their relationship later.

"Sorry, you'll have to forgive my rudeness," Celeste said, eyes still a bit wide. "I didn't think I'd see Alistair again, not in this lifetime."

I grit my teeth, annoyed at myself for a glimmer of anger that sparked when Celeste used Ash's given name. I didn't think he let anyone call him that, and the fact that the voluptuous witch did it so casually made me want to strangle her with the nearest hookah. Ash also looked uncomfortable. He'd taken a seat on a chair across from Celeste and his knee bounced up and down like a grasshopper in a frying pan.

"So, you two used to date?" I asked.

"Yes," Celeste said at the same moment that Ash said, "No."

"Whatever," I muttered.

"I suppose we never actually dated," Celeste purred. "It's not like we ever left my room."

She licked her lips and I started scanning the room for vampires. I'd give anything for a bunch of monsters to stake about now.

"Knock it off, Celeste," Ash said with a sigh. "It was one time and the next day you were already throwing yourself at Chadwick."

I gasped and turned to see Celeste's olive skin turn a sickly shade of gray.

"Yes, we all make mistakes," she said, voice soft.

"You chose Chadwick over Ash?" I asked.

"Not for long, if I remember correctly," Ash said. "Didn't you go after Sheila, our supply truck driver, the very next day?"

Celeste gave a "what can you do" shrug and took a sip of her drink. She frowned and set the glass down with a clatter of ice cubes.

"Jen...Jenna, be careful of Chadwick," she said.

Bile rose in my throat, and Celeste's drink suddenly looked awfully tempting.

"Bit late for that, love," Ash said, frowning at Celeste.

"Oh, by the Goddess!" she said. "I should have known from your aura. I am so, so sorry. I should have warned you about Chadwick sooner."

"It's not your fault," I said, though it did chafe a bit that if she hadn't been so high on drugs when we met, she might have thought to warn me. Which reminded me, why wasn't she back at the infirmary? "But I have to ask, how did you escape Martens? Didn't he have you in the infirmary, um, drying out?"

"Benjamin doing an intervention?" she asked. "Now that's a laugh."

I frowned, obviously missing something, and for a moment I wished I was back in Harborsmouth. Our Guild, like any family, had a few of our own dysfunctional members, but nothing like this, and at least there I knew what people were talking about. Here in Bruges, I had no frame of reference to go on. These people had a history together, a history that I wasn't a part of.

"Why is that so funny?" I asked. "Martens is your doctor, and he said he was going to help you kick your addiction."

I frowned at the hookah at her elbow and turned back to the witch, but I didn't have a chance to learn more about Martens.

"Jenna," Ash whispered. "At your three o'clock."

I turned to the right to see a gorgeous man, with dark hair and pale skin, helping an inebriated woman toward a doorway at the back of the room. He nodded to another pale skinned man with long blonde hair, and the blonde slipped in behind them as they passed out of the room. *Shit.* The vamps were on the move.

CHAPTER 27

"Vamp magic is often nullified by crossing moving water."

-Jenna Lehane, Hunter

Following the two vampires and their intoxicated victim wasn't easy. It's hard to be stealthy with a witch, who won't stop ogling your hunting partner, tagging along. Not only was she running her eyes up and down Ash like he was a damn ice cream cone, she was also muttering incantations under her breath. If she hexed us in the middle of our hunt, I was going to be pissed.

"Cut it out, Celeste," I growled, keeping my voice low. We were keeping our distance from our target, but vamp hearing was much better than human. "I will not allow you to sabotage our mission because of something that happened between you two in the past. Whatever bullshit is going on between you and Ash, it's time to bury it."

"I thought we did that already," she said with a wink. "Right, Ash?"

For the love of Athena, did everything with the witch have to come back to sex? Ash sighed and rubbed the back of his neck.

"Give it a bloody rest, Celeste," he said. "Jenna is right. It wouldn't kill you to at least try to be professional."

She pouted, but shut up. *About time*, I thought, shaking my head. I would have insisted that Celeste stay behind, but I didn't like the idea of leaving her alone at the Van Haecke Maleficium and if these vampires took their prey where I was thinking, her magic may be necessary in order to follow.

I frowned, keeping pace with our target. As much as I hated to admit it, we needed the witch.

The vampires turned a corner and I smiled. These bloodsuckers were predictable. The vamps were heading toward the place where I'd been ambushed last night, but as they began to walk across the stone bridge, the woman in their arms started to struggle.

"Their control over the woman is slipping," Ash said.

I nodded. Vamp magic is often nullified by crossing moving water. It's one of the reasons I was so surprised to find such an infestation of fangheads here in Bruges. A canal city seemed like an unlikely place for them to congregate.

"Let's do this," I said. "On my mark. Three...two..."

We wouldn't get a better chance than this. With the vamp's magic diluted by the canal below their feet, the woman they'd selected for their dinner had a better chance of survival. I drew two stakes and shifted my weight onto the balls of my feet, a slow smile spreading across my face. When you're fighting for your unlife, it's hard to keep your food from running away.

"One."

With a grunt, I bolted after the vampires. In my peripheral vision, I could see Ash keeping pace with me, his sword raised over his head. He would have looked like an avenging angel if it weren't for that foolish hat on his head.

I'd lost sight of Celeste, but I could hear her chanting at our backs. My experience working with users of the Craft was limited, but I knew enough to realize that she was only now doing the ritual, Drawing Down the Moon.

If she was calling on the moon for power, that meant she'd left the guildhall without even charging her magic batteries. The Mandragora had muddled that woman's brain. She'd gone to a vamp owned club without preparing for a fight.

Good thing we didn't need her help.

I lunged forward, crashing into the vampire on the left, effectively tearing the struggling woman from his grasp. The vampire went down hard, but he was already recovering from the shock of being attacked. Now that they knew we were here, we'd lost the element of surprise, but that was okay. I had more tricks up my sleeve.

I ripped a glass bottle of holy water from my skirt and threw it at the vampire. It hit his head and shattered, splashing holy water all over his face. The vampire's handsome glamour dropped and he shrieked, wiping frantically at his crumbling flesh.

I ducked, as he blindly slashed out with his claws, and rammed a stake through his heart. The vampire stopped moving, all except for the places where the holy water was eating away at his mummified head.

I turned my back on the incapacitated vamp and scanned the opposite side of the bridge. Ash was circling the other vampire, but the bloodsucker was using the woman as a shield. I glared at the vampire as Ash and I darted in and out, testing his defenses.

We had to find a way to take out the vampire without harming the sobbing woman in his vice-like grip. I drew another bottle of holy water from my battle skirt, but as it turned out, I didn't need it.

With a satisfied whoop, Celeste got off a spell, and the human woman dropped to the ground like a sack of rocks. If the desired effect was for the vampire to lose his grip, it had worked. I just hoped the woman was still alive.

The vampire spun away from Ash's sword, the strike missing by less than an inch. As Ash brought his sword back up, the vampire flung himself toward the side of the bridge. If he jumped over, we'd lose him. A smirk twisted his lips and I knew he'd figured that out as well.

In a blur of motion, he sprinted toward the stone wall that lined the sides of the bridge. I lunged, trying to head him off. I wouldn't have succeeded if it hadn't been for Ash, cutting the vamp off at the knees.

The vamp shrieked and I bared my teeth in a fierce smile. *Gotcha.*

But before I could stake the vamp, or draw my sword and take his head, Ash grabbed my arm making me jump.

"Sorry, love," he said, wincing at the way I flinched. Damn, I was still a bit twitchy after my run-in with Chad last night. Ash nodded toward Celeste and gestured at the other side of the bridge. "You may want to take a step back."

I frowned, but joined Ash halfway across the bridge. There I dug in my heels, refusing to go any further. Vamps are fast healers, and there was no way in hell I was letting this bastard get away.

"Aesh deamhan fola animus mundi," Celeste chanted. "*Loisg!*"

The vampire burst into flame. Within seconds his body was nothing but grimy ash and dust. My fingers itched to sift through the ash for my trophies, but the fangs would have to wait. I ran over to check on the fallen woman, my skin still hot from the blaze.

I dropped the bottle of holy water and felt for a pulse. It was hard to tell over the beating of my own rapid heartbeat, but after a few seconds I breathed a sigh of relief.

"She's alive," I said, rocking back on my heels. "But I don't know what we're going to tell her when she wakes up."

"Her?" Celeste asked. "She won't remember a thing, not after that spell I dropped her with."

"Not bad, Dubois," Ash said looking over the fallen woman and the drifting pile of ash across the bridge.

I had to agree. I still didn't like Celeste, but she'd proven herself useful.

"Next time give me some warning," I said, flashing a smile and nodding toward the sooty smear where the vampire had burned. "I'll bring marshmallows."

"Mmmm, that would be fun," she said, licking her lips.

I turned my attention to the vamp I'd staked. There wasn't much left of his face, but I was never one to take chances. I drew my sword, but before I brought it down on the vamp's neck, I rolled him over with my booted foot. There, on the small of his back, was a familiar mark.

"He's from one of those sodding vampire factions we faced off against last night," Ash said, coming up beside me.

I rubbed my temples, pushing away a headache. Ghosts were starting to flow out of the buildings that lined both sides of the canal, edging closer as they were drawn by the vampires' final deaths.

"What I don't get is why there are so many predators in Bruges," I said. "It's not like it's a large city. I expect this sort of thing in London, New York City, L.A., or back in Harborsmouth, but not here. Are we sitting on a nexus point?"

That was the reason why Harborsmouth was so infested with supernaturals. They were attracted to the power generated at the point where the lay lines intersected, creating a magical crossroads in the center of Harborsmouth.

"No, but I agree that there's an evil in Bruges just below the surface," Celeste said. "My coven has a theory that the good of the Holy Blood must be balanced by the evil of the monsters who dwell here."

It was an interesting theory, but it didn't get us any closer to ridding the city of predators.

"Well, let's go shift the balance," I said. "We're practically standing on the vamp's doorstep. Might as well pay them a visit."

After calling a cab for the woman who was still dazed from Celeste's spell, we climbed down the embankment on the other side of the canal and entered the tunnel beneath the bridge. Unfortunately, our visit was cut short.

"I can't break through that ward," Celeste said, shaking her silky hair from side to side. "Not without preparing some serious spells."

"How much time will that take?" I asked, eyeing the exit. More vampires could show up any minute, and with that door closed we'd be boxed in with no means of escape.

"I need more than time," she said. "I need my grimoire and spell components."

I sighed. I guess it wouldn't hurt for us all to stock up on weapons and information.

"Come on," Ash said, sheathing his sword. "Let's get you two back to the guildhall."

After climbing up the embankment, I paused, holding up my phone.

"I'll be right there," I said. "I need to make a call."

CHAPTER 28

"Never suffer a vamp or his greedy cronies to live."
-Jenna Lehane, Hunter

Darryl was waiting for me in the archives. Ash wanted to gather more of his weapons, so we agreed to split up for now. I had a nagging suspicion that he'd asked Celeste to stick with me like glue while he was gone. The witch had insisted on walking me down to the archives door, but when she started to enter the archives itself I raised my arm to block the way.

"I'm in good hands," I said. "Go get your spell components. I'll be fine."

"You sure?" she asked.

"I'm sure," I said. "And Celeste? If Chadwick shows his face, call me."

She waggled her fingers and winked.

"Don't worry about me," she said. "I still have enough moon energy to give Chad a zap or two where it hurts."

We shared a conspiratorial smile and she left. My steps were light as I moved farther into the archives. It was nice knowing that where Simon Chadwick was concerned, Celeste and I had each other's backs.

"Was that our girl Celeste?" Darryl asked, tilting his head to the side. "I haven't seen her around the past few days. Was startin' to think she had a new boyfriend or girlfriend takin' up her time. It's not you, is it?"

"God no," I said with a snort. "Celeste is okay, but she's also a basket full of crazy. Plus, I'm not into girls."

"Good to know," he said with a wink.

Darryl might be blind, but he could still flirt up a storm. I blushed and took a seat by his work station, letting the chair scrape the floor so he'd know right where I was and that it was time to put on our thinking caps. I put my boots up on his desk and took a deep breath.

"I have a puzzle for you," I said.

Darryl's lips curved in a sly grin.

"You know I loves me a puzzle, darlin'," he said. "Go on, shoot."

"Okay, first I've been noticing that some of the vampires I've staked are marked with a symbol like a lion while others are marked with a fleur-de-lis," I said. "And all of these kills have been within the city walls, so probably within the same territory."

"Interesting," he said, rubbing his chin.

"So, knowing that, here's my question," I said, letting my boots drop and leaning forward. "If you've got some vamps dumping bodies and making sloppy kills and ghouls carefully dumping bones in the same city, what does that tell you?"

"I'd say you have two groups of vamps, which those lion and fleur-de-lis markings seem to support," he said. "One nest of careful vamps with ghouls who do their cleanup for them, and a second group of vamps who don't care, or don't fear, the consequences."

"My thoughts exactly," I said, pounding a fist into my other hand. "So tell me, based on the history of Bruges, what two vamp factions come to mind."

Darryl's scarred eyes widened and his chair squeaked as he jerked away from the desk. He shook his head and got to his feet.

"Oh shit, you have got to be kidding me," he muttered.

"What?" I asked. "What is it? You've figured something out."

I bounced to my feet, ready to badger Darryl until he told me everything he knew.

"Sit back down, girl," he said. "Let me think."

I managed to wait five grueling minutes before asking another question.

"So, who are the vamp big wigs in town?" I asked. "You got a Master of the City here, or is this unclaimed territory?"

Darryl frowned, the expression tugging on the pink scar tissue around his eyes. I sat across from the archivist on an old, threadbare velvet chair that had seen better days. I tried to ignore the wire spring poking me in the ass and focused on Darryl. If I fidgeted, he'd hear the couch start squeaking, and I didn't want to distract him.

Darryl may have most of this library memorized in that head of his, but that didn't mean retrieving it was easy. I needed that information, and I wasn't about to do anything else to jeopardize getting it. I'd already pestered him with too many questions. I held myself as still as a gargoyle.

"Bruges has a Master of the City, alright," he said. "Same bastard has been this city's vampire master since he was Count of Flanders back in the 13th and 14th centuries."

He frowned, but he started walking further into the archives and waved for me to follow.

"Come on," he said. "There's something you've got to see."

I followed Darryl through a maze of bookshelves and into a dark, dusty room in the back. When a blind man tells you there's something you need to see with your own eyes, you listen.

I jumped, but it was only Darryl snapping on a series of sconce lights throughout the room. The gaslights had been converted to electric, the threat of fire too great in a library filled with dry parchment. Dust motes shimmered in the air giving each bulb its own personal halo. I hesitated before entering the room, fighting against instinct.

The room was old, obviously part of the original structure, built into the very foundation of the guildhall. My heart raced as I scented the hint of mildew in the musty carpets and traces of dust along the shelves lined with books. There were underlying signs of neglect here that made the rest of the archives feel homey by comparison.

It was that same neglect that set off my alarm bells. Most humans can't see ghosts, but that doesn't mean that deep down they aren't aware of their existence. On the surface we may not care about cold spots, or places that seem to shroud themselves in shifting shadows, but our animal brains can feel the wrongness. It's that animal part of our brains that make us sidestep places that are haunted, shutting off rooms or abandoning entire buildings.

This room had all the signs of being avoided, but a cursory search turned up no sign of ghosts. There must be some other reason Hunters abstained from using this part of the archives. I hurried to catch up with Darryl, my boots kicking up little clouds of dust from the carpet.

Darryl stopped in front of a painting that hung over an empty, soot stained fireplace and folded muscular arms over his chest.

"Should I know what we're looking at?" I asked.

The painting was creepy, like the man in the portrait was laughing at me. It was also older than dirt.

"That is Guy Dampierre, the vampire Master of the City," he said.

Even if I hadn't known that the supernatural existed, I might have guessed after examining this ghoulish painting. Dampierre sat astride his horse amidst a battlefield strewn with dead bodies. Hundreds of human corpses lay tangled with the lifeless husks of their mounts.

Forcing myself not to turn away, I realized that every man and beast sported the same disturbing wounds. Their throats had been viciously mauled. Even more sinister was the fact that the only blood depicted in this battle was on the hands and faces of the victors—Guy Dampierre and his men.

Surrounded by all of this, Guy Dampierre faced the painter with a look of cold satisfaction on his blood stained lips.

"Seems like a nice guy," I said, voice dripping with sarcasm. "We should invite him over for tea."

Darryl snorted and shook his head.

"Even during his reign as the Count of Flanders, he would have opted for blood over tea," he said. "The Hunters' Guild kept close tabs on the House of Dampierre, and there is evidence that Guy may have been turned as early as 1251 AD."

"How did it happen?" I asked. "Was he attacked?"

"No," Darryl said, shaking his head. "The fool chose to become undead. In a plot to murder his brother and gain control of the seat of power here in Flanders, Guy unearthed the secret of his father's bloodline. When he discovered that the House of Dampierre had a long history of undeath, he chose to become a vampire in order to gain the power he wanted."

"He chose to be a walking corpse just so he could rule over Bruges and the surrounding area?" I asked. "That's...that's...insane."

Most vampires are turned against their will, chosen as a power play in a deadly game between monsters. They were pieces on a game board, pawns that may someday become masters, but pawns just the same.

"True that," he said. "I won't argue that the bastard's elevator don't go all the way to the top, but his actions make more sense in context. You see, it all started when the Holy Blood was brought to Bruges."

Darryl got that glazed over look he got when he was retrieving data from memory, and I knew he must have read about Dampierre in the years before his injury.

"Constantinople was sacked during the 4th crusade, led by Baldwin I in 1204," he said. "Holy relics were secreted away to safety in Western Europe. The Holy Blood was no exception. It was brought to Bruges with the help of Baldwin I and the Knights Templar. Baldwin was killed before ever leaving the Holy Land, but his daughter, Margaret II, Countess of Flanders, oversaw the installment of the Holy Blood in the basilica here in Bruges."

I nodded, not that he could see me.

"I visited the Basilica of the Holy Blood my first day in Bruges," I said. "I heard a little of the history behind it," I said.

"What you probably don't know is the connection between the blood and the vampire Master of the City," he said. Darryl frowned and scratched his neck, clearing his throat. I flicked my eyes back to the gruesome painting. A connection between Guy Dampierre and the Holy Blood? That couldn't be good. "You see, the Holy Blood was brought here in secrecy and was believed to be safe until Margaret married her second husband, William II of Dampierre. According to archivists of that time, there was a darkness that haunted the House of Dampierre, and although the city thrived, the Holy Blood remained hidden until his death in 1231."

"You think Margaret didn't trust her new husband?" I asked.

"That's my best guess," he said. "Unfortunately, she was a little too trusting of her sons."

"Guy Dampierre," I said.

"Bingo," he said. "Believing the city to be safe, Margaret allowed the Holy Blood to finally be venerated in the basilica soon after her husband's death. It looked like the danger from the House of Dampierre had been averted, but in 1251 her first son William III was murdered by hired assassins. The death of Margaret's first son shifted power to the second son, Guy Dampierre."

"Three guesses who ordered the hit on Guy's brother," I said, rolling my eyes.

"Yep, Templars who were here at the time traced the money trail back to Guy, but there wasn't much they could do," he said.

"Why not?" I asked.

I knew that the Hunters' Guild traced its roots to the Knights Templar. So it was no surprise that most of our original archives were scribed by Templar archivists. What surprised me was that they hadn't done anything to take out a vampire who so obviously was planning to take over the city.

"The Templars were here to watch over the Holy Blood, not interfere with local politics," he said.

"But..." I started.

"No, listen," he said, holding up one of his large hands. Damn, if Darryl wanted to, he could palm my skull like a basketball. I shut up. "Dampierre was smart. He didn't go around killing humans and dropping them on the Templar's doorstep. Even when he wanted his brother dead, he had someone else do his dirty work for him."

"He wasn't a rogue, so the Templars didn't step in," I said.

My hand went to my necklace and caressed the fangs that hung beneath my shirt. As Hunters, we didn't kill indiscriminately, but if I had my say, we'd change our charter. "Never suffer a vamp to live," had a nice ring to it.

"Guy became Count of Flanders," he said, nodding. "Bruges entered a Golden Age of international trade, but Guy's relationship with the commoners was strained due to his preference for nocturnal meetings, and a rumor that he'd made a deal with the devil. The powerful merchants of Bruges, however, didn't seem to care where Guy's luck came from, so long as it continued to make them wealthy."

Bile rose in my throat and I swallowed hard. Maybe that rule should be, "Never suffer a vamp or his greedy cronies to live." It didn't roll off the tongue, but it sure as hell was a smart rule to live by. I had no sympathy for men like those merchants who supported monsters like Dampierre. The only difference between the merchants and the vampires was that one group grew fat on profits, while the other became engorged like ticks on the blood of the innocent. Either way, they bled the commoners dry.

"So Dampierre and his posse of vampires and greedy merchants ruled the city, which was the goddamned envy of the outside world," I said.

I'd seen enough in the guidebooks and souvenir shops to know that during Bruges' Golden Age it was one of the most prosperous trade ports in the world. But behind the lace markets, towering cathedrals, and the Van Eykes lurked something sinister. In fact, if you look at the later work of Hans Memling and Hieronymus Bosch, it is clear that all was not well here.

"Yes, but he didn't rule unchecked," he said. "Dampierre may have had most of Flanders in his pocket, but he still had enemies."

Darryl took two measured paces to the left and turned to face the wall at our backs. I spun on my heel and sighed. Just as I suspected, another creepy painting hung on the wall. This one depicted two men, one wearing a crown while the other stood just behind him at his shoulder. There was obviously a difference in rank between the two men, but they also shared something in common.

They both had dead eyes and twisted smiles.

"Let me guess, vampires," I said.

"Yes, Dampierre's territory continued to grow, encompassing most of medieval Belgium, but he had a rival enemy in France," he said.

"Who are they?" I asked, moving closer to the portrait.

"Philip IV, King of France, and ruler of House Capet, sometimes known as 'Philip the Fair' and his man Jacques de Chatillon," he said with a frown.

The freaking King of France?

"Please tell me you're kidding," I said.

I recognized the pattern on Philip's cape. It was the same fleur-de-lis pattern that he'd branded his vampires with.

"I wish I were, girl," he said, shaking his head. "On my momma's grave, I swear I wish it were anyone else."

"I take it that Philip the Fair wasn't given that name for his winning personality," I said.

"No, he was nicknamed the Fair because of his handsome appearance," he said. "One of his contemporaries, Bernard Saisset said, 'He is neither man nor beast. He is a statue,' to describe him, which about sums it up. The man was a coldhearted bloodsucker with a throne."

His "handsome appearance" would most likely have been due to vamp glamour. My stomach twisted. A vampire on the throne? What a nightmare.

"You said this guy was Dampierre's nemesis," I said.

"Yes, in 1284 Philip tried to gain control of Flanders, and the battle over the city of Bruges between Guy and Philip officially began," he said. "Ten years into their power struggle, Guy arranged the marriage of his daughter Philippa to Edward, Prince of Wales. This should have granted Dampierre the support of the English crown, but Philip thwarted those plans. He had his men kidnap Philippa and bring her to Paris where she was thrown into prison."

"Was Philippa human or vampire?" I asked.

"The Templars believed her to be an innocent," he said.

"So she was just another pawn in this game between Guy and Philip," I said.

"Looks like that was the case," he said, nodding. "But that's not the worst of it. Philip wanted Guy's territory, so he sent his man Jacques de Chatillon to rule over Bruges."

"The other guy in the painting," I said.

Darryl nodded.

"With Philip's backing, Jacques became governor of Bruges, and Guy went into temporary hiding," he said. "But the merchants rebelled and Jacques had to request more troops to cement his position as Philip's puppet governor. Unfortunately for Jacques, Philip sent a human army, an army that never had the chance of a fair fight against Guy's vampire militia."

"What happened to the French army?" I asked.

"The Bruges Matins happened, one of Belgium's bloodiest massacres," he said. "On May 8, 1302, Dampierre's men snuck into the homes where the French troops were garrisoned and drained every Frenchman while he slept. Over two thousand men died that night. The only French survivor of the Bruges Matins nocturnal massacre was Jacques de Chatillon."

"Because he wasn't human," I said.

Darryl nodded.

"Jacques escaped and returned to Paris," he said. "In retaliation, Philip sent an army of elite cavalry, but again, Guy used his vampire militia to defeat the huge invading army. Philip's army far outnumbered Guy's militia, but it was mostly human. The long ride to Bruges couldn't be limited to nightfall, which made sending large numbers of vampires difficult. On July 11, 1302 Dampierre's militia defeated

Philip's army of over eight thousand men in the Battle of the Golden Spurs."

"Golden spurs?" I asked.

"There were so many French cavalry dead that the battlefield was covered in thousands of golden spurs," he said.

"The painting," I said, turning back to the portrait of Guy Dampierre. "Dampierre was there that day."

"Yes," he said. "The history books sometimes say differently—Philip was King of France and used his position of power to spread rumors that Guy was a prisoner of the throne—but in fact, the only Dampierre prisoner was Guy's daughter, Philippa."

"What happened to her?" I asked.

"In 1306 the poor girl died in a French prison," he said with a frown. "After Philippa's death, Guy Dampierre, Count of Flanders, disappeared from public life. He was said to be dead, and some believed the rumor that Philip had finally imprisoned him, but Guy's sons, the later Counts of Flanders, were all said to bear a striking resemblance to their father and Philip's troops were repeatedly repelled from the city."

"So to keep the humans from asking too many questions, like how he continued to look so youthful, Guy switched identities taking on the role of his sons and grandsons," I said. It wasn't an unusual practice for vampires as deeply entrenched in one city as Dampierre had become. "But what happened to King Philip?"

"After his men were slaughtered during the Bruges Matins, and his armies defeated at the Battle of the Golden Spurs, Philip turned his attentions away from Bruges and the House of Dampierre, and focused his hatred on the Knights Templar," he said.

So, Philip went from having a hard-on for control of the city that housed the Holy Blood to obsessively destroying the Templars, the order of knights who were sworn to protect it. A coincidence? I think not.

"What reason did he give for attacking the Templars?" I asked. "And am I the only one who thinks it's weird that Philip went after the militaristic religious order that eventually became the Hunters' Guild?"

"Philip didn't just go after the Knights Templar," he said, nostrils flaring. "He destroyed them."

"But how?" I asked. "The Templars were trained in battle and knew how to fight vampires."

"By deceit and treachery," he said. "On October 13, 1307, Philip had hundreds of Templars arrested, accusing them of heresy. These men were tortured, and forced to make false confessions of witchcraft and demon worship. He had Jacques de Molay, the last Grand Master of the Temple, burned at the stake."

"My god, he started the Burning Times," I said.

Darryl nodded, hands clenching into fists.

"Eight months after the death of Jacques de Molay, Philip conveniently died in a hunting accident," he said.

He used finger quotes for "died", and I got the hint. Like Guy Dampierre before him, Philip faked his death but continued his despicable unlife.

I swallowed hard.

"So there really are two factions here in Bruges," I said. "Those marks, the lion and fleur-de-lis—it's Guy Dampierre and Philip IV."

One had killed tens of thousands of men to maintain control of Bruges, while the other had annihilated the Knights Templar and sparked the Burning Times. They were here, in Bruges, and they were fighting again.

"Yep, we've got two master vampires in a turf war," he said.

Oh shit.

CHAPTER 29

"A good Hunter knows exactly what resources she has at hand."

-Jenna Lehane, Hunter

Ash paced nervously up and down the sidewalk in front of the guildhall.

"You okay?" he asked as I came down the stone steps.

I hurried over to where he waited, eager to get on with the hunt.

"I'm fine," I said. "No sign of Chadwick. I just got off the phone with Celeste and she should be right down. I told her to meet us out here."

The door opened and Celeste sashayed across the street to meet us. Even in her hunting gear, she looked sexy as hell. Her long, silky, black hair was tied up into a topknot that accentuated her almond shaped eyes, and the leather body armor she wore over a black body suit fit her like a second skin, showing off her curves to perfection.

I avoided looking at Ash, not wanting to see where his attention was. I didn't feel like peeling his chin up off the pavement. I couldn't imagine any man not watching the show Celeste was putting on. Trouble was, I was pretty sure it was the witch's default setting. As far as I could see, Celeste had made an art out of being sexy.

I grit my teeth and did a mental inventory of my weapons. I didn't really care if Ash ogled Celeste, but if she became a distraction during battle, we could all end up dead. That was not how this was going to play out.

"Sorry I'm late," Celeste said, coming to a stop just inside my comfort zone. The woman had no respect for personal space. "I couldn't find my grimoire."

"Maybe if you stopped smoking Mandragora, you wouldn't have that problem," Ash muttered.

Celeste was standing close enough that I'd have been able to smell the drug on her breath, but there was no sickly sweet scent of Mandragora. Even so, her pupils were abnormally large.

"So, did you complete your rituals?" I asked.

If her pupils were dilated from holding too much magic, I wouldn't have to start knocking heads together. Not that keeping Celeste in line should be my job. I wasn't her doctor, her friend, or her boss. When Master Peeters returns from Brussels he was getting an earful. What kind of Master allows their Hunters to become addicts?

"Oh yes," she said, arching her back as she stretched. "Hecate has been most generous."

"And your spell components?" I asked. "You brought everything you need for raiding a vamp nest?"

Celeste tugged on her ear, poking her tongue in her cheek.

"I think so?" she asked with a shrug.

I frowned, narrowing my eyes at her and trying to keep my hands off my blades. A good Hunter is always ready for a fight. A good Hunter knows exactly what resources she has at hand. A good Hunter does not guess and shrug the question off when going into battle.

"Check," I said my voice hard. "After my talk with Darryl, I can assure you that you want every damn spell in your arsenal."

Celeste sighed and rolled her eyes, but started checking her pockets. Ash leaned toward me, eyebrow raised.

"Learn anything new, love?" he asked.

"Yes," I said, stomach churning. "Two badass ancient vampires are in a turf war and we need to put the fangbangers down before any more innocent humans get caught in the crossfire, or become rations for their troops."

Who needs an energy bar when you had grab-and-go tourists? Freaking vampires.

"Bloody hell," Ash said.

Celeste's eyes widened and her hands started to shake as she checked her gear.

"A bloody Hell is exactly what this city will become if we don't do something to stop them," I said. "We need to take them all out."

"So what's the plan, love?" he asked.

"We'll target Dampierre's nest first, entering through that warded door we found, and then scour the city for the remaining rogue vamps that belong to Philip," I said. I rubbed the fangs on my necklace, a slow grin tugging at my lips. "I'll go to the ends of the earth if I have to. Some of these vamps are the same bastards who annihilated our brothers, the Knights Templar. Let's return the favor."

Fangs clicked together and I went through the old mantra, saying the words under my breath. *Chicago, Milwaukee, Harborsmouth, Harborsmouth, Harborsmouth, Bruges, Bruges...* Hmmm, I was collecting so many trophies, pretty soon I'd have to start stringing fangs into bracelets. Heck, after we wipe out the Dampierre and Capetian clans, I can make myself a beaded curtain or two.

"And it's just us?" Ash asked, pulling me from my thoughts. He rubbed the back of his neck, eyes shifting to the front door of the Guild. "You didn't ask the others for help?"

"No, it's just us," I said. "Darryl said that Martens is down in Gent with his daughter, and Zharkov is also out of town securing large amounts of C-4 for the armory."

There was no point discussing Lambert and Chadwick. Darryl's blindness made him a liability in the field. There was no way he could come with us to raid a vampire nest. And there was no way that I'd trust Chad with my back. No. Freaking. Way.

"It's true," Celeste said. "I stopped by their quarters on my way out. Their rooms are empty and the hearse is gone. It's a shame about Aleksey. He really loves making people scream."

She licked her lips and I swear her eyes dilated even further. I clenched my jaw and turned to Ash. If we were going into the lion's den, there was one more pit stop I had to make.

"Okay, we just need to stop by my hotel so I can grab the rest of my weapons," I said. "Come on, I'll fill you in on the rest of my plan while we walk."

"We're really going to go after the vampire Master of the City and all of his underlings?" Celeste asked.

"Yes, and when we've purged the House of Dampierre we're going after House Capet," I said.

"Two vampire masters?" she asked. She tilted her head as if giving that some thought. "Sounds like my kind of fun."

"You always did like taking on two at a time," Ash said.

By Athena, if the vamps didn't kill me, these two were going to drive me bat shit crazy. I sighed and started walking toward the Vandenberghe Inn. At least I'd get a moment's peace in my hotel room while I weaponed up.

CHAPTER 30

"Puncture wounds are a bitch."
-Jenna Lehane, Hunter

Ghosts peered out at us from every window as we made our way to the inn where I'd stashed my gear. I ignored their stares and whispers. Something had set them off, but it didn't take much to agitate some spirits. I didn't think much of it until I turned onto my street and my eyes caught sight of one crucial detail that made my heart start to race.

The door to the inn was open, hanging askew, ripped partly off its hinges.

"No," I gasped.

Within seconds my sword was in my hand and I was running down the street and up the inn's front steps. Sofia and Nicolas were good people. I would not let them die because I'd been foolhardy enough to lead the monsters to their doorstep.

"Jenna, wait!" Ash yelled, but I never slowed.

I dove through the half open door, kicking it hard, and bringing my sword up in a defensive move to block the fangs launched at my jugular. I shoved the vamp off and shifted my weight as he staggered into the shadows cast by the one flickering bulb over the reception desk.

There was a trail of blood smeared across the floor, but I didn't have time to investigate. I was too busy fighting for my life.

Claws lashed out from where another vampire had been hiding behind the door. Judging from the way the bitch was shrieking, I'd pissed her off with that kick to the door. I hoped she'd caught a few wooden splinters in the chest, but if not, I could remedy that situation. I had a splinter with her name on it.

I smiled and palmed a wooden stake, never lowering my sword.

"Come on you bloodsucking hag," I said.

The female vamp hurled herself at me and instead of pushing her away like I had her partner, I let her inside my

guard, and dropped my sword. She smiled, flashing her fangs,
convinced that she had me. With the vampire gloating and
distracted by the sword at her feet, I sidestepped, grabbed her
shoulder, and pulled myself onto her back. She let out a
frustrated wail and threw herself onto the floor, back first. We
went down hard with me grappling like a psychotic spider
monkey.

Before she could throw me off, or smack my head into
the floor again, I reversed my grip on the stake in my hand and
yanked it toward me, jamming it through her chest and into
her heart. The woman's cries cut off mid-wail, paralyzed by the
stake in her heart. I rolled her over, retrieved my sword, and
sprang onto my feet.

As I burst up out of my crouch, I gripped my sword with
both hands and brought it up between the legs of a third vamp.
If I thought the chick's screams were loud, this guy had gone
supersonic. Glass panes started shattering and I continued to
bring my sword up, kicking the vampire in the back. He went
down onto his knees, facing the open doorway, still screaming.

I'm pretty sure I just tore him a new asshole, literally.

I snickered and spun to check on the first vamp, but Ash
was already on him. As I watched, he severed the vamp's head
from his body. Turning away from the cloud of ash and dust
now surrounding Ash, I tore my sword through the air, but it
hit only more ash as a ball of flames winked out.

The absence of screams made my ears feel like they'd
been stuffed with wool. I scanned the lobby, but there didn't
appear to be any more vampires in the room with us. Celeste
walked in and smiled down at the circle of smoldering carpet.
Apparently, that last kill was the witch's handiwork.

I shook my head and stomped out the flames. I didn't
think Sofia and Nicolas would appreciate us burning down
their inn.

I was assuming that they were alive because I wasn't
ready to face the alternative. If the innkeepers were dead, it
was my fault.

"Try not to use flames inside," I said. "We're not here to
burn the place down."

"He wouldn't stop screaming," Celeste said with a pout.

I shook my head. I could try to explain to Celeste that it
would be inconsiderate of us to do any more damage to the
Vandenberghe family's inn, but I suspected that the woman

didn't much care about anything that didn't give her pleasure. I sighed. Some people weren't worth reasoning with.

"Just try not to burn the place down," I said.

I turned to where Ash was collecting fangs from the floor. For a moment, my hands clenched. *Mine*, my brain screamed as he picked up the fangs from my kills. But they weren't my kills. Ash and Celeste had delivered the killing blows, and the one I'd staked through the heart was still alive, undead, whatever.

By Athena, working with other Hunters made my head hurt. Or maybe that was from getting my head slammed against the floor while still suffering a minor concussion.

"Here," he said, handing over both pairs of fangs. "I...I thought you might want these."

"Um, thanks," I said, fixing my face into a bored expression. I shoved the fangs into my pocket, eyes falling to the blood smears that traveled behind the reception desk. "Let's clear this place and check for survivors. Celeste? Stay here with this one and watch the door. Keep our exit clear."

"Can I play with her?" she asked, nudging the female vamp with the pointy toe of her boot.

"Not yet," I said.

Celeste sighed, but I ignored her. We might need the vamp chick's help finding Sofia and Nicolas. I wasn't ready to give up on them. They were still alive, they just had to be.

"I'll take the downstairs," Ash said. He rounded the reception desk and I held my breath.

"Clear." He caught my eye and shook his head. "They're not here." He pulled a tagged key from a hook behind the counter and tossed it to me. "I'll check their apartment."

"I'll take the upstairs," I said, catching the key. "Good hunting."

Calf and side aching, I hurried up the stairs. My leg was wet and I was pretty sure I'd pulled a few stitches. Puncture wounds are a bitch.

At the first landing, I used the master key to unlock the door to my right. I held my breath as the click echoed up and down the hall. The place felt empty and I fought the traitorous tears that blurred my vision.

I wiped angrily at my eyes and grit my teeth. I was a Hunter. Death happened in our world. If the Vandenberghes were dead, I'd mourn their loss when the mission was over. Not a second sooner.

With a steadying breath, I swung the door open and strode into the room, sword held high. There was no one lurking behind the curtains, no monsters beneath the bed. I checked the bathroom, stabbing before pulling the shower curtain back, but there was no one here. The room was empty.

I continued to search the other four rooms on each floor. When I came to my own, I hesitated. Claw marks scored the door's surface and the lock was broken. The vampires had followed my scent all the way up to my room.

The monsters had sniffed me out.

The big question was, were the monsters still here? I held my breath and listened, but there were no sounds coming from behind the door. I shifted my weight to the balls of my feet and on the exhale, I kicked the door open.

Sword held high, I stormed into the room. I was ready for a fight, but the only monster in the room was me—the creep who'd brought destruction down on this room and possibly its owners. I did a thorough check of the bathroom as well, but the vampires had gone, leaving the room in ruin.

It was a good thing I hadn't been asleep when the vamps made their attack. To say the bed was in tatters would be a gross understatement. The sheets and mattress were shredded, pink mattress stuffing pouring out of deep gashes like frothy entrails. The headboard stood like a gravestone, the claw marks that marred its surface an epitaph written in a dead language.

"Clear," I whispered into the darkness.

Stepping over a broken chair, I pawed through the pile of empty drawers and torn drapes. I shook my head and let out a frustrated groan. I'd hoped to retrieve my backup stakes and the first aid kit I'd left open on the desk, but there was nothing left.

Thankfully, I hadn't packed before coming here the other night in my flight from Simon Chadwick, and since that night I hadn't had time to move my stuff over from the Guild's dorms. I sighed and headed out to the landing, pulling the clawed door shut behind me. I was going to pay to cover the damages just as soon as I saw Sofia and Nicolas.

With any luck, the happy couple would be downstairs having tea with Ash, laughing about the break in, and considering themselves lucky. Please let them be okay, I prayed. *Please, please, please.*

"Clear," I yelled down the stairs. "The upstairs is clear. I'm coming down."

I held onto that pleasant fantasy, but as I stepped into the bloodstained lobby, I knew it wasn't true. There was no laughter here, only dust, ashes, and blood. Ash raised an eyebrow, but I shook my head.

"No sign of the Vandenberghes," I said.

"Looks like the bloodsuckers took them out the back," he said. "But from the looks of it, Sofia and Nicolas put up one hell of a fight."

I slumped against the reception desk and let my head drop into my hands.

"This is my fault," I said.

"It's nobody's flippin' fault," Ash said.

I dropped my hands and looked him in the eye.

"The vampires followed me here," I said. "I never should have come."

Ash reached up to tuck a piece of hair behind my ear.

"Chadwick didn't give you much of a choice," he said.

I pulled away and headed for the door. I appreciated that Ash was trying to make me feel better, but he was wrong. We always have a choice.

I made the wrong one.

CHAPTER 31

"A Hunter can never have too many weapons."
-Jenna Lehane, Hunter

"Let's kill us some vamps," I said, stalking toward the canal.

I'd hoped to grab a few more weapons from my room, but what gear I had would just have to do. With possible hostages in the mix, we were now on an even tighter timetable than before. I was going to do everything possible to find Sofia and Nicolas and kill every vampire in my path along the way. The fact that we needed to take out the vamps before the war between House Dampierre and House Capet turned the streets of Bruges into a charnel house was a bonus.

I reached into my leather jacket, pulled out a broken chair leg, and started whittling it down to a point with my jackknife as I walked. Ash raised an eyebrow and pulled out one of his own.

"Great minds think alike," he said with a wink.

I nodded. A Hunter can never have too many weapons.

"If some crappy old chair legs make you a great mind, then I must be a freaking genius," Celeste said.

She pulled a miniature crossbow from her satchel of spell components, and I almost clapped my hands like a kid on Christmas morning. At least, I think that's what normal kids do on Christmas. I wouldn't really know.

Her fingertips lingered on mine as she handed the weapon over, and she leaned in close.

"You're thinking that you could kiss me about now, am I right?" she said, parting her lips in anticipation.

"Bloody hell, Celeste," Ash said with a frown. "That's my line."

I sighed and latched the crossbow into a quick release thigh holster between the panels of my battle skirt. Leave it to these two to ruin the moment. I swear they could suck all the joy out of the city with one petulant look.

"Thanks for the crossbow," I said. "I didn't even realize my stuff had arrived."

I'd asked Master Janus if I could have a few of my custom weapons shipped over. Apparently, he'd succeeded in pulling the necessary strings to get them into the country.

"It was in your room," she said with a shrug.

I narrowed my eyes at Celeste and frowned.

"When were you in my room?" I asked.

The pistol sized crossbow was mine, a gift from Jonathan after one of our nastier fights. He'd carved a wolf howling at the full moon and a stick figure girl with her hands over her ears into the butt of the stock as a joke. Rooming with a werewolf definitely had its downsides, especially on the full moon. It's amazing I never shot him with his gift.

"I stopped by when I went looking for Benjamin and Aleksey," she said. "Don't worry. It's not like I went through your panties. I just thought you'd like your weapons."

For all I knew, she'd snuck into my room and stole the crossbow for herself, but right now I didn't care. My fingers traced the carved wood strapped to my leg and for the first time tonight, the muscles in my shoulders relaxed. Handling a familiar weapon can be like coming home.

"You think to grab my quiver of bolts?" I asked.

"Oh, I think so," she said, biting her lip and rummaging through her bag. She was one of the most disorganized witches I'd ever met, a trait that did not inspire confidence. I just hoped she could find what she needed to blast the vampires into dust—and not her allies—when it counted most. "Here, I found it!"

I grinned as she pulled out the compact quiver. The quiver was filled with custom iron-filled, silver-tipped wooden bolts. Each bolt had a cross carved into the shaft and had been dipped in holy water. Those bolts would slow both faeries and the undead, but they were particularly useful against vampires.

I snapped the quiver into place, finished whittling the tip of the chair leg, and strapped my new stake onto the opposite thigh.

"Are we going to kill us some vamps?" Ash asked, looking from me to Celeste and back again. "Or are we just going to stand here all night, fondling our weapons?"

"I vote for killing *and* fondling," Celeste purred. "Not necessarily in that order."

"Stay sharp," I said. "This isn't a game. The three of us are all that stand between the people of this city and the bloodsuckers."

Celeste pushed out her bottom lip, but she kept her mouth shut. Smart girl.

We made it down the embankment and through the iron grate without trouble—a fact that made me twitchier than usual. Celeste sent a ball of witch light to float above our heads, and my eyes darted to every wavering shadow. Even with the magically warded door in front of us, this felt too easy. After our previous clashes with the local vampires, there should have been guards posted at every entrance to their nest.

Had Philip's vamps already taken out Dampierre's men? Normally, I'd have cheered the French vampires on, but not now. Before putting the last vampire back at the inn out of her misery, I'd rolled her over and checked her lower back. The lion brand marked her as House Dampierre. When I withdrew the stake enough for her to answer my questions, she'd only laughed in my face, but that was alright.

I already had my answer. Sofia and Nicolas had been taken by Dampierre's men. If there was any chance that the innkeepers lived, then I'd likely find them down in the sewers. So long as Philip's men hadn't come and exterminated every last vampire and human feeder in House Dampierre's nest.

The only heartening fact was that the door ward was still functioning.

Celeste drew a circle and placed candles at each cardinal point. After lighting the candles with a touch from her fingertip, she closed her eyes and began chanting. My skin tingled and the marks beside the door began to glow.

"*Oscail!*" Celeste shouted.

My ears popped and a gust of air put out the flames of the red, green, and black candles at her feet. I bounced on tiptoe, trying to get a better look.

"Did it work?" I asked, keeping my voice low as I raised my crossbow and aimed it at the door.

In answer, the door swung open, belching the rotting stench of the grave.

CHAPTER 32

"A Hunter's work is never done."
-Celeste Dubois, Hunter

Ever leave a ham and mayo sandwich in your gym locker? Ever open that locker at the same moment a toilet backed up and overflowed steaming shit all over your gym socks? Well, the smell pouring out of the sewer tunnels was worse than that. Magnify that putrescence by a thousand and add in the stink of a charnel house and you have some idea of what it was like where I was standing. My eyes burned, and I struggled not to gag.

But that wasn't the worst of it.

Along with the foul stink came a swarm of angry vampires. They were on us like pixies to salt. Fortunately for us, I'd brought my favorite fly swatter.

I got off one shot with my bow before the vamps closed the distance and I switched to my sword. I took the first vampire's head off cleanly and kicked the second in the knee, sending him sprawling into Celeste's firing range. A flash of heat warmed my back, and a fierce grin tugged at my lips. *Ashes to ashes, dust to dust, baby.*

Vamp number three wasn't so easy. These front line troops were made up mostly of young vampires, but even the ill trained can get lucky. Bones, some with bits of cartilage intact, littered the floor surrounding the door and as I lunged to the side, I stepped onto a rib cage. My boot caught, slowing my movements by a mere second.

But when your opponent has the speed of an immortal predator, a second is all the advantage he needs. The vampire surged forward, and my blade missed his neck, instead becoming lodged in his shoulder. I kicked out at the vamp, trying to withdraw my sword, but it held fast. *Shit, shit, shit.*

The vamp gnashed its fangs so close to my face that I could smell its carrion breath over the stink of sewage. I swallowed hard and reversed my grip on the sword, struggling to use it as a lever to push the vamp out of biting distance, but he was strong and more of his friends were clawing their way through the doorway, trying to join the party.

So much for swatting flies. If I couldn't fend off this vamp one handed, allowing me to draw another weapon, I was going to become this creep's Slurpee.

Luckily for me, Ash had a fly swatter as well, and he wasn't half bad at using it. With a roaring battle cry, Ash took the head off a vampire to my right. The vampire in front of me turned his head a fraction at the sudden cloud of ash and dust, and I used the distraction to my advantage.

The usual hand-to-hand combat tactics don't apply when fighting vampires. Unlike humans, vampires don't have a lot of functioning pain receptors. That's the problem with fighting the undead. You stomp on top of a human's foot, and they crumple to the ground. Do the same to a vampire, and they just try to eat your face. But there were ways to level the playing field.

My hand dipped into my jacket and before the vampire knew what hit him, I'd staked him through the heart. When it comes to fighting vampires, I prefer the classics. In this case, it was a sharpened chair leg through the heart.

"A little piece of justice from the Vandenberghe Inn," I quipped.

The vampire didn't laugh, didn't even blink, but that was okay. He was paralyzed after all.

I pushed the vampire to his knees and gripped the hilt of my sword with both hands, yanking it free from his shoulder with the grinding sound of metal against bone and the snap of mummified cartilage. I grinned. This guy's tendons might be like old shoe leather, but that had to hurt—even with a lack of pain receptors.

More vamps were pouring through the doorway, and without hesitation I put a boot on the vampire's shoulder and launched myself over his body and onto the party crashers. The young vamps were standing shoulder to shoulder, and I took two heads with one swipe of my sword. Amateurs, now they were just making it easy.

Within seconds, I'd evaluated and targeted their weaknesses. But before I could finish them off, I felt a cool touch and Ash's breath in my ear.

"Want some help, love?" he asked.

I shook my head with a grin.

"Not really," I said. "But you're welcome to watch and learn."

I rushed forward and took the head cleanly from a vamp's shoulders. Before his friends could react, I spun and took two more heads. The remaining vamps hissed and rushed toward me, but I'd anticipated that. I jinked left and dove into a low crouch, bringing my sword parallel with my shoulder and cutting two of the vamps off at the knees. They'd heal, eventually, but maiming slowed them down.

Using the forward momentum of my strike, I ducked my head and tumbled, catching a vamp on the chin with the heel of my boot and snapping his head back at an unnatural angle. A broken neck wouldn't kill a vampire either, but that's okay. Now I was just having fun.

A smug smile on my lips, I came to my feet and, without even looking behind me, swung my sword in an arc. With a pirouette, I turned to watch three more heads fall. The vampires turned to ash before the heads ever hit the ground.

I started wiping my sword on one of the vamps I'd staked earlier, and Ash clapped his hands. I blushed, heat rising to my face. I wasn't usually so cocky, but then again, I didn't often have an audience. Still, I probably shouldn't have shown off when lives were at stake.

"Not a damsel in distress," Ash said, looking me over. "I'll remember that."

I shrugged and turned to survey the dead and dying. At least now I knew where the missing guards were. Dampierre was smart—not surprising since he was over seven hundred years old—and had pulled his men inside to defend the nest from invaders while keeping their flank protected. But that hadn't worked out as he planned. Not unless he'd wanted a pile of ash on his doorstep.

Ash lifted his scarf to his face, covering the smile on his lips, and I held my breath as we finished off the last of the downed vamps. I'd have to come back and sift through the ash for fangs later. Sofia and Nicolas might still be alive. My trophies would just have to wait.

"Celeste," I said, grimacing at the grit that coated my teeth as I spoke. Pieces of dead vampires choked the air. "Any luck finding the Vandenberghes?"

She'd crafted a poppet of mandrake root using hair that Ash had collected from the couple's apartment. I'd growled when she first lifted the mandrake root from her satchel, wondering if she was going to light up and smoke it, but instead she'd carved the root into a humanoid shape and used candle wax to attach Sofia's and Nicolas' hair to its head and pressed a purple gemstone tied with a blue thread into its center.

According to the witch, the poppet would let her know when we were close to the Vandenberghes—so long as they were still alive.

"Nothing yet," she said, shaking her head.

Her silky black hair and olive skin were untouched, a magical field keeping her pristine. I grimaced and turned to Ash, who also looked suspiciously clean for someone who'd just battled over a dozen vampires. Celeste was probably keeping the dirt and grime from touching him as well. I guess I was the only one not worth the effort.

I strode into the sewer tunnel and winced.

"I sure wish I had your affliction right now," I said, turning to Ash as he came up beside me. The tunnel was wide enough here for three people to walk abreast, four if they didn't mind touching the curved stone walls. I, for one, was steering clear of the damp surface caked with centuries of blood and excrement.

"What affliction would that be?" he asked. His eyes flicked to Celeste, and she shrugged.

"Having no sense of smell," I said, wrinkling my nose. "This place stinks worse than troll farts."

"Ah," he said, a slow smile on his lips. "Not everyone can be as perfect as me."

I snorted and gestured down the tunnel.

"Come on," I said. "Stench or no stench, we've got work to do."

"A Hunter's work is never done," Celeste muttered.

Ash gave her a sideways glance and winked.

"You have no sodding idea," he said.

Celeste let out a throaty laugh, and I gripped my sword hard as I turned to trudge down the tunnel. I frowned as I dodged puddles of reeking effluent. By Athena, I couldn't wait until this job was over. As soon as the Vandenberghes were safe topside and the city was cleansed of both warring vampire clans, I was asking for a transfer.

Anything would be better than this assignment. Hell, even being stationed in a desolate Siberian outpost would be better than working in this city. At least there I had a better chance of working solo—and if there was blood, piss, and shit, at least it would be frozen solid.

CHAPTER 33

"A true Hunter doesn't balk when asked to wade through a moat of rotting corpses and liquefied feces."
-Jenna Lehane, Hunter

The tunnels twisted and turned, branching off repeatedly in multiple directions. If it hadn't been for my request that Celeste leave a magical beacon at each crossroads, a bit like Hansel and Gretel's breadcrumbs, we'd never find our way back out. As it was, the growing heat of the place was making my chest tighten.

If we ended up cooked in some hag's oven after sloshing through all this filth, I was going to be pissed.

My foul mood was made worse by the increasing stench brought on by the heat, and the fact that every vamp we'd killed in the past twenty minutes had turned to mud as their ashes mixed with the slop that ran down the center of the tunnel. That was a lot of fangs down the toilet. I was willing to do a lot to retrieve my trophies, but scooping up puddles of excrement like some feverish miner panning for gold was not one of them.

"Celeste?" I grumbled. "You getting anything?"

Her poppet had wiggled its arms and chirped about five minutes ago, and since then I'd badgered her with questions. Apparently, the crude effigy had made a connection to the Vandenberghes' *spiritus mundi* or vital life force. As of five minutes ago, at least one of the innkeepers was still alive. There was a chance we might be able to rescue Sofia and Nicolas.

But a lot could happen in five minutes.

"By Hecate, it's only been a few minutes," Celeste said with a sigh. I frowned at an approaching crossroads and the witch rolled her eyes. "Fine, I will try to speak with the poppet."

She pulled a flask from her satchel and, holding the root in the palm of her hand, she poured red wine into its mouth. At least, I hoped it was wine. I was sick to death of blood.

I fidgeted, shifting from foot to foot. We needed to keep moving, but if we took the wrong turn, we could lose all chance of finding the Vandenberghes alive. Ash came alongside me, eyes flickering up and down the tunnel and back to the poppet in Celeste's hand.

The magical root twitched as the wine soaked into its skin. Celeste walked over to the intersection and slowly waved her hand to the left, but nothing happened. I grit my teeth and watched intently as her hand continued to move. When her hand shifted to indicate the tunnel to the right, the poppet did a lot more than twitch.

It screamed bloody murder.

"Bloody hell, Celeste," Ash muttered.

He brought his sword up, and I raised my crossbow to lay down cover fire. I was getting low on wooden stakes, but the wooden bolts filled with iron and tipped with silver would paralyze a vampire just as effectively. In the ever narrowing tunnels, there was barely room to swing a *cat sidhe* let alone two swords, hence my current preference for the crossbow.

I held my breath, waiting for the rush of lightning fast feet as they sped toward us, but all I could hear was the scurrying of rats. Then again, my eardrums were still recovering from the poppet's onslaught.

"You could have warned me that thing would start crying like a banshee," I muttered.

Celeste shrugged and wrapped the poppet in a piece of cloth. It looked like a rudimentary doll in a blanket.

"I forgot," she said with a shrug.

I bit the inside of my cheek to keep from yelling at her and turned down the tunnel to the right. At least now we knew which tunnel to take. We also had another piece of vital information. One or both of the Vandenberghes remained alive, for now.

The tunnel straightened, giving me clear line of sight for a change. Confident that there were no vampires lurking ahead of us, at least not in the next hundred yards or so, I took off at a run. Celeste grumbled, but she and Ash soon followed on my heels. We made good time racing down those tunnels.

Right up until the path was cut off by a bubbling river of steaming crap. I'd deny it to the death, but a whimper may have escaped my lips as I came to an abrupt halt.

The dungeons where the vampires took their prisoners must be somewhere up ahead. The poppet had screamed that this was the right path. As much as I didn't like it, I had no choice. I had to keep moving forward. *Come on, Jenna, suck it up*, I berated myself. But my feet had turned to lead weights.

Hunters are stoic. Hunters put the needs of others above their own. A true Hunter doesn't balk when asked to wade through a moat of rotting corpses and liquefied feces.

I've never regretted my decision to take my vows and join the ranks of the Hunters' Guild. But right then as I stood there, looking for another way across that steamy river of filth, I was questioning my career path—because I sure as hell was balking.

"That's never going to come out," I groaned.

Bubbles rose to the surface of the slow moving river and popped, releasing more noxious gases into the air. If I ever made it out of here alive, I was going to have to burn every piece of gear I had with me. I swallowed hard and squared my shoulders, but Celeste tapped me on the back before I took another step. The witch flashed me a sly smile, and I halted, toes an inch from taking the plunge.

"I might be able to help with that," she said, wiggling her fingers.

"I *knew* you were using a spell to stay so clean," I hissed.

I would have yelled, but sound echoed this far down in the tunnels. We'd already pressed our luck earlier with the screaming poppet. The sewage was covering our scent from roaming vampire patrols, but if we wanted to retain the element of surprise, we had to communicate with whispers and hand signals.

Not that I wanted to take a deep breath down here. The gases would probably make me pass out, and I'd rather be dead than face down in a river of sewage and vamp leftovers.

"It's just a little air magic," she said, preening like a cat.

"So you can keep that stuff out of my gear?" I asked, pointing at the sludge.

"That will be more difficult, but yes," she said. "Just be sure to keep your head above the surface. You too, Ash."

She turned to Ash, and he raised his hands and backed away.

"Just because I have no sense of smell doesn't mean I want to go swimming in that shite," he said.

"Don't worry, you'll make it across without a speck of that stuff on you," she said. "Get to the other side quickly and I can shield all three of us with an air spell. Jenna, just remember what I said about keeping your head above the surface. The air flowing over your skin creates a seal, but that's a problem if it has to cover your face. It's air magic, not an oxygen mask."

"Got it," I said with a nod. "Just let me know when your spell is ready."

She drew a circle in the filth at our feet with the toe of her boot and pulled two candles from her satchel. Another bubble burbled to the surface, belching more gases into the air. My eyes widened as realization dawned, and not a moment too soon. I grabbed Celeste's hands and shook my head.

"No fire," I said, flicking my eyes to the burbling sewage. "I don't think you want to light those candles."

She frowned and rolled her eyes.

"Why not?" she asked.

"Because you'll send us to kingdom bloody come," Ash said.

I nodded.

"If there's enough methane built up in these lower tunnels, any open flame could cause an explosion," I said. "I don't know about you, but I'd rather not learn what it's like to be a bullet shot down the barrel of a gun."

"Not the analogy I'd use, considering our present situation," Ash quipped.

Celeste gaze clouded and she blinked.

"Oh," she said.

"Can you still do the spell?" I asked.

"I think so," she said. "But...it might not be as effective."

Some protection was better than none. I nodded and gave her an encouraging smile.

"*Aer bhac gaoith*," she whispered.

Celeste brought her thumb and middle fingers together, pointing toward me and Ash with her pinkies. Next, she shook out her hands and waved her fingers as if indicating wind or sideways rain. My skin began to tingle and a warm breeze caressed my skin.

"It's working," I said.

Celeste dropped her hands to her sides, and Ash flashed me an impish grin.

"Ladies first," he said, gesturing in front of us.

"What a gentleman," I grumbled.

I wrinkled my nose and gingerly stepped down into the sludge, keeping my arms out for balance. The liquid came up to my waste, but my legs and feet remained dry. Celeste's spell was functioning as planned.

I'd made it halfway across when Ash and Celeste joined me. On my next step, I stumbled as my foot came down on something the size of a dead cat. I wobbled, but managed to stay upright. My crossbow didn't even take a fatal nosedive.

Wading through sewage gave a whole new meaning to being up shit's creek.

Once I was on the other side, I pulled myself up and onto the tunnel floor. The smell was bad enough to make my eyes burn, but when I stood and brushed at my skirt with my free hand, it came back dry. I started to smile, but before I could thank Celeste for the spell, I heard footsteps running toward us.

"You have got to be shitting me," I muttered. "Hurry up, you two. We've got company."

"I've heard of shit hitting the fan," Ash said. "But this is bloody ridiculous."

He struggled to pull himself up out of the moat. Once he was out, he turned around to give Celeste a hand, but she just gave him a scathing look.

"Remember, Celeste," I whispered. "No fire magic."

"Why not?" she asked. "I like fire magic."

Athena give me strength. Mandragora use had seriously damaged that woman's brain.

"Trust me," I said. "No flames. No sparks. No goddamned fire balls. Got it?"

"Fine, fine," she said, giving a one armed shrug as she came up beside me. "Whatever."

I cut off my retort as the vampires rounded the corner. If Celeste didn't listen to me, then at least we'd take out a bunch of vamps as she blew us all up. I let off three shots in succession, reloading fast and furious.

After the third downed vamp, I slammed the bow into its thigh holster and drew my sword. There wasn't much room here, but if I could flank these vamps, it should give Ash and me both enough room to fight. If not, I would be down to using handheld stakes and my trusty combat knife. I'd still be able to take out vamps, but it would get messy.

Severing a vampire's head from its body with a combat knife is slow, grueling work. It takes time and determination to saw through the thick layers of leathery sinew, not to mention the spine. That's why I ducked and ran down the tunnel, dodging vamps and bumping into the tunnel wall, like a psychotic game of pinball.

At the back of the posse, I spun and launched myself at the rear guard. I took off his head with a laugh. Ash let out a whoop of pleasure, and we proceeded to cut through the vampire patrol like weeds. We met in the middle with me covered in dust and ash, and him flashing me a wide smile.

"Well, that was fun," he said, tipping his hat back on his head at a jaunty angle.

"Whatever," Celeste muttered.

She swiped at his hat, attempting to knock it off his head, but miraculously missed. Maybe his hat was spelled. There was no other rational reason for it to remain on his head.

I smiled at Ash, but my lips soon pulled into a frown as I took note of the number of vampires we'd just faced.

"They're traveling in larger numbers," I said. "Come on. We must be getting close."

I hoped that we'd be in time to save the Vandenberghes. Being alive didn't mean that they were unharmed. My throat constricted as my mind conjured all of the atrocities that could have befallen Sofia and Nicolas since their abduction.

There were much worse things than death.

CHAPTER 34

"Hunters protect the innocent from monsters, no matter the personal cost."
-Jenna Lehane, Hunter

We hurried down the tunnel, careful to keep our steps as silent as possible on the damp floors. After dispatching two more vampire patrols, we descended to a rocky outcropping overlooking a cavern filled with the moans of living prisoners.

Welcome to Hell.

We'd stepped inside a goddamned Hieronymus Bosch painting. In fact, Bosch had spent time in Bruges. Perhaps the local vamps had invited the artist down here as an honored guest. Since he'd lived to recreate this place in his paintings, he obviously hadn't been a prisoner. It didn't look like the vampires' human feeders had much hope of escape.

Iron cages hung from the ceiling, and prison cells, with iron bars that were built into the stone walls of the cavern, held the dead and dying. A larger pen seemed to be used as an exercise space, or perhaps for when there was a glut of prisoners. Either way it was more suited for cattle than humans, though PETA would have had a field day if that were the case.

A low growl rumbled deep in my throat. No creature deserved to be treated this way.

Thankfully, House Dampierre appeared to be low on rations. The dungeon was obviously equipped to handle more human feeders, but fighting with Philip's men had probably curbed trips into the city to stock the nest's larder. Though I knew that it could have been much worse, the whimpers and groans coming from below were still hard to stomach.

At the moment, the place was half empty, with only a few occupied cells and a body dangling from one of the walls at a painful angle. I hoped that the person shackled to the wall was dead. If not, they'd be in excruciating pain whenever they regained consciousness.

I was going to free these people—the ones who still lived—but first I needed a plan. If I ran down there without knowing what kind of numbers I faced, then I might as well fall on my own sword. The vampires had the home advantage. It'd be smart to remember that.

I swallowed hard and scanned the dungeon for guards. It wasn't easy. The undead have perfect night vision and they obviously didn't take the comforts of their prisoners into consideration. The cavern was cloaked in darkness, broken only by an eerie luminescence coming from patches of some type of glowing subterranean fungus.

Identifying targets by the light of bioluminescent fungi is not as easy as it sounds. The glow radius was often less than a meter. It was like trying to keep score of a hockey game in a pitch black arena, using only a handful of glow sticks. The best way to determine guard activity was to patiently watch for a silhouette to pass in front of one of the mushroom clusters.

I grit my teeth, keeping my breathing slow and even, and tracked the movements of the dead. It wasn't easy, not at all, because the vampires weren't the only dead in the cavern.

The entire place was swarming with ghosts.

Tormented souls, spirits of the dead writhing in agony, choked the dungeon. Their numbers were so great that I couldn't tell where one ghost began and another ended. Vampires had been feeding on, torturing, and murdering their prey in this place for centuries.

That kind of shit left a mark.

I squinted, ignoring the spectral forms as I counted vampires. *One, two, three, four...* What the hell? It was while I counted the fourth vampire that I noticed a peculiar phenomenon. The ghosts, moving as one ectoplasmic mass, shifted in the presence of a vampire.

After that, it wasn't difficult to track the guard's movements. I just wish I had better news to report.

"Fifty-three," I whispered. "And that corpse on the throne? Pretty sure that's Guy Dampierre."

Guy Dampierre, the ancient master vampire. I couldn't see Ash, but I could feel his body go rigid.

"The Master of the City, here?" Ash asked. "Bloody hell."

We might be in the bowels of the city, but apparently this was the heart of House Dampierre's nest. For some reason, that seemed fitting.

"Where?" Celeste asked, her voice a husky whisper.

"There's a ledge, similar to this one, but larger," I said. "It forms a balcony overlooking the dungeon...at your two o'clock."

The quick intake of air let me know when she'd found it. It wasn't so difficult, once you knew what to look for. More than half of the vampires were amassed there at their master's feet.

"So, what's the plan?" Celeste asked. "You do have a plan, don't you?"

"It's a work in progress," I said with a shrug.

"Great," she said. "We're going to die."

"Shut up, Celeste," Ash muttered.

"Hey, will that poppet start screaming again if it gets close to the Vandenberghes?" I asked, nudging Celeste's shoulder to get her attention.

"Um, yes, as long as there's a crossroads...a place where there's a choice to be made on which direction to travel," she said.

"Good, that's good," I said, nodding eagerly. "When we reach the cavern floor, I want you two to turn left toward that block of cells. Celeste, when you reach that spot where the path branches near the largest pen, wave the poppet in either direction. It should start screaming its head off. As soon as the poppet starts screaming, drop it and run toward the cells."

Celeste let out a heavy sigh.

"We're using a root as a distraction, that's your plan?" she asked.

"At least some of the guards should head toward the noise," I said. "When they do, you flank them and take them out. Just remember, no fire magic."

It wouldn't do us any good to reach the prisoners if Celeste blew us all up before we got them out.

"You're no fun," she muttered.

"Where will you be?" Ash asked.

This was the tricky part, convincing my companions that we'd be better off splitting up. It wasn't a sensible plan, but it would ensure the best chance of survival for Ash, Celeste, and the prisoners. That was good enough for me.

I was a Hunter. Hunters protect the innocent from monsters, no matter the personal cost. I'd taken a vow, and now was my chance to put that promise to the test.

"Someone needs to hold back the guards and take out Dampierre," I said.

I managed to say the entire sentence without my voice wavering. Go me. I was proposing a single Hunter battling more than two dozen vamps. That alone would be difficult. Add a seven-hundred-year-old master vampire to the mix and this became a suicide mission, plain and simple.

"No flippin' way," he said. "I won't let you kill yourself."

"Just try to stop me," I said.

I lifted my crossbow to shoulder height and took off down the tunnel, leaving Celeste's gasp and Ash's cursing behind me. It was better this way. I was no good at sentimental touchy feely crap.

I never did like goodbyes.

My boots hit the cavern floor without making a sound, a spongy moss absorbing my footsteps. I grinned, baring my teeth. I was going to take down as many vampires as possible. I wouldn't have chosen a cavern stinking of sewage and death as the place I'd take my last breath, but I didn't regret that this was what I was about to do.

I always knew that this was how I'd die. It had just been a matter of time.

Using the sea of ghosts to find my targets, I took down three vampires before anyone noticed any trouble. That was me, trouble with a capital T.

A vampire rushed toward me, knocking the bolt I shot at him and deflecting it away from his chest. Shit. I stopped running, hoping to increase the odds of a heart shot, when the poppet's cry rang out.

To my left, all hell broke loose. Still rushing toward me, the vampire snapped his head in the direction of the screams, and I took my shot. Four vamps down, only fifty more to go. And that last one, the Master of the City?

He was mine.

I took up position behind a whipping post, using it as a partial blind, and picked off vamps as they rushed toward the prisoners' cells. That little poppet sure made one heck of a distraction, even better than I'd hoped. The vampires probably didn't have much experience with attacks this far inside their defenses.

It was like shooting fish in a barrel.

I'd downed over twenty vamps when I ran out of ammo. All I had left was my lucky bolt, the one that Jonathan had given me with the crossbow for luck. Not bad. Not bad at all.

I switched to my katana and, leaping over paralyzed vamps, I started cutting a path to the throne. Vampires are selfish, but sooner or later one of these creeps would probably realize that helping his brothers by removing the wooden bolts from their hearts would be mutually beneficial. Until then, I had a chance at Dampierre.

I wasn't going to waste it.

I raced forward, ignoring the burn in my leg and the warm, wet trickle of blood that oozed into my sock and pooled in the heel of my boot. Unfortunately, I wasn't the only one who'd noticed that I'd popped my stitches. Three vamps in the throes of blood frenzy launched themselves at me. They moved lightning fast, too fast for my human eyes to follow, but I was good at estimating trajectories.

I swung my sword based on where I calculated they would be. I used speed and distance, and swung, taking off two of their heads and slashing the third across the chest. See kids, you really do use algebra outside of high school. I laughed, and let my momentum propel me to the left and out of the vampire's reach.

It hissed and lunged at me, claws outstretched. I took off both hands at the wrist and kicked him in the stomach. The vampire staggered, and I brought my sword back up and took off his head.

My eyes flicked to the throne, but the vampire sitting there didn't so much as twitch. Either he didn't deem me worth his trouble or he was having trouble deciding what to do with the annoying little gnat that had invaded his home.

Some vampires are like that. I guess the passage of time is different when you live millennia. But whether his seven hundred years had made him cocky, or slow to make a decision, I didn't hesitate.

I ran up the steps, chest heaving, and swung my sword. The clash of weapons rang out, but the corpse still sat rigidly in his throne. Good god, I was fighting a statue.

With a sigh like gases escaping a bloated corpse, Dampierre came to his feet. He moved stiffly, but no matter how fast I slashed and stabbed, I couldn't get inside his defenses. Dampierre might look like he was half asleep, but he knew his swordplay.

If I was going to win, I'd have to fight dirty.

Dampierre pressed the attack, taking the offense, and my muscles burned. Losing ground with every strike, I staggered and shifted my sword to one hand. The tip wavered, my arm growing fatigued, but I maintained a meager defense as I used the other hand to draw a bottle of holy water.

I tossed the holy water at Dampierre expecting a reprieve, but it didn't come. He was either too ancient to feel its effects, or was too far gone to notice the holy water burning his face and chest. Instead of shrieking and clawing at his melting chin, Dampierre slammed into me with such force that I lost all feeling in my right arm.

My sword dropped to the ground, the hand that held it going numb. Heart racing, I reached for my combat knife, but my ankle rolled as the sole of my boot came down on a discarded skull. I lost my footing and staggered backward, collapsing to one knee.

I was going to die.

Instead of seeing my life flash before my eyes, the world seemed to slow. It only prolonged the agony of defeat. Dampierre's sword was coming toward me, and there was nothing I could do to stop it. I was a Hunter, but he was a seven-hundred-year-old master vampire. I just wasn't fast enough.

I sent up a prayer that if this was to be our deaths, that the vampires made it quick. The thought of Sofia, Nicolas, Ash, and Celeste rotting in this place brought tears to my eyes. But before a single tear could fall, Dampierre's sword shot toward me...and into Ash's chest.

Ash, the fool, had thrown himself in front of Dampierre's blade. My vision blurred, but I'd seen the entire thing at close range. There could be no mistake. It was a killing blow. That much was obvious.

Alistair Ashford was dead.

CHAPTER 35

"It's the things outside our control, the problems you can't solve with a bow or a sword, that are the hardest to accept."

-Jenna Lehane, Hunter

"No!" I screamed.

I screamed with every fiber of my being. I screamed with rage, and fear, and loss. And as anger bloomed hot within my chest, it burned away the fatigue and pain. My right arm might be useless, but I was still in this fight.

I would make Dampierre pay for killing Ash, and then I'd wipe out every last bloodsucking son of a bitch in this god forsaken hellhole.

Fumbling awkwardly with the thigh holster, I managed to retrieve my crossbow with my left hand, raise it to Guy's chest, and fire a wooden bolt into his heart. My aim with my left hand wasn't as good as my dominant hand, but at point blank range it was an easy shot.

The bolt sunk into Dampierre's heart and he froze, becoming a statue once again. But that wasn't good enough. He'd killed Ash. *Dead, dead, dead...*

I shook my head. No time for gibbering. I could fall apart later. For now, I would take Dampierre's head and rescue the survivors. Later, when this was all over, I would mourn Ash.

I holstered my crossbow, wincing as feeling started to return to my right side, sending pain down my right arm. I grit my teeth, shook my hand, and grabbed my sword. I lifted it to Dampierre's neck and glared, nostrils flaring.

"If I had my way, I'd disembowel you with my bare hands and make balloon animals out of your intestines," I said. I choked on a laugh as it bubbled up out of me. It sounded harsh, as if it flayed my throat on the way to my mouth. "Lucky for you, I don't have the time."

I swung my sword and severed Dampierre's head from his body. He was gone in a puff of ash. It was too kind a death for someone who'd sat here overseeing the murder and torture of countless people—for the monster who'd killed the honorable man who'd fought by my side.

I knelt down and sifted through the ashes for Dampierre's fangs. When I found them, I gripped them so tightly they cut into my palm. It was the same hand I'd sliced just a week before, and it sent a jolt of pain down my fingers, but I just smiled. I welcomed the pain.

Finally, I zipped the fangs into an inside pocket and stood, brushing the powdery remains from my hands. I shuffled over to Ash's fallen body, breath hitching in my throat as I crouched beside his remains. I never did learn why he'd left the Hunters' Guild, but it didn't really matter. He'd proven himself to be a man of honor and courage.

I reached down to take his hat. It was a silly sentimental token, but the only piece of him I could carry out of this place. With prisoners to rescue, his body would have to be left behind.

"I always knew you fancied my hat," Ash said.

I gasped as he reached up and took my hand. His skin was cool against mine, but he was alive. I pulled my hand away and stumbled backward, awkwardly crawling and falling on my butt. I blinked rapidly and shook my head.

"You were d-d-dead," I stuttered.

Leather clad legs moved into my field of vision and I flinched, but it was only Celeste.

"Tell her," she said.

Her voice was hard, and I looked up to see her frowning at Ash.

"Tell me what?" I asked.

My eyes flicked around the cavern, but all of the vampires were gone, either dead or escaped. Celeste had freed the prisoners and had left them huddled around one of her witchlights. The humans looked dazed—a bit like how I felt.

I turned back to Ash, and he winced. Oh god, Celeste wanted Ash to say goodbye. It's the only thing that made sense. He might still be hanging on to life, somehow, but he had Guy Dampierre's sword protruding from his chest. If we moved him, he would die. If we left him here, he would die. There was nothing I could do to stop his death. It was just a matter of time.

It's the things outside our control, the problems you can't solve with a bow or a sword, that are the hardest to accept.

I'd thought that seeing Ash die the first time was painful, but this—sitting here and waiting for it to happen—this was worse. But I'd let him have his deathbed confessional. It was the least I could do for someone who had saved my life.

"I didn't mean to keep it a secret, love," he said. "It just kind of happened that way."

"Keep what a secret?" I asked, blinking away tears.

Ash reached down and gripped the sword protruding from his chest with both hands, and I gasped.

"No!" I cried.

But before I could reach him, he'd pulled it free and tossed it to the ground. There was no blood on the blade. His clothes weren't bloodied or torn. There was no sign of a wound at all.

"I'll give you two a moment," Celeste said, patting my shoulder as she sauntered away.

I blinked at Celeste and back to Ash. Ash, who was alive. Ash, who just pulled a sword from his body without any blood. Ash, who sat up and leaned toward me, a pleading look on his face.

"Please, love, try to understand," he said.

Suddenly, I did understand. Ash's ability to stay clean. His knack for stealth. The way women walked past without a single look.

That last bit should have clued me in the first day we'd met. As much as I'd tried to ignore it, Ash was gorgeous. In a city that appreciated beauty, he should have been drawing stares. Except that wasn't possible.

People didn't see Ash. The only people I'd ever known to interact with him were me and Celeste—and she was a witch with ties to the spirit realm. I covered my mouth with my good hand, afraid I was going to be sick. Yes, I did understand. The truth had been there all along.

Ash was a ghost.

CHAPTER 36

"Ghosts are flimsy shadows, remnants of strong emotions left behind."
-Jenna Lehane, Hunter

"You're a ghost," I said.

I stumbled over the words. I tried not to make a habit of conversing with the dead, and yet here I was, discussing the fact that Ash was a ghost, a spirit, a specter. By Athena, I'd spent this past week hanging out with a dead man.

"Yes, love, I am," he said.

"How?" I asked, shaking my head. "How is any of this possible?"

"You can see ghosts, love," he said. "You try to hide it, but I've watched your reactions to their presence."

"Yes, but...they don't look real!" I said. "Ghosts are flimsy shadows, remnants of strong emotions left behind. They don't manifest whole. They are not flesh and blood, and they can't do the things I've seen. Even poltergeists don't have enough power to swing a sword the way you do. Is this some kind of trick?"

But I knew this wasn't a joke. Even Ash wasn't foolhardy enough to attempt a prank like this in the heart of a vamp nest.

"I am not going to argue philosophy, but I can assure you that I am real," he said. "Though as you've already witnessed, I'm no longer flesh and blood."

He gestured at his unmarred chest.

"If you aren't flesh and blood, how did you stop Dampierre's blade?" I asked.

"I don't know," he said, letting out a heavy sigh. "I wish I had answers for you. All I know for certain is that I wandered this city for two years with no one except Celeste the wiser. Not that she reacted well to my appearances."

Two years. He'd haunted the witch for two years. No wonder she turned to Mandragora.

"How can Celeste see you?" I asked. "Is it because of her magic? Because I've known witches who don't even believe in ghosts."

"Celeste has always had an affinity for moon spells and spirit magic," he said. He grimaced and looked away. "But I think it was our ties that allowed her to see me."

"Oh," I said, picking at the layers of soot and blood on my hands. "I thought that was just a onetime thing."

He met my gaze, and cocked an eyebrow.

"Not those kinds of ties, love," he said. "Celeste and I were partners, *hunting* partners, until I was drained by a rogue vampire. I think she blames herself, though it wasn't her fault. The bastard came out of bloody nowhere."

Ash had been drained by a vampire? Suddenly his affinity for flamboyant scarves made more sense. He may not suffer new injuries as a ghost, but he'd still have the wounds inflicted at the time of his death. Wearing a scarf would keep those telltale wounds hidden.

"Wait, so you were a Hunter when you died?" I asked. "I thought you left the Hunters' Guild."

"I said that I was no longer a member of the Guild, which was true," he said with a shrug.

"And when you said that the Guild wouldn't welcome someone like you, you meant they wouldn't welcome a ghost, not a former Hunter," I said.

Ash nodded and I winced. He really hadn't been able to come inside the guildhall, at least not by the front door. The building, except for the basement and underground parking structure, had been warded against the dead.

"It must have been lonely," I said.

"It was bloody boring," he said. "I tried to leave the city, but I always ended up right back in Bruges."

"Like the day we met," I said. "That's why you were on the train. You were trying to leave."

"I was, but I didn't mind being in Bruges once you turned up," he said. "Imagine my surprise when you could see and hear me."

"But you grabbed my hand," I said.

I thought back to that day and shook my head. I don't know how Ash managed to manifest so fully, but he hadn't appeared so to everyone. That cyclist had ridden his bike clear through him.

"Oh god," I groaned. "The old ladies in the church."

I'd yelled at Ash when he'd started doing the chicken dance in the Basilica of the Holy Blood, but it must have looked like I was yelling at the elderly women who were sitting behind him.

"Like I said, death became much more interesting since your arrival," he said.

He pulled himself to his feet and reached down to help me up. I hesitated, but took his hand. What the hell? I tried not to encourage ghosts, but Ash wasn't like the others. That much was clear.

"Come on," I said. "Since I'm not rid of you yet, you might as well make yourself useful. We've got prisoners to take topside, and there could still be vamps down in these tunnels."

"You wound me," he said in mock horror. "I'm nothing more than an extra pair of hands."

"Athena, give me strength," I muttered.

But I couldn't hide the smile. It was nice to have Ash back, even if he wasn't alive in the normal sense.

"You know, I heard most of what you said while I was incapacitated," he said.

I groaned and stared ahead toward the huddle of sobbing humans.

"You were prepared to make balloon animals out of someone's intestines for killing me," he said. "I'm flattered."

"It didn't mean anything," I said.

"Whatever you say, love," he said.

"Then I say, get your ass over there, and start getting these people on their feet," I said.

Ash gave me a wink and a mock salute and hurried over to help Celeste who was tending injuries. We'd defeated Guy Dampierre and his nest of ruthless, murdering vampires, but I didn't kid myself.

This mission was far from over.

"We better get moving," I said, looking over our ragtag group of survivors. "I know you've all been through a lot, but..."

A shadow broke away from the wall on the far side of the cavern. The prisoners we'd just rescued couldn't see the vampire from where they sat huddled together. Heck, I could barely see it, the vamp was moving so fast. I reached for my sword, since my crossbow was now completely out of ammo, but Celeste stepped in front of me, waving her fingers in the air as if playing an invisible game of cat's cradle.

"*Dóiteáin!*" she shouted.

Too late, I realized what she intended. I threw myself on top of the human prisoners, knocking them to the ground and using my body as a shield. A wave of super-heated air hit me like a steam train, knocking the wind out of my lungs and leaving my skin burning as if someone had taken a flame thrower to my back.

In a way, someone had—and that someone was only now realizing her mistake.

"Oops," Celeste said.

At least she had enough smarts to sound embarrassed, though smart and Celeste were not two words I'd expect to use in one sentence—not after the stunt she just pulled. I'd warned her about using fire when we were so far down in these tunnels. We were just lucky that we were in the large, high-ceilinged throne room when the explosion happened. If we'd been in the narrow tunnels, we'd be dead right now.

Since those were sewer tunnels, pieces of my dead corpse would probably have shot up into some poor fool's toilet. I let out a heavy sigh. Celeste was a goddamned menace.

"I could have sworn I said not to use fire magic," I said, pulling myself to my knees and shaking my head.

"Bloody hell, Celeste," Ash said. "Lay off the pipe. That shite is eating your bloody brain."

It was true. I'd noticed Celeste's memory slips, but until now her mistakes had been relatively minor. Today she could have killed somebody—a lot of people, in fact. The knowledge that the humans we'd just freed from the vampires could have ended up dead from the witch's mistake, sat heavy on my chest.

My hands balled into fists at my sides and I took two slow, calming breaths before turning to face Celeste. What I saw at the far end of the cavern stole the air from my lungs for the second time tonight. As expected, the vampire had been turned to ash along with a number of pieces of old furniture. But that wasn't what held my gaze.

I stared at the giant pile of rubble and swore.

"There goes our exit," I muttered.

CHAPTER 37

"Vampires don't always take the best care of their undead servants."
-Jenna Lehane, Hunter

Never bring a forgetful, addle-brained witch with a penchant for fire spells into a warren of sewer tunnels.

Celeste's fire magic had ignited the buildup of explosive gasses in the tunnel nearest the attacking vampire, the same tunnel we'd already cleared of vampire patrols. The explosion had brought down part of the ceiling, blocking the mouth of the tunnel.

She had sealed off the route we'd taken to enter the cavern, removing our safest way out.

"I guess we need to find ourselves another way to the surface," I said with a heavy sigh.

I just hoped that the vampires had a back door out of this place. Otherwise, we had a whole lot of digging in our futures.

I straightened and checked the humans for visible signs of injury. They appeared startled, but unharmed by the blast. That was one blessing at least. If we had to carry these people out of here, we wouldn't be able to keep our weapons drawn. Since we'd be venturing into unknown territory, I didn't doubt we'd need to be ready for a fight.

There was no saying what evil still lurked down in these tunnels.

I strode to the one remaining exit, a pitch-black, narrow hole in the opposite wall. The faint glow from the nearest phosphorescent fungus wasn't bright enough to penetrate the inky darkness. I swallowed hard and clicked on my flashlight. Squinting and blinking rapidly, I waved the beam of light inside the opening.

It took my eyes a minute to adjust, and what I saw when the tunnel came into focus wasn't much of an improvement. The opening was large enough for us all to stand upright, but we'd have to walk single-file. This was no public works project. From the scratch marks in the damp earth, it appeared as if the vampires dug this tunnel with their bare hands—like a newly born vamp clawing its way out of the grave.

Now that was a cheery thought.

Ash and I took point, with Celeste bringing up the rear. I'd rather have Ash at our backs, but the humans couldn't see him, and we needed someone to keep them moving. Ash wouldn't be able to help with the humans, because he was a ghost.

I was still having trouble wrapping my head around that fact. Thankfully, the nest of ghouls we stumbled into kept my mind off the fact that Ash was one of the living impaired.

Ghouls may not have vampire speed, but they were damn persistent and difficult to kill. That doggedness was why their vampire masters created them in the first place.

Vampires create ghouls as slaves to do their bidding. Unlike vampires, these revenants are spawned when a vampire turns a corpse, rather than someone with a pulse.

Thankfully, ghouls can only be sired by very old, very powerful vampires. Unfortunately for us, Guy Dampierre was about as ancient as they came. He had ghouls aplenty and they were all intent on one thing—eating the flesh from our bones.

When a ghoul rises, it has very little mental functioning beyond the innate need to feed on human flesh. This suits the vampires just fine. They use their putrescent slaves as servants, and if a servant pleases them, they feed them their blood-drained table scraps. The service of ghouls who are neglected by their masters ends when their bodies rot beyond usefulness.

The ghouls coming at us were in various states of decomposition. If I'd thought the sewers were bad, this tunnel smelled even worse.

"Celeste, keep those people back, and whatever you do, don't use any fire magic!" I yelled. "Ash, go for their heads."

"I know how to kill a bloody ghoul," he said.

More of the creatures began crawling out from alcoves that had been carved into the walls at shoulder height, scuttling out of the holes like cockroaches eager for a meal.

"Good, 'cause we've got company," I said.

A ghoul that had probably been a teenager when he'd died limped toward me, baring his teeth. I raised my sword as he lunged at me with a snarl. On closer inspection, he didn't have much of a choice when it came to showing his teeth. He was missing anything resembling lips and most of the flesh from his cheeks was being eaten away by blow fly larvae.

I swung at the ghoul's neck, intending to take off his head, but my sword caught on his tattered hoodie. I shifted my weight and slanted the blade up at an angle which took off the top of the creature's head. A chunk of scalp, writhing with maggots, hit my boot and I gagged. But I didn't have time to puke my guts out.

The ghoul was still coming at me.

The only sure way to kill a ghoul with a blade is decapitation. A head shot with a large caliber gun loaded with silver shot will also work, but I was fresh out of both. The airlines frown on firearms in a girl's luggage, and silver shot was expensive. I'd have to make do with decapitating the monsters with my sword.

That would be a whole lot easier if the shuffling corpses weren't trying to chew my face off.

Ghouls aren't like movie zombies, though a past encounter with humans is probably where Hollywood got some of their ideas. A ghoul bite won't turn a human—only a vampire can create a ghoul—but a bite from a rotting corpse could still be deadly. Sepsis, staph infection, and necrotizing fasciitis are just a few of the bonus prizes that may come along with a ghoul bite. I'd rather take my chances with a rabid Pit Bull.

A ghoul latched onto my ankle, attempting to gnaw through my boot and I jumped.

"Damn it!" I shouted, shaking my foot, but the female ghoul held on tight. At least, I think she was female. She was so decomposed, it was hard to tell.

"Need a hand, love?" Ash asked.

He held up a severed hand and I snorted.

"No thanks, I got this," I said.

I swung my sword a second time, taking off the first ghoul's head. I threw myself back against the nearest wall, kicked at the female ghoul with my other booted foot, sheathed my sword, and drew my combat knife. It would take longer to cut through the ghoul's neck with my knife, but it was safer than using my sword. With the ghoul latched onto my ankle, I was likely to take off my own foot if I used a longer blade.

I ducked, narrowly missing the grasping hands of the creature in the nearest alcove, and drove the knife into the female ghoul's neck. She kept on gnawing away at my boot.

Pesky ghoul.

Grabbing her hair in one hand, I tried to hold her head still as her body thrashed around. Her arms ended in stumps at the elbow, so her attempts to claw at me were futile. She was also missing both legs at the hip, hence trying to gnaw through my ankle instead of my skull.

I don't know what happened to her arms and legs. Perhaps another ghoul ate them. Vampires don't always take the best care of their undead servants. Who cared if your pets cannibalized themselves when you could just make more?

I grit my teeth, sawing at the ghoul's neck. Rotting flesh fell away in chunks, but the spine wasn't so easy to sever—not with the woman continuing to gnash her teeth and chomp at my leg. It took a few more kicks to crack the bone, and a hell of a lot of sawing, but the head finally came free from the ghoul's body.

Foamy spittle flew from her mouth as I tossed the head aside, and not a moment too soon. The ghoul from the alcove had climbed its way out and was dragging his way toward me. I was pretty sure the creature was eyeing my boots like they were a goddamn Slim-Jim. Who knew leather boots were so tasty?

I drew my sword and brought it down in a sweeping arc, chopping off the ghoul's head.

"Incoming," Ash said with a grunt.

I was still down on one knee, so I rolled, narrowly avoiding a head coming at me like a cannonball. The skull hit the wall with a sickening crack and tumbled over to rest on the ground beside me. A spider scuttled out of an empty eye socket and I snorted.

I know just how you feel, buddy.

I'd been uprooted from my home and tossed over to a foreign country where, so far, nothing had gone easy. But unlike the spider, I couldn't just find another skull to crawl inside and start filling it with my new family. No, spiders had it easy. They didn't have to protect a dozen innocent humans while trudging through a rough hewn crypt filled with the flesh-eating undead.

And have I mentioned the smell? Now I knew why some of the city's streets had such a foul odor, and it wasn't just the sewers.

We continued to battle the ghouls, carving up the rotting, animated human flesh like a Thanksgiving turkey left too long at room temperature. Like the holidays, I survived, but it wasn't an experience that I wanted to repeat anytime soon.

After we cleaned out the servant's quarters, we made it through the rest of the tunnel without too much trouble. Celeste was partially responsible for the ease of our escape, which was a good thing for her since I hadn't forgotten that she was the reason we couldn't leave the vampires' nest the same way we'd come in.

Though her power was waning, Celeste managed to use her magic to calm the humans we'd saved and convince them that they were the victims of a mugging gone wrong. I was glad that we didn't have to deal with frantic people, but the smiles on some of their tear streaked faces were creepy.

The tunnel dead ended beneath a wooden trap door. The rungs of a ladder bolted into the wall appeared to be our only means of escape.

"Celeste," I said, waving her forward. "Can you sense anything?"

The front door to the vamp nest had been magically warded against intruders. I didn't know if opening this door from the inside would trigger any traps, but it was better to be safe than sorry, especially when we had more than our own lives to worry about.

"It feels…blocked from the other side," she said. "Just a minute."

Sweat beaded on Celeste's forehead, but she kept her eyes closed and hands raised palms up. After a few minutes, she nodded and opened her eyes.

"Is it clear?" I asked.

"It should be," she said.

That was as much assurance as I was going to get. I shimmied up the rickety ladder and shouldered the trap door. I was prepared for a fight, maybe even a mundane trap or two.

What I saw in the hidden, underground room was not at all what I expected.

CHAPTER 38

"Hunters can't afford distractions."
-Jenna Lehane, Hunter

Two ghosts, a man and a woman, were inside the small room, humping like bunnies.

"Is that a nun and a flippin' priest?" Ash asked, coming up behind me.

I jumped, heat rising to my face.

"Apparently, this room wasn't always part of the vampires' underground railroad," I said.

Nope. At one time, this room had definitely been the place of a scandalous tryst. Not that it mattered.

I shook my head and hurried past the amorous ghosts. Hunters can't afford distractions, no matter how bizarre or ridiculous, so I continued to look for a way out. The tunnel had been steadily climbing upward, and if the draft I was feeling was to be believed, we were close to the surface.

I shone my flashlight along the wall and stopped when I caught sight of a tapestry moving slightly. If we were in luck, the movement would be from that same draft I'd felt, rather than the movement of rodents. I'd seen enough rats to last a lifetime.

"Help me move this bench," I said, waving Ash over.

"Looks like a church pew," he said. "Bloody strange for a vampire bolt-hole."

I just shook my head and we dragged the heavy wooden bench across the floor. I had no idea where we were, or why the vampires had clawed a tunnel to this place.

"Look," I said, pulling the tapestry back to reveal a small door.

It was sized for hobbits, but I wasn't about to complain. I ran my fingers along the seams of the door, looking for a way to open it.

"Step back, love," Ash said.

I sighed and moved to the side. Ash took two steps back and ran at the door, slamming into the dry wood with his shoulder. The door shuddered, and after three more tries, it burst open.

Ash was surprisingly solid for a ghost. He claimed that he only manifested fully when he was close to me, and I wasn't sure if he was flirting or telling the truth.

Dust motes filled the air, but it was obvious that we'd found another tunnel. I groaned and shook my head. I was sick to death of tunnels. What I wouldn't give for the sun on my face.

"Go tell Celeste it's safe to start bringing people up," I said. "I'll search the tunnel for a way out."

I rubbed the back of my neck and surveyed the tunnel. Aside from the dust, it was clean. It was more of an underground, stone passageway than the kinds of tunnels we'd been trudging through—the kind found in old forts and castles.

At the end of the passageway, I found another trapdoor set into the ceiling. I climbed up a set of handholds, drew my combat knife, took a deep breath, and pushed upward. The shriek of the old metal hinges set my teeth on edge, but I smiled as I pulled myself up into an old room that held nothing but an old bed frame and chamber pot.

The faded silhouette of a cross still hung above the bed, but that's not what made me smile. There was a small window on the far wall. I ran to the window and looked out onto one of the city's canals.

We made it. We were free.

CHAPTER 39

"Hunters are trained to put the needs of others above our own."
-Jenna Lehane, Hunter

According to Ash, the vampires' tunnel had brought us to the Spookhuis, an infamous haunted house. The irony wasn't lost on me. The Spookhuis was actually made up of two buildings that at one time had been joined by an underground passage. One building had been a monastery, the other a nunnery. The passageway had been intended to provide the nuns access to the monastery's chapel, but one priest and nun found another use for it.

The popular story is that the priest felt remorse for his sins of the flesh, and one night murdered the young nun. If that was true, the two had made up in the afterlife. Either way, the buildings had developed a reputation for being haunted and were sold off, eventually becoming abandoned.

I didn't really care—we'd found our way out of the vamp nest and our human charges were alive. I was dead tired, but my footsteps were light as we made our way to the guildhall.

Once we reached the guildhall, we left Ash outside—since ghosts couldn't pass through the door wards—and took the men and women down to the Guild infirmary. I'd called ahead, rousing a grumpy Doc Martens who'd only just returned home after returning his daughter to her boarding school. If I thought he'd sounded irritated on the phone, it was nothing compared to his mood when we walked in with a dozen patients, all of us stinking of the sewers.

"And what am I supposed to do with all of these people?" he asked.

"Let them use the shower in the back, give them clean clothes and a bed, and tend to their injuries," I said, narrowing my eyes at the doctor.

"That's my shower," he complained, but he started assessing injuries and pulling out supplies. Hunters are trained to put the needs of others above our own. It's a hard habit to break, even when we're not feeling so generous. "What happened to these people anyway?"

"They were the victims of a mugging," Celeste said. "There was a street gang wearing masks to scare people into giving them their money. The gang was using the sewers as their hideout and had forced these people to follow them while they stole their valuables. Thankfully, we were out for a walk and heard a scream."

It was farfetched as hell, but the vampire's former prisoners seemed to accept the lie. I grimaced at the glazed eyes and vacant looks. Sofia and Nicolas, who we'd found alive and mostly unharmed, didn't even seem to recognize me. It was as if they were all sleepwalking. I bit my lip, wondering what would happen when they all woke up from this living nightmare.

I inched my way over to Celeste and gave her a sidelong look.

"I thought memory spells were illegal," I said, keeping my voice low.

She shrugged and waved a hand toward the men and women waiting their turn with Doc Martens.

"The vampire venom and blood loss already made them susceptible to suggestion," she said. "I just encouraged them to believe a plausible lie, one that would explain their injuries and disorientation. Would you rather they know the truth?"

I shivered, a chill running icy fingers up my spine.

"No," I said. "Thank you. You helped save these people from more than death in that dungeon."

"I just wish it was enough," she said.

I cocked an eyebrow at Celeste, but she shrugged and shook her head. I wondered if it had anything to do with what Ash had said earlier. Celeste had been his partner, but she hadn't been able to prevent his death. She'd taken it hard, and I couldn't help but wonder if she was still punishing herself for what she perceived as her ultimate failure.

"These people aren't the only ones who owe you a debt," I said. "You helped save their lives and save this city from a clan of vicious killers. If you're willing, I'd be honored to have you at my side as I take out the remaining vampires."

Her eyes widened and a smile flickered across her face.

"Help you take out Philip's men?" she asked. She nodded and pulled out her phone. "I'd like that. But first I need to rest and to have a chat with my coven. I'm going to call a circle. They don't approve of me being a Hunter, but they're still my sisters. They deserve to know what happened here. I'll be back by nightfall."

I smiled. If Celeste was back by nightfall, we could begin our hunt for Philip's remaining vamps as soon as they awakened and made the mistake of walking this city's streets.

Watching Celeste leave, I sidled up to Martens. He frowned, but continued to hand out bottles of water to his patients.

"How are they doing?" I asked, nodding toward Sofia and Nicolas.

"Not bad for the victims of a mugging by a gang of delinquents who enjoy dragging their victims through the sewers," he snapped.

I rubbed my face and yawned. I didn't have the energy to argue with Martens. He was angry, I got that, but this was his job. If he didn't like it, then he shouldn't have signed up for it.

"I should get cleaned up, but...if there's anything I can do for them," I said.

"No," he said, shaking his head. "You look like hell Jenna. Go get some rest. That's an order."

"Okay, thanks Doc," I said. "And Doc? Call me if there's any change."

"Fine, now go, Lehane," he said. "You're stinking up my infirmary."

Wasn't that gratitude for you? I raid a vamp nest, put down a rabid master vampire, and help rescue a dozen human prisoners, and when I make it topside I get told I stink. I snorted and shook my head. Good thing I didn't do this job for the glory and recognition.

CHAPTER 40

"Being a Hunter isn't always glamorous. More often than not it involves wading through blood, shit, and tears."
-Jenna Lehane, Hunter

I trudged up the steps, out of the guildhall, and onto the street where Ash was waiting. Did he get tired? Did ghosts sleep? Even when my mother's ghost had watched over me as a kid, I hadn't thought to ask.

"Come on," Ash said. "Let's get you some chocolate waffles."

I shook my head.

"I'm supposed to go home and rest, doctor's orders," I said.

"He said you have to rest, but he didn't say you couldn't eat first," he said. "If you don't start getting some calories, you're going to fade away until you're a bloody spook like me. Hmmm…maybe you should continue your ridiculous fasting. Can you imagine? We could be the dead version of Bonnie and Clyde. I can picture the haunting spree now."

Great. Ghost humor. I was never getting used to this.

"Is there even a place that serves waffles at five in the morning?" I asked. The sky was still pitch black, since sunrise in Bruges this time of year wasn't until seven. Most people would still be in their beds. "Plus, no one in their right mind is going to let me inside their restaurant looking and smelling like this."

I looked like a coblynau who'd climbed straight up out of the mines, but Ash was right. As tired as I was, I was too keyed up to sleep yet, and my stomach was growling. I couldn't remember the last time I ate.

"I know a place," he said.

Of course he did. Ash had spent the past two years floating around the city of Bruges with nothing better to do—until he'd met me and become a real boy, like freaking Pinocchio. Except there was a difference, because as real as Ash seemed to me, even now that I knew he was a ghost, most other people couldn't see him. It was hard to wrap my mind around.

Maybe a stack of sugar and carbs would help fuel my brain and clear out some of the cobwebs. I gave up and followed Ash.

The waffle place turned out to be an all night waffle stand, and though the guy working behind the counter gave me a disgusted look, he did serve me. I took my "celebratory waffles" as Ash called them over to a bench and dug in with no regard for diets and optimal nutrition. Chocolate had never tasted so good.

I was eyeing the cup that the melted chocolate had come in, considering licking it clean, when someone tossed a coin into it.

"Hey, what the hell!" I shouted.

The man's eyes widened and he hurried to blend in with the growing crowd. The Burg and Markt squares were often busy, but it was barely five-thirty in the morning and buses were beginning to drop off tourists in droves. I'd ignored it while eating, but the sound of luggage being rolled across cobbles was a constant. The place was so packed, I was lucky to have scored the bench I was sitting on—the bench most of the tourists were avoiding like the plague.

"They think you're homeless, love," Ash said with a smirk. "Think about it. They can't see me, but not one person has tried to share this bench with you."

I groaned and let my head drop into my hands.

"I really do stink," I said.

"I wouldn't know," Ash said with a shrug. "The benefits of being dead. But you do have some rather vile muck on your boots, and about an inch of vampire ash coating your hair. Plus, you keep talking to your imaginary friend."

I shook my head—kicking up an embarrassing cloud of dust—and straightened, ignoring the burning in my cheeks. Ash just smirked. Apparently, he thought being my imaginary friend was hilarious.

"Come on," I said. "I need a shower and about three days of sleep."

The sugar high that I was currently on wouldn't last. I'd be lucky if I made it to my bed without passing out.

I winced, the memory of my hotel bed coming to the surface unbidden. Crap. As much as sleep beckoned, I had a long morning ahead of me. The vampires had torn my bed to ribbons and trashed my room. Not to mention the Vandenberghes' blood left smeared across the lobby floor.

I groaned and Ash raised an eyebrow. I was about to tell him about the cleaning job that loomed in my future, but I felt a flash of recognition at one of the faces in the crowd.

"What is it, love?" he asked. "You look like you've seen a ghost."

That might have been funny a minute ago, but not now. The man I'd seen over Ash's shoulder was no innocent tourist. I'd seen this monster recently in a centuries old painting, and he hadn't aged a day. I'd know that face anywhere.

It was Jacques de Chatillon, the lone French survivor of the Bruges Matins nocturnal massacre, Philip's right hand man.

"This way," I said, grabbing Ash's arm and dragging him through the crowd.

People looked at me strangely, but I didn't care if it seemed like I was talking to myself. Philip had sent Jacques de Chatillon to rule over Bruges once before, and I was going to make sure that once again he was cast out of the city— preferably in a bag of street sweepings.

Ash and I pushed our way through the crowd. Well, I pushed and he sometimes floated through the tourists, although from the way he twitched, I didn't think that was his favorite option. He may only be solid when touching me, and vampires, and some inanimate objects, but passing through humans looked like it hurt. Apparently, being incorporeal had a down side.

"How come you can touch vampires?" I asked.

I turned my head back and forth struggling to keep Jacques in sight. The distance was growing between us, but no matter how fast we ran I couldn't outpace the vampire. My only hope was that he'd stop somewhere soon so we could close the distance.

"Because they're dead," Ash said.

I suppose that made sense. My feet were sore from running on cobbles, and my calf was screaming at me to stop, so I distracted myself with the puzzle that was Alistair Ashford.

"So, how can you touch me?" I asked. "I'm not dead."

"That I don't know," he said.

"Oh," I said lamely.

I'd hoped he'd have more answers.

"Are you going to tell me why we're running, or is this some evil plan to burn off those waffle calories?" he asked.

I stopped and spun in a circle, but the vampire was nowhere in sight. I pounded my fist against the nearest building. I'd lost him.

"Jacques de Chatillon, he was here," I said. I growled in frustration. "*Was* being the operative word, since I lost him."

"Jacques de Chatillon, Philip's second in command?" he asked.

"Bingo, that's the one," I said. "Damn. Look, I have to stop by the Guild later to check on Sofia and Nicolas. There's a picture of Jacques down in the archives. I'll borrow the painting and ask Celeste to do a tracking spell. Maybe we can figure out what Jacques is up to and put a stop to it."

Philip's right hand vamp was in Bruges. It was time to take him out of the equation and wrap this up like a Christmas present. This mission wouldn't be over until I cleared out every last bloodsucker from this city. Taking out the leaders would hasten that.

"You were lucky to spot him at all in this crowd," Ash said. "At least now we know he's here leading Philip's men. It's a damn sight more than we knew before."

An older couple clipped my heels with their suitcase, and I clenched my fists so hard that my nails bit into my palms.

"Why is it so damned crowded?" I asked. "Is it half priced frites day or something? Where did all these people come from?"

I was rambling, but it was better than cracking heads when there are no monsters within easy reach.

"Day after tomorrow is Ascension Day," he said, still looking around for any sign of the vampire. "Or rather, tomorrow is."

We'd spent a long time down in those sewers. Another hour and the sun would be rising over the city.

"And?" I asked.

I was tired, I was bleeding, and the sugar buzz had worn off. I started limping back toward the inn, where I faced at least two more hours of bagging up debris and scrubbing floors before I could grab any sleep. I was in no mood for riddles.

"Over fifty thousand people come to Bruges each year on Ascension Day for the procession festivities," he said with a shrug. "It'll get a mite busier before the day is out."

"Well the timing sucks," I said with a scowl.

"I'll be sure to complain to the tourist board," Ash said.

Fifty thousand people? That had to be double the local population. Not the kind of complication you want when you're hunting monsters. I'd try to keep the violence from spilling onto the busy city streets, but there was never any guarantee when dealing with bloodsucking vampires.

"So what is this whole procession thing?" I asked. "Some kind of street carnival?"

If there were going to be parties in the street, I was wearing ear plugs to bed. It would give the monsters an edge whilst sneaking up on me, but that was a chance I was willing to take if this was some kind of Belgian Mardi Gras.

"It's the Holy Blood Procession," he said. "It's basically a parade with men in medieval costumes. Then there's a bit of street theater—sometimes they do a passion play, which is not as fun as it sounds—followed by much rejoicing and everyone cramming into the pubs."

I shook my head. I was definitely wearing ear plugs all weekend. I was so tired that even my eyelids ached. Too bad I still had an inn to scrub clean.

Ash and I spent the rest of the morning washing away the evidence of the attack on Sofia and Nicolas. There were no other boarders staying here at the inn, but I couldn't risk someone showing up and seeing something in the light of day. With fifty thousand revelers flooding into the city, most hotels would be at maximum occupancy. Tourists were bound to come here in hopes of renting a room.

Plus, the place needed to be spotless when the couple returned home, and I was hoping that would be soon. So we grabbed gloves, bleach, and garbage bags and set to work.

Being a Hunter isn't always glamorous. More often than not it involves wading through blood, shit, and tears. The upside is that I'd become something of an expert at cleaning up the messes the monsters leave behind.

When we were done, there wasn't a trace of evidence to prove that an assault had ever happened. I suppose if I ever needed extra cash, or a new job, I could try my hand at crime scene cleanup. It's always good to have a backup plan.

"The place actually sparkles," Ash said.

"If you make a vampire joke, I will stake you with this mop handle," I said, leaning against the back of the Vandenberghes' couch. "Don't think I won't."

We were standing in Sofia and Nicolas' apartment. When we started there'd been blood all over the floor—lots of it—since the vamps had dragged the Vandenberghes' bleeding bodies through the apartment on their way out the back door.

"I wouldn't dream of it," he said.

"Speaking of dreams," I said, stifling a yawn. "It's time I follow Doc's orders and get some sleep. See you in the morning?"

"It is morning," he said. "But yes, I'll stop by once you're up."

I put away the mop and bucket and shooed Ash toward the door.

"Jenna," he said. "You did good today."

I shook my head.

"I screwed up in more ways than I can count," I said. "But thanks."

"You staked Dampierre, a notorious seven-hundred-year-old master vampire, led a raid to clean out a huge nest of bloodsucking vamps and flesh eating ghouls, rescued human prisoners, and stuck around to clean up a supernatural crime scene," he said. "Bloody hell, woman. Learn to take a compliment."

He walked out the door without looking back. I locked up and climbed the stairs to my room, a small smile on my lips.

When he said it like that, it sounded like a victory.

Chapter 41

"If you can't find your balance, you can kiss your ass goodbye."
-Niall Janus, Master Hunter

I expected to toss and turn all morning, but apparently the exertion of the hunt and the following hours of cleanup had pounded my nightmares into submission. I slept like the dead.

Damn good thing too, since I had a busy evening planned. I needed to visit the infirmary to check in on Sofia's and Nicolas' progress, then convince Darryl to loan me documents from the archives, and get Celeste to cast a locator spell to help me find a needle in a stack of freaking needles.

Once we had Jacques' location, we could plan out tonight's hunt. I wanted to rid the city of the remaining vampires, and I had a hunch that I'd find the House Capet clan vampires wherever Jacques was hiding out.

As much as I wanted to rush off for the wholesale slaughter of House Capet vampires, I knew enough to go through my usual training routine, waking up fully, and finding my balance. As Master Janus was fond of saying to new recruits, "If you can't find your balance, you can kiss your ass goodbye."

I stretched and moved through my katas, testing the new stitches I'd given myself, and working through the stiffness I'd acquired from sleeping on the floor. I hadn't been able to replace my room's furnishings, not at the ungodly hour we'd returned to the inn, and the mattress was beyond repair. I'd bagged up the shredded fabric and mounds of stuffing, and used the remains of the curtains for a pillow. As soon as I could, I'd order what I needed to make the room new again. So long as I kept renting the room and kept a "Do Not Disturb" sign on the door, the Vandenberghes should be none the wiser.

That didn't make the guilt any harder to shake.

"I'm so sorry," I whispered as I left the room.

I'd never forgive myself for leading the monsters to the Vandenberghes' doorstep, and I vowed never to make the same mistake again.

I made it to the infirmary by eight o'clock, just in time to interrupt Benjamin Martens' dinner.

"For the love of Pete, let me eat in peace," he growled around a mouthful of bacon cheeseburger.

I wrinkled my nose and nodded over his shoulder toward the curtained off rows of beds.

"How are they?" I asked.

I tapped my foot as Martens pointedly ignored the question. After about five minutes, the room began to spin and I realized I was holding my breath. I crossed my arms, made an effort to breathe, and focused on the blotch of mustard on Martens' nose as I waited for his response. It was better than watching the ketchup and grease dripping from his burger like blood and plasma onto his desk blotter.

"Better than can be expected," he said, as he chewed the last bite of his burger.

He gave a one armed shrug and wiped his face with a paper napkin. The sound as he dragged the napkin against the bristles of his five o'clock shadow grated on my nerves, but I kept a straight face as I asked, "And Sofia and Nicolas Vandenberghe?"

"The Vandenberghes are doing fine," he said. "They're a little shaken up, but they should be able to go home later tonight. I've been sending folks home once they wake up, but those two were still asleep last I checked."

Sofia and Nicolas were going to be okay, thank God.

"Let me know if they need anything, and if there's any extra costs involved in caring for these people, bill it to me," I said.

The Hunters' Guild was sworn to protect humans from the monsters, but I hadn't asked Chadwick's permission before bringing House Dampierre's prisoners to the infirmary. I hadn't followed protocol, and Martens knew it. If anyone was going to have to face Master Peeters about any incurred costs, it would be me. I might as well offer to cough up the money now, before Martens sent the bill up the food chain.

There went the money I'd been saving for replacement rounds for my SIG semi-automatic pistol and a custom KA-BAR tactical knife. It's not like the human military or outdoor survivalists need their blades tipped with silver and iron, or their firearms loaded with silver, iron, or wooden bullets. Well, not that they know of. It sure would make my job easier if they did.

My point being, you can't buy the necessary weapons for hunting the fae and the undead in your local Walmart. Good weapons, the kind that kept my ass from becoming grass, weren't cheap, and from the look on his face, Martens was about to drain my bank account dry.

I sighed and shook my head.

"I'll be down in the archives if you need me," I said.

"Got a new lead on the House Capet vampires?" he asked.

"Let's just say I have an interest in art appreciation," I said with a wink.

He grunted and turned back to his desk and its scattered piles of paperwork. I had to go up to the ground level before crossing the lobby and descending down the stairs to the archives. It gave me time to formulate a plan for convincing Darryl to break the rules and allow me to remove an ancient painting from the Guild's collection. I rubbed my neck and sighed.

It wasn't going to be easy.

Chapter 42

"Note to self; don't try to sneak up on a blind Hunter."
-Jenna Lehane, Hunter

By the time I made it to the archives, I'd decided to borrow the painting without asking. It's often easier to ask forgiveness than ask permission. I opened the door slowly, without so much as a creak, and tiptoed inside the archives. Darryl wasn't behind his desk and I let out the breath I'd been holding. Good so far.

Walking carefully, I crossed through the main chamber and into the musty room in the back. But when I lifted the painting of Philip and Jacques from the wall, I felt the cold edge of a blade at my throat.

Note to self; don't try to sneak up on a blind Hunter.

"Did you really think you could come in here without me knowing?" Darryl asked.

He shifted into my peripheral vision, allowing me to see that, though his voice was hard, his lips twitched in amusement.

"Look, Darryl, I can explain," I said.

"Girl, I don't want to know why you're trying to steal Guild property," he said.

"Earlier this morning..." I said.

"No," he said, holding up one large hand and lowering the sword in the other. "I really don't want to know. I'm going to go to my desk and sharpen pencils real noisy like, and if you and that there painting aren't here when I'm done, then there's no way a blind man could have known what you were up to. Now is there?"

"I'll bring it back," I said.

"Don't want to know," he said.

Darryl padded off to the front of the archives, and I waited for him to start up the pencil sharpener before so much as blinking. When I tiptoed out past his desk, Darryl was pushing pencils into the electric sharpener, a smile playing along his lips. I shook my head and tiptoed out of the archives.

For once, something had gone easier than expected. I should have known the proverbial shit was positioning itself to hit the fan with the greatest possible impact.

CHAPTER 43

"You keep throwing yourself in front of the monsters, and you'll find out soon enough that life is short."

-Alistair Ashford, Hunter

I made it out onto the street to where Ash was waiting without encountering another Hunter. I took that as a good omen.

"You made it out without a sword in the gut," Ash said with a nod. "Well color me impressed."

"Actually, Darryl made it pretty easy," I said, gingerly setting the bottom edge of the painting's frame on the sidewalk and balancing it against the side of a stone building. "At least, he did once he established that I wasn't pulling the wool over his eyes. At a guess, I'd say he's a bit touchy about being underestimated."

"Lambert let you waltz out of the archives with a priceless painting?" Ash asked, eyes widening.

I shrugged.

"He knows I'll do my best to bring it back," I said. "I wouldn't take it if it wasn't important."

"No, love, you don't do anything selfish," he said. "That much is obvious."

"You make that sound like a bad thing," I said narrowing my eyes at him.

Now it was Ash's turn to shrug.

"You keep throwing yourself in front of the monsters, and you'll find out soon enough that life is short," he said. "Take it from me. Live a little while you still can."

I snorted.

"Because that's working out so well for Celeste," I said. "Speaking of which, I need to give her a call about working a locator spell. I tried calling earlier, but it went straight to voicemail."

I pulled out my phone and dialed Celeste. I wasn't sure if she was back yet from her meeting with her coven, but hopefully she'd have her ringer on. Once again, I was in luck.

Celeste picked up on the third ring, her voice groggy. I
just hoped that she was catching up on her sleep, not hitting
the Mandragora. If she kept smoking that stuff, she was going
to burn away the last wedge of her Swiss cheese memory.

"Wake up, sleepyhead," I said.

"Is it time for our hunting date, already?" she asked.
"By Hecate, I'm tired."

"You here at the guildhall?" I asked, tipping my head
back and hoping she was upstairs in her room. I had no idea
where her coven held its circle, and I didn't feel much like
waiting.

"Yes," she said with a yawn. "You here already? I can
be down as soon as I get dressed. Unless you want to join me
in my room..."

Celeste's voice went low and sultry, and I cringed. I
started pacing the sidewalk, making sure not to bump into the
painting I'd borrowed from the archives. The last thing I
needed was getting Darryl on my bad side.

"I'm outside with Ash," I said. "There's been a change of
plan. I might have a lead on the House Capet vamps."

"What do you need me to do?" she asked.

From the rustle of fabric, it sounded like Celeste was
finally getting out of bed. Good. The sooner we located
Jacques, the sooner we killed ourselves some vampires. The
city would be safe again, and I'd probably have enough fangs to
string myself another necklace. All in all, it would be a win-
win.

"I need you to do a tracking spell on a vamp," I said.

"That's going to be difficult," she said.

"Why?" I asked, shaking my head. "I have his name and
a picture of him from an old painting. Isn't that all you need?"

I'd seen tracking spells done on vamps before, and
though the results could be unreliable, I knew we had enough
to give it a try. We couldn't just sit around and wait for
Jacques de Chatillon to fall into our laps. I'd been lucky to spot
him in the crowd before, and I knew better than most that good
luck always runs out eventually.

"It's not that," she said with a sigh. "My magic is tied to
celestial movements. And as my sisters reminded me during
my visit this morning, there's an eclipse tomorrow."

My ears pricked at the mention of an eclipse, and something niggled in my brain. Wasn't there something else happening tomorrow?

"Ash, that procession that's causing all the crowds," I said. "Isn't that tomorrow?"

I wasn't sure how much of our conversation he'd overheard, but his brows drew together as he nodded.

"Aye, love," he said. "The procession is tomorrow."

I'd been pacing the sidewalk, but I stopped dead in my tracks.

"When does this parade happen?" I asked. "Is it before sunrise, or after sunset?"

Ash shook his head.

"No, love, the Procession of the Holy Blood is held every year at two-thirty in the afternoon," he said. "They've been holding the festivities at the same time for centuries. Why, what are you thinking?"

"Celeste, what time is this eclipse?" I asked.

"Two-forty," she said.

Shit. My gut was telling me that it was no coincidence that a group of vampires had tried to invade House Dampierre's turf so close to an eclipse. An eclipse that took place at the same time as a party that had something to do with the Holy Blood.

"Ash, what's the significance of the procession?" I asked. "What happens exactly?"

"It's the one time each year that the Holy Blood is removed from the lockbox in the basilica and paraded through the city streets," he said. "Like I said before, it's a big deal. Pilgrims and tourists come from all over the world to be a part of the celebration."

"They remove the real Holy Blood from the safety of consecrated ground, and parade it around the city?" I asked. "Are they nuts?"

"It will be under armed guard," Celeste said, making me jump. I'd nearly forgotten she was still on the line.

"Well, I hope it's locked inside a Pope Mobile filled with Holy Water, or we have a problem," I said.

"Bloody hell," Ash muttered.

Bloody Hell was right. Pieces of the puzzle came together, and I didn't like the growing picture, not one bit.

The Holy Blood was the relic that started the feud between House Dampierre and House Capet, the same item that the Knights Templar brought from the Holy Land and put into the safekeeping of the Basilica of the Holy Blood. Philip obviously had his greedy eye on it seven-hundred years ago, and he'd waited until the one moment when the Holy Blood would be outside of consecrated ground under the cover of darkness—when vampires can walk the streets.

It would have taken a lot of planning and even more patience, but I didn't doubt that this was all part of the master vampire's plan. What are a few centuries when you're immortal?

Not that Philip hadn't made other attempts to gain access to the Holy Blood in the past few centuries. A chill ran up my spine as I remembered the stories of Van Haecke, who had been a chaplain in the Basilica of the Holy Blood back in the nineteenth century. The man was rumored to have become a Satanist after his encounters with a woman who'd arrived in Bruges from Paris. I seriously would not be surprised if Philip sent Berthe Courriere in an effort to corrupt Van Haecke and goad him into desecrating the church that housed the Holy Blood.

Philip hadn't succeeded, at least not fully. Van Haecke had fallen to the dark side, but the Basilica of the Holy Blood remained a place where vampires could not tread. But that hadn't stopped the vampire master—and now his men were here to finish the job they'd started centuries ago.

The vampires were clever, but they hadn't counted on us uncovering their evil plot. That, at least, gave us the element of surprise. If we were going to take advantage of that, we needed all hands on deck for this. It was time to call in the troops.

"Celeste, can you take down the ward keeping spirits from entering the guildhall?" I asked.

"Sure," she said.

"Good, do it," I said. Taking down the wards would allow Ash to join us. He might be a ghost, but he was also a Hunter. I wanted him with us. "When you're done, call Zarkhov and ask him to meet us in the archives. Ash and I will meet you there."

"What about Martens and Chadwick?" she asked.

"Martens is busy with the patients we brought him last night," I said. "I'll fill him in later."

"And Chadwick?" she asked.

"Screw Chad, we do this without him," I said. "I want people I can trust at my back."

"Okay, give me a few minutes to get the ward down," she said. "Alistair should be able to tell when I'm done."

We hung up and I stared at the ghosts that floated up and down the street. I wouldn't need Ash to tell me when the wards were down. I had my very own detector right here. My ghost posse had followed me out of Dampierre's dungeon, and I'd been ignoring them ever since. But they sure would indicate when the wards were down.

I just hoped they didn't rattle too many chains while we were inside.

CHAPTER 44

"Hunters protect the innocent from monsters."
-Jenna Lehane, Hunter

"You're telling me the vampires are going to try to steal the Holy Blood, the Sangreal, the Holy Grail?" Darryl asked.

We'd gathered in the archives, me, Ash, Darryl, Aleksey, and Celeste. As I suspected, the horde of ghosts had followed me inside, but so far they seemed to be behaving themselves. Ghosts with restraint, who knew? Celeste rubbed her arms, but otherwise no one seemed to give the ghosts much notice.

They were all too busy listening to Darryl's tirade.

"Yes," I said. "But you're just kidding about it being the Holy Grail, right? Isn't that supposed to be a cup or something?"

"No one knows for sure, but there's plenty of scholarly debate," he said. "*Sang real* means Holy Blood and *san greal* means Holy Grail, so you can see where things get complicated."

The archives suddenly felt way too small for five Hunters and a couple hundred ghosts. My chest was tight, and someone had replaced my knees with Jell-O.

"You're saying that Philip is after the Holy Grail," I said. "That's his end game."

"What I'm saying, girl, is that it's a possibility," he said.

Athena save us all.

"Looks like we're on a Grail quest, love," Ash said.

Zarkhov blew out a whistle and smiled.

"That mean I get to blow shit up?" Aleksey asked.

I hated to encourage that eager gleam in Zarkhov's eyes, but the truth was that I needed his help. Vampires are highly flammable, and Celeste's magic would be limited due to the eclipse. We'd need our pyromaniacal demolition expert's skills before the day was through.

But I didn't have to like it.

We had a city filled with innocent humans. Collateral damage was a major concern, even without explosives. Add

Aleksey into the mix and things could get messy. But if it was the only way to keep the Holy Blood safe, and prevent the deaths of millions, I'd do what needed to be done. I'd known that when I'd called this meeting. I just hadn't considered all the ramifications until now.

I leaned my head back and groaned.

"Aleksey, darling, I believe that's a yes," Celeste said.

I lowered my head to take in our ragtag group of Hunters and nodded. Celeste was pressed up against Aleksey, trailing her nails along his chiseled jaw and eyeing him like he was the last goddamned ice cream cone in the desert. The Guild didn't discourage fraternizing amongst Hunters, but I suddenly wished they did, so I could throw the book at them.

We were in the archives, and there were a hell of a lot of books lying about. My fingers twitched, but I looked away from Celeste. If groping Zarkhov kept her head in the game and a Mandragora pipe out of her hands, then so be it.

"We all need to take part in this hunt," I said. "Darryl, you're up first. I need to know everything you have on Jacques, Philip, and the Holy Blood. And make it fast."

Unfortunately, there were no Cliff's Notes for centuries of historical facts, hearsay, and scholarly conjecture. Darryl did his best to summarize what Guild archivists knew, but much of the information, especially what we pulled from Grail legends, was contradictory.

It was a long night.

We stayed up pouring over the archives, raiding the armory, and sketching out plans for the following day. When tempers began to flare, I suggested we take a break and reconvene at dawn. It would give everyone a few hours to rest up, since we had an even longer day ahead of us tomorrow.

Though with Celeste's tongue in Zarkhov's ear, I highly doubted those two would be getting much sleep. I shook my head and went back over my notes. I wasn't planning on getting any rest either. There was still too damn much to do.

We needed a solid plan.

There was no way to stop the procession. It wasn't the kind of event that scheduled a rain date, not that we could change the weather. Celeste claimed that making it rain was impossible today, even if her entire coven lent their magic to the spell. Zarkhov's suggestion to call in a bomb threat was met with more enthusiasm, at least until Darryl recalled a

similar threat making the papers a decade ago. The people of
Bruges hadn't cancelled the procession then, so there was no
reason to believe they'd do so now.

Zarkhov's offer to follow the threat up with a real
bombing was unanimously vetoed. Hunters protect the
innocent from monsters. We don't bomb parade routes filled
with tourists, not when there are other alternatives. If we did,
we'd be no better than the rogue paranormals we hunted.

So we were left with the duty of guarding the Holy
Blood along the parade route. I wanted to rail against the
longstanding tradition that might place the Holy Blood,
possibly the Holy Grail if Darryl was to be believed, into the
hands of vampires. But there was no point in raging about it.
Plus, doing so would make me a hypocrite.

The Hunters' Guild was steeped in old lore and we held
to our own centuries old traditions. We had plenty of ancient
ceremonies and rituals that would make most modern
outsiders roll their eyes, but we continued to do things in the
old ways. Adhering to those traditions was part of what bound
us together, made us strong.

"You alright, love?" Ash asked.

He'd stuck around when the others had gone to their
beds and, since I doubted that ghosts needed sleep, I'd let him.
Sometimes we need more than tradition to stay strong as we
stand in the path of the coming storm.

"I'll be alright when this is over," I said. "How about
you? It must have been weird being back here again, around
your former Guild brothers."

With Celeste's help, I'd convinced the others that the
ghost of Alistair Ashford, their fallen comrade in arms, was
indeed here with us. For a group of Hunters who go around
policing supernaturals, they were surprisingly reluctant to
believe me. Faerie ointment doesn't make the dead, or the
undead, visible to mortal eyes, and the ability to see ghosts was
rare. If it hadn't been for Celeste backing me up, and more
than a few floating objects that they couldn't explain, I'd
probably still be trying to make my case.

"I'm sure they would have been a mite happier if they
could have seen me in the flesh," he said. "But then again, who
wouldn't?"

Ash winked and I snorted. He always did see the
positive side of things. I smiled and turned back to my notes,

determined to try his approach. Maybe if I focused on the positive aspects of our mission, I'd be able to figure out how to make this right.

There was still so much we didn't know, but at least we had a good idea of when the vampires would strike. The eclipse only gave the bloodsuckers a seven minute window of darkness to make their move. If they stuck around after that, they'd end up how I ate my steak—burned to a crisp.

From the vampires' limited timetable, I could estimate the point at which the attack would take place on the parade route. There were variables—length of speeches, speed at which the procession moved—but I was confident that the Holy Blood would not leave Burg square before the eclipse began. That was our point of contact.

I pulled out a map of the city center and overlaid a public works blueprint showing all sewer drains, manhole covers, and fire hydrants. With the nearby canals, multitude of sewer access points, and numerous buildings, there were just too many places where the vampires could enter the square. We couldn't guard them all.

That was when the fire hydrants caught my eye, giving me an idea. I grinned as my fingers traced trajectories.

"We'll be waiting for you, bloodsuckers," I whispered, staring at the map. "Prepare to get hosed."

CHAPTER 45

"A Hunter's work is never done."
-Jenna Lehane, Hunter

Martens called around ten in the morning to let me know that the last patient had been released from the infirmary. He obviously intended to close up shop and sleep for the next week. Too bad that wasn't a possibility. Martens may be a doctor, but he was also a Hunter, and as we all knew, a Hunter's work is never done. He might as well get used to it.

"I'm glad you called," I said. "We've got a situation."

"Give me a break, Lehane," he said. "I've been pulling double shifts ever since you stepped foot in Bruges. What is it now?"

"The vampires are going to make a move on the Holy Blood during the procession today," I said. "We'll need your help to keep the relic safe."

The line went so silent, I wondered if Martens had fallen asleep.

"Doc, you still there?" I asked.

"Y-y-yes, shit, yeah, I'm here," he said. "What's the plan?"

I told him some of the basics. I didn't want to overwhelm him with all the details, but he needed to know our intent to stop the theft of the Holy Blood, while protecting as many humans as possible.

"They're going to make a grab for the relic today between fourteen and fifteen hundred hours," I said. "I'm guessing that will place the procession inside Burg square when the vampires make their move. It's going to be wall to wall people, so collateral damage is a concern."

"You want me there for triage?" he asked.

"Yes," I said.

He sounded relieved and I had to wonder the last time this guy had seen actual fieldwork. Martens was a Hunter, but as the Guild's doctor he may have managed to avoid facing conflict in recent years. After the loss of his wife, I guess I couldn't blame him.

His reaction made me confident that I was giving him the right role in all of this.

"Minimizing casualties will be your priority, but you can also be our eyes and ears inside the crowd," I said. "If you see a vamp, radio it in. We'll be wearing ear pieces for this run."

"Okay," he said with a sigh. "I'll be leaving soon then. I need time to gather the necessary medical supplies and get them in place."

"I can send Aleksey over with your ear piece and radio transmitter," I said. "But Doc, before you go, I need one more favor."

"Why am I not fucking surprised?" he asked. "What is it this time?"

"I might need your help restraining Simon Chadwick," I said.

The line went silent again, but this time I waited for Martens to process my request. Even I had to admit it was a lot to take in.

"That's insubordination," he said.

Master Peeters, for some unfathomable reason, had put Chadwick in charge during his absence. Knowing Chad, he'd volunteered for the job. It was the kind of move he'd make. Simon Chadwick might be a judgmental, chauvinistic ass, but he was also driven.

Problem was, with Chadwick as our interim boss, going against him was a serious offense. I believed in doing what would save the most innocent lives—it seemed the truest way to uphold my vows—but not everyone would feel that way. Chadwick wasn't the only Hunter with a strict adherence to rules and red tape. I just hoped that Martens could be swayed to see things my way.

"I know," I said. "But he's a liability."

Chad wasn't a team player. He was a control freak who got off on dominating those he believed were inferior. If he discovered what we were up to, he'd shut down our operation and ask questions later. That was a risk we couldn't take.

He was also my means of getting close to the Holy Blood.

Once I'd established my plan for intercepting the vampires, it became clear that we needed a Hunter at ground zero. It was the only way to ensure the Holy Blood didn't get snatched in the ensuing chaos. But getting close to the relic wouldn't be easy.

That's where Chad came in.

Each year a group calling themselves the Brotherhood of the Holy Blood was given the honor of carrying the relic during the procession. Chad was one of these thirty-one men. The Hunters' Guild maintained a presence within the Brotherhood and, due to his noble blood, Chadwick was our current inside man.

"What makes you think I can help you restrain Chadwick?" Martens asked.

"Call it a hunch," I said.

"Fine, Lehane," he said. "Meet me in the lobby in five. We might as well get this over with."

Martens hung up and Ash quirked an eyebrow at me.

"What are you up to, love?" he asked.

"Chad's going to let me march in his place today," I said.

"I highly doubt that," he said, shaking his head.

"I can be very persuasive," I said, rolling one of my knives over my knuckles.

"Still, it won't be easy to get Chadwick to give up his spot in the procession," he said with a frown.

It was true that Chadwick would probably toss his own mother under a bus for an opportunity to show off his role within the elite Brotherhood of the Holy Blood, but my trip to House Dampierre's dungeon had given me an idea.

When I killed Guy Dampierre, I'd helped to set thousands of ghosts free from that room of death and torture. But hundreds more had remained. I'd felt their lingering presence this evening as I walked the streets from the inn to the guildhall, swirling around me in curiosity and confusion.

I'd stolen the focus of their rage, and now I intended to give them a new target. One Simon Chadwick, chauvinist and attempted rapist, would do nicely.

"Oh, I don't know about that," I said, an evil grin tugging at my lips. "I think Chad is about to have a very, very bad day."

CHAPTER 46

"A Guild divided against itself will perish."
-Jenna Lehane, Hunter

Facing Chad was not how I wanted to spend my morning. I didn't trust him, and part of my brain still gibbered in a dark corner at the thought of what he tried to do to me, but I was running low on options. The Blood of Christ in the hands of vampires could not be good. If the vampires got an upper hand in the coming war, more innocents would die. I couldn't let that happen.

"Any idea where Chadwick is now?" I asked.

Martens was pacing the lobby, a medical satchel slung over his shoulder. I convinced Ash to stay behind with Celeste in the archives, but I hadn't come empty handed. I'd brought my weapons and a bag containing a coil of rope, just in case. But my real weapons were the vengeful ghosts I'd just encouraged to go haunt Chad's ass.

The horde of spirits raced up the ornate staircase, so I was guessing that Chad was either in the dormitory or the mess hall.

"Probably getting into his costume," Martens said. "That replica armor is a bitch to put on, and he broke his finger in a training accident this week. It's going to take him awhile to get ready."

Convenient that. I grinned, flashing my teeth. I'm pretty sure I was the one who broke Chad's finger, and that sure as hell was no training accident, but I refrained from taking the credit. Martens already thought I was bad news.

When we reached the hallway outside Chadwick's door, I could hear a commotion coming from inside. Martens raised an eyebrow, and I shrugged. I hadn't explained my ability to interact with ghosts, there hadn't been time. Plus, I had no idea if my plan would work.

I'd hoped to put Chad off balance by sending a pack of angry ghosts his way, but I had no guarantees that the spirits would do as I asked. With a few exceptions, I'd made a habit of ignoring the dead. To say that I was in new territory here was an understatement.

I rapped on the door and held my breath.

"W-w-who's there?" Chad asked from inside the room.

"It's me, Lehane," I said. My voice didn't quiver half as much as Chad's did and I raised my chin and reached for the doorknob. "Open up."

"Bossy little bitch," Chad muttered. "Go away. I'm not feeling well."

"Then I guess it's a good thing I brought the doctor with me," I said in my most cheery voice.

I felt the lock click beneath my hand, and I opened the door. What I saw as we stepped inside brought a smirk to my lips, and I had to cough to stifle a laugh.

Chad was flailing around as if surrounded by a swarm of pixies, but I knew better. It wasn't the annoying insects of the fae world flitting around his head. Nope, Chad was plagued by ghosts.

Karma's a bitch that way.

When he noticed me staring, Chad lowered his hands and forced his arms down at his sides. He scowled down his nose at me, but at the moment he wasn't all that imposing. Chad's face twitched, and as we moved further into the room, he shivered and rubbed his arms as he crossed them over his chest.

"Sorry to hear you've come down with something," I said, not meaning a word of what I said. "Flu is it?"

Chad shook his head and reached for the costume that lay spread out on his bed.

"P-p-probably j-j-just something I ate," he said as he fiddled with the catches on the shining breast plate.

Martens caught my eye and tilted his head toward a book on Chad's nightstand. It looked an awful lot like a Satanist bible.

I stiffened. Was Chad our traitor? Had he been continuing Van Haecke's work to try to desecrate the church for the vampires? It didn't seem to jive with what I knew of Chad, but then again, maybe his holier-than-thou attitude was a cover. Maybe he was just plain evil.

I could get on board with that theory.

The rusalka, Natasha, had said we harbored a traitor in our midst, but I was hoping that her comment had been typical fae manipulation, a way to get us Hunters chasing our own tails. Then again, as much as faeries enjoyed twisting the truth, they are incapable of telling bald-faced lies. Out of every Hunter I'd met, Chad was the most likely suspect.

I narrowed my eyes and turned back to Chad, moving forward to get his attention. Now more than ever, I needed to take his place in today's procession. If Chad was working with the vampires, there was no way we could allow him to be that close to the Holy Blood.

Plus, a Guild divided against itself will perish. We had to have solidarity amongst our team if we were to win this fight.

"You're obviously not feeling like yourself today, Chad," I said. My words were kind, but my voice was iron. "How about we send another Hunter in your place?"

Chad's head jerked up, and he glared at me, righteous fury in his gaze.

"No, this is my solemn duty," he said. "I earned the right. I will not let a...an illness get in the way."

Duty? Doing his duty meant watching the backs of his Guild brothers and sisters. It wasn't a dress up party where grown men vied for status. It sure as hell didn't mean attempted rape, or treason against the Guild.

"Simon Chadwick, I am ordering you to the infirmary," Doc Martens said, moving forward. "And if you don't hand over that costume, I will knock you out and carry you there."

Martens held up a syringe, a wicked gleam in his eye. Damn, the doctor was a scary guy when he was grumpy. I made a mental note to send him a fruit basket when this was all over.

"It's alright," I said, raising a hand to Martens. "I've got this."

I turned back to Chad. As much as I'd enjoy knocking Chad out with a solid punch to that pompous face of his, I was going to try to do this without a fight.

"You're right, Chad," I said. "Protecting the Holy Blood is serious, which is why you need to stand down."

"I don't...I just..." he stuttered. With his disheveled hair and wide eyes, he resembled a lost child, but I didn't back off.

"It is your duty," I said. "Stand down."

His shoulders sagged and he let the replica armor drop to the floor with a clang. Martens took his arm and led him out of the room. At the door, Chad turned.

"But who will you find worthy enough to take my place?" he asked.

Oh, I already had a replacement, but ol' Chad wasn't going to like it. Not one bit.

"That's easy, Chad," I said. He tilted his head and I felt a slow grin slide across my face. "You're looking at her."

Chad let out a strangled cry, but his attempt to lunge at me was short-lived. His eyes glazed over and he slumped against Martens.

The doctor sighed and shook his head as he withdrew the hypodermic needle.

"I'll get this one situated in the infirmary before I head out," he said.

"Thanks, Doc," I said. "How long you think he'll be out?"

"Until tonight, I'd wager," he said. "Not long enough."

"Why do you say that?" I asked.

We only needed Chad out of the way until we defeated the vamps. If he was unconscious all day, we were golden.

"Chadwick's going to be pissed when he wakes up, thanks to you," he said. "You better watch out when he comes to." I shrugged and he shook his head. "Was that really necessary, telling him a woman was going to take his place?"

"Yes," I said, holding his gaze.

"Never easy with you, Lehane, is it?" he asked.

I snorted.

"No," I said, beaming. "It never is."

CHAPTER 47

"Hunters keep most humans in the dark in order to prevent fear and chaos."
-Jenna Lehane, Hunter

I stood in the heat of midday, sweat rolling down my back beneath the shining armor and white tabard emblazoned with a bright, red cross. Although I blended with the other members of the Brotherhood of the Holy Blood, I'd made some modifications to my costume. I'd replaced the replica armor with the real stuff, which meant the gleaming metal would deflect weapons and fangs.

It also made it heavy as hell.

I rolled my shoulders, wincing at the many aches and pains I'd developed over the course of the past week. When all this was over, I was going sleep for an entire day. Either that, or I'd be sleeping for eternity. I was hoping for the former.

I checked in on the radio I was wearing, confirming, once again, that my team was in position. We'd only have one chance at this, hence the double-checking. The eclipse was scheduled to begin in eight minutes and, make no mistake, when day turned to night, the vampires would come. I could feel it in my bones.

"Position check," I said, keeping my voice low.

The head of the procession was just beginning to exit the Basilica of the Holy Blood, but I, and the other costumed members of the Brotherhood, had not yet passed through the threshold of the church and out into the noise of the awaiting crowd. I didn't want to risk the curiosity of the other guards by talking loudly to myself.

Not that I was too worried about the Brotherhood of the Holy Blood.

At one time, the Brotherhood had been comprised of skilled knights who vowed to keep the Holy Blood safe. It was their annual duty to guard the relic as it was paraded through the streets of Bruges. But from the look of the pudgy men in their fancy dress shoes, trained knights had been replaced by other pillars of the community such as lawyers, bankers, and politicians.

I was willing to bet that the last time someone with the necessary skills had assumed a role as guardian, this armor and tabard was still in fashion. I shifted my weight from foot to foot as I waited for my team to check in.

"Lambert, check," Darryl said.

"Dubois, check," Celeste said.

"Zarkhov, check," Aleksey said.

"Martens, check," Benjamin said.

"Lehane, check," I said.

Five Hunters and one ghost against an unknown number of vampires who were being led by Philip's lieutenant, Jacques de Chatillon, a vamp so old, he died his first death centuries before the Burning Times. It wasn't the best odds.

Not with a crowd of humans to protect.

I fidgeted with my fang necklace as the door to the square grew closer. I walked beside the ornate palanquin on which the relic was displayed. Two members of the Brotherhood of the Holy Blood hoisted the poles of the palanquin onto their shoulders, solemnly carrying the relic like pallbearers. I'd offered to work crowd control, which put me close to the relic, while keeping my hands free for my weapons.

My armor wasn't the only thing I'd replaced with the real thing. The sword, daggers, and crossbow I carried were real, so were the wooden stakes tucked beneath my tabard. If a vampire got within my reach, I'd take him out.

We Hunters don't normally expose the secrets of the supernatural world, but not for the same reasons as the fae and the undead. The supes want their existence to remain a secret for the sake of self preservation. Hunters keep most humans in the dark in order to prevent fear and chaos. No one wanted another Burning Times, no one sane anyway.

That was why I'd use the pageantry of today's event in our favor. If the crowd witnessed a costumed knight decapitate or stake a vampire, they'd think it part of the street theater they'd come to expect from this event. See a vampire burst into a cloud of ash? They'd explain it away as sleight of hand and amazing special effects.

Most humans can't handle the fact that they share their world with monsters who have been here long before man crawled out of the mud, created his first crude weapons, and started making himself a nuisance. Humans fear what they can't explain. So the brain has developed coping mechanisms that help keep man in the dark.

That's why children and the mentally ill see more than the rest of us. Children haven't fully developed those coping mechanisms yet, and the coping mechanisms of the mentally ill have become damaged.

It also helped that faeries and the undead hide their true appearance beneath a magic glamour. If humans managed to see vampires during the darkness of the eclipse, the vamps were likely to look like uber attractive twenty-somethings—not walking corpses. For the undead, that glamour helped to camouflage the visage of a killer from their unwitting prey.

Today it might also help to prevent a riot.

I blinked rapidly, eyes darting through the crowd as we stepped out onto the Burg. The noise was even louder than I'd expected. The cheers of the crowd reverberated off the cobbled square and the stone buildings that enclosed the Burg, creating an almost deafening din.

Once again I was glad of the high tech ear pieces that Zarkhov had provided from the armory. If we'd relied on cell phones or standard issue walkie-talkies, we'd have total radio silence right now. Instead, I could continue to hear status reports above the cheers of the crowd.

Everyone on my team had a job to do, no matter what suspicious thoughts made my chest tight. The rusalka's words still rang in my head, but I shook it off. Chad wouldn't wake for a few more hours, and I had Zharkov working away from the action. They were the only two I thought might be capable of that kind of treachery, not that I wanted to believe the faerie's accusations at all.

But the memory of Martens nodding toward the Satanist bible on Chad's nightstand was still fresh. I grit my teeth and tried to stem the growing paranoia. I couldn't afford the distraction, and there wasn't much else I could do to control the situation. If there was a traitor in our midst, we'd find out soon enough.

I scanned the crowd, hand heading toward my sword. It was on my hip in plain sight, one of the many benefits of being part of the procession. I was fully armed and ready for battle.

A children's dance group was performing ahead of us, their costumes bedecked with colorful fabric streamers that twirled through the air as the dancers spun in circles. A choir was singing ahead of them, but they were already passing out of the Burg square, taking their music with them.

I eyed the sky nervously. The eclipse would begin any minute now. I'd done everything I could think of to put into play a plan to keep the relic out of the vampires' clawed hands and protect as many innocents possible. I swallowed hard, my mouth going painfully dry. I just hope I wasn't forgetting something.

The square darkened, and there was no more time for worrying. The eclipse had begun, rapidly swallowing the sun. It was time for action.

Amidst *oohs* and *ahs*, the crowd pointed to the sky, but I kept my eyes on the square. I scanned rooftops, doorways, and the spots where the archive's maps indicated manhole covers and sewer grates. I didn't know where the vampires would make their grand entrance, but I was sure of one thing.

They would come.

CHAPTER 48

"Hunters working a security detail learn early on that you keep one eye on what you're guarding and the other eye on the crowd."

-Jenna Lehane, Hunter

The eclipse began, and the attention of every guard was on the sky. As I'd feared, there were not enough eyes on the phial. It was a rookie mistake, another indication that these men had never been trained as guardians.

Hunters working a security detail learn early on that you keep one eye on what you're guarding and the other eye on the crowd. If today was any indication, you shouldn't stare directly up at an eclipse. It gave the monsters an edge, and these humans were already at a disadvantage.

I inched closer to the relic, jostling my way forward through the crowd. I came abreast with the relic as darkness fully descended and temporary night fell on the city. I drew down the night vision goggles that I'd retrofitted into my helmet, the world switching to shades of green.

"Now!" I shouted.

Darryl, Celeste, and Benjamin were posing as maintenance workers, and on my order they let loose with fire hoses, pointing them above the crowd.

They worked in two teams. It took both Celeste and Benjamin to handle the hose on the Eastern side of the square. To the West, Ash and Darryl were working together.

Ash turned the water on and helped guide Darryl's brawn, telling him where to aim the hose. If you'd told me a ghost and a blind man would make a great team, I would have laughed. Now it just made perfect sense.

I'd been surprised when Darryl asked about the other person in the archives earlier today, but when I realized he could hear Ash, albeit faintly, the revelation had given me an idea. We needed more Hunters in the field on this mission, and with Ash's help, Darryl was the strongest man we had out there.

Also, Ash's ability to manifest grew weaker the farther he moved from my position. I didn't know why, another question for later, but it meant pairing him with Darryl gave him a chance to aid in our mission, even if he wasn't directly at my side.

Of course, he could move fast if I needed him as backup. The fact that he could literally move through the crowd gave him an advantage the other Hunters didn't have. It was like having two pieces on the game board instead of one.

My team let loose with the fire hoses, aiming them high above the crowd. We didn't want to knock people over, just get them wet. The water would only be an annoyance to the gathered humans. In fact, in the darkness, they may even mistake it for a passing shower. Heck, some of them probably think this is all part of the show. But those hoses weren't spraying regular old H2O.

They were spraying holy water.

Inhuman shrieks rose up from my two o'clock and seven o'clock. The holy water helped to pick the vamps out in the crowd and, judging from their positions, they were descending on the relic in a pincer move.

I kept my sword raised, scanning the crowd for the vamps. Too late, I caught movement on the opposite side of the palanquin. In a blur of movement, a gloved hand reached out and snatched the phial from its resting place inside the larger, ornate reliquary and replaced it with a replica. It was so dark, and it happened so fast, the guards bearing the weight of the palanquin didn't even notice.

With a growl, I ducked under the palanquin and between the two guards. I nearly did a header, having to adapt to the weight of my armor, but managed to keep my feet under me as I ran.

"The wine has left the cup," I said. "I repeat, the wine has left the cup, moving east. Dubois and Martens, we're heading your way."

I felt the displacement of air, just before the claws grazed my chin. A vampire had come up from behind and was trying to tear out my throat. I'd been expecting company. I jinked left, away from the clawed hand, and spun. In one smooth movement, I severed the head from the vampire's body, turning her to dust and ash. A few people coughed, but that was it. No one noticed the vamp's second death. They were still too busy looking at the sky.

But that distraction wouldn't last. A countdown in my goggles let me know that the vampires were running out of time—and so were we.

If we didn't retrieve the Holy Blood in the next three minutes, the vampires would go to ground, and the relic would be on its way to France. I couldn't let that happen.

I heard someone cry out as they fell to the pavement and I ran. I'd lost sight of the vampire I'd been chasing, but that had to be him up ahead. My leg burned and the ache in my side sent waves of nausea to grip my stomach, but I pushed myself to run faster.

"Martens, Dubois, do you see anything?" I asked.

I had to be right on top of their position, but the witch and the doctor were nowhere in sight.

"Yes, vampire to your three o'clock," Martens shouted. "Don't let that bloodsucker get away!"

Celeste didn't check in, and I just hoped she was alright. I still wasn't sure how many vamps had entered the square, but I'd given our Hunters orders to protect the innocent bystanders. If the witch wasn't chasing down the vamp who stole the relic, then maybe she was helping to protect the humans.

"Copy that, Martens," I said. "I see him."

I caught sight of the vampire, recognizing him from his portrait. I wouldn't forget those cold eyes. It was Jacques de Chatillon. I put on a final burst of speed, following him into a narrow side street that angled away from the Burg.

"I'm heading down Hoogstraat," I whispered, aware that the vampire had supernatural hearing and was probably listening for pursuit.

"Da, copy that," Zharkov said, his voice faint over the pounding of my heart.

The vampire passed a familiar bric-a-brac shop and a hotel and turned onto Mallebergplaats. It was a short, narrow street with only a few eateries on one side and the brick sides of large hotels on the other. In the blink of an eye, he was already nearing the end of the street where it would merge with Philipstockstraat to the west, Twijnstraat to the east and Wapenmakersstraat to the north. If the vampire made it past that corner, he'd have access to the rest of the city, and I'd likely lose him in the warren of medieval streets.

I yanked the night vision goggles from my eyes and ducked.

"Zharkov, now!" I shouted.

The end of the narrow street exploded in a riot of light and color. Twirling sparklers spun above a cake of crackling fireworks. Jacques wasn't making it down that street, not unless he liked his body extra crispy.

The Russian had come through. He'd remotely detonated the fireworks, his pyrotechnic display working exactly as we'd planned. He'd had to rig every egress out of the Burg, since we had no idea which way the vamps would run, but the man had done it. I smiled. That meant Zharkov was probably one of the good guys after all.

I knew the traitor was Chad, but it was good to have that theory confirmed. But this was no time to celebrate.

The vamp spun around with a hiss. His eyes had turned to dark pits and his fangs elongated, but I didn't hesitate. I gripped my sword and charged forward, keeping my eyes low. I didn't need to get snared in his gaze, not now, not ever.

I raised my sword, but instead of taking his head I aimed for the chest. He slashed at my arms, clawed hands scrabbling for purchase, but I ignored his attempts to tear me apart and focused on driving my sword up under his rib cage and through his heart.

He stopped moving, freezing in place.

I'd filled the groove of my sword with a wood paste earlier today, but I drew a wooden stake from my belt and drove it through the vampire's heart for good measure. With a smile, I patted down the pockets of the Frenchman's stylish, for the sixteenth century, suit, but soon my lips turned downward.

"Where is it?" I demanded.

The vampire couldn't move, but I could see the laughter in his eyes. He didn't have the relic. I'd chased the wrong bloodsucker.

The Holy Blood, the Blood of Christ, the Holy Grail was gone.

Chapter 49

"There are many ways to subdue a man on the run."
-Jenna Lehane, Hunter

"Shit," I muttered.

"Can you repeat that?" Zharkov asked.

"You okay, girl?" Lambert asked.

I lifted a small, portable incendiary device Zharkov had whipped up for me and placed it against Jacques' chest. With a spark, the vamp went up in flames. It was a better death than he deserved.

Too bad killing vampires didn't solve everything. Jacques was dead, but the Holy Blood was gone.

"I'm okay, but we have a problem," I said. "Jacques didn't have the relic."

I sifted through the pile of ash with my sword, grabbing the shining fangs as I checked in with my team, and ran back down the street. It had all taken mere seconds, but my heart was pounding.

Where was the phial?

I raced back into the Burg, eyes scanning the crowd. What the hell? The vamps were all dead and the sun was coming out, so who had the phial?

I shook my head. It didn't make any sense.

That's when I saw Doc pushing through the crowd, running in the opposite direction, trying to leave the Burg.

"It's Martens," I said. "He's our traitor. Keep eyes on him, I'm going in."

I knew that he could hear every word, but we didn't have time for establishing new channel frequencies. He was the traitor. He had to have known that I would come for him, sooner or later.

As the sky brightened, the procession began to move again, and the crowd cheered them on in earnest. The darkness was chased away by the sun, but there were still monsters among us—and some of them were human.

How could Martens have sided with the vampires? By giving the Holy Blood to Philip and his men, he was selling out humankind. He was delivering a weapon into the hands of our enemies. I would not—could not—let that happen.

Breathing hard, I pushed through the surging crowd. Bodies pressed in from all sides and I used my armored elbows to full effect. I didn't enjoy injuring civilians, but a few bruises were better than the alternative.

I drew my combat knife as I closed in on Martens. There was no room to safely swing a sword and projectile weapons, were out of the question in this crowd. I was skilled with a bow, but nobody is that good of a shot. It was just too damned risky.

I clenched my jaw, wishing I could use my crossbow. Martens was nearly out of the square.

I put on a burst of speed, my heart pounding faster than my booted feet on the cobbles, and reached for Martens with my free hand. I spun him around by the collar of the municipal uniform he still wore and slammed him against the wall of the nearest building.

With a snarl, he rammed a blade into my side. He was aiming for my kidneys, but the chain armor I wore beneath the larger chest plate deflected the blade from my side. If I'd been wearing costume armor, I'd be gasping my final breaths.

Not that it didn't hurt. Martens knew of my injuries, and he'd aimed his knife at the same side that the vampires had torn open with their claws. Unfortunately, I didn't have time to register the pain.

Martens was already swinging another short blade at me. Without hesitation, I stabbed him in the gut, keeping my combat knife between us. The crowd was focused on the procession, but there was no need to be sloppy. This was something no one needed to see.

"Why?" I asked, voice raw.

There was so much in that one question. Why had he betrayed the Guild? Why run when he knew I was coming for him? Why try to stab me?

I never would have used deadly force if he hadn't pushed me to it. There are many ways to subdue a man on the run. My stomach twisted as warm liquid soaked the fingers wrapped around my blade.

"You w-w-wouldn't understand," he wheezed.

"Try me, Doc," I said. "You swore an oath, as a doctor, and as a Hunter. How could you betray the Guild?"

He sneered, spittle dripping from his lips.

"The Guild?" he asked. "What did they ever do for me? My wife gave her life for the Guild, and what is her legacy? I can barely afford my daughter's tuition, but the Guild doesn't care—all it does is take."

"So this was what, revenge?" I asked. "I'm sorry your wife died, but that's a risk every Hunter takes. It's not a reason to hand over the power to the vampires. Do you think they'd make any better masters?"

I grit my teeth. We all lose people. We all fall on hard times. It was no excuse.

"No," he said, spitting blood at our feet. "No, but at least the vampires are honest about being monsters. They threaten you to your face instead of stab you in the back."

I didn't agree with him, but Martens was swaying on his feet. I needed to keep him talking. Darryl, Ash, Celeste, and Aleksey would be on their way. In fact, Celeste should have been here by now. She'd been with Martens when the procession began.

A chill ran up my spine.

"What did they threaten you with, Doc?" I asked. "And where's Celeste?"

"Philip will come for my daughter," he said. "You must give him the phial..."

"I'll take care of it," I said.

Philip had kidnapped and killed Guy Dampierre's daughter back in the 14th century. He'd done this before. Unless someone stopped him, he'd likely do it again.

Ash and Darryl came to my side, Ash leading the way. Darryl was out of breath, but Ash just looked worried. I guess when you're a ghost, you no longer have to breathe.

"He's in bad shape, love," Ash said. "We've got to get him back to the infirmary."

I shook my head.

"There's no time, not with this crowd," I said. "Help me get him on the ground, and hand me his medical bag."

With Ash and Darryl's help, I managed to move Martens into the adjoining courtyard and onto the ground. I pulled off my tunic and wadded it around the knife protruding from his stomach. I knew I had to staunch the bleeding, but I had no idea if I should remove the blade or leave it where it was. Hopefully, Doc could give me some pointers once I got his pain under control.

"Here," Ash said, handing me Martens' medical bag.

I unzipped the bag with shaking hands. At the top of the bag was the Holy Blood, confirming once again that Martens was our traitor, not that we needed any more proof. His confession and attempts to kill me were damning enough.

I lifted out the phial, slipping it carefully into a pocket beneath my armor, and continued to dig through the bag. I tossed items onto the cobbles, fingers scouring every pocket and compartment, but there were no life saving medical supplies inside. The black leather bag was packed with a change of clothes, cash, two plane tickets, and Benjamin Martens' passport. He had planned to run, probably with his daughter, and hadn't even come to the square with the medical supplies necessary to heal any of our wounds. He never intended to help us when the vampires attacked.

Ironically, we were now lacking the tools to save his life. Poetic justice? Perhaps, but I couldn't help thinking about that little girl waiting for her dad to pick her up for the vacation he'd promised.

"Someone call Clara's boarding school," I said. "Make sure the kid is okay. When Philip doesn't receive the phial, he might make good on his threats to hurt Martens' daughter."

"I'm on it," Darryl said.

"Clara?" Martens asked. His breath rattled in his chest, and blood coated his lips.

"Don't worry, Doc," I said. "We'll keep your daughter safe."

"Promise," he rasped.

"I promise," I said.

Martens let out a sigh, and I watched the life leave his eyes. I held my breath and waited for his ghost to appear and give me hell for taking his life, for robbing his daughter of a father, but he never came. Benjamin Martens was gone.

I let out the shaky breath I'd been holding, and blinked away hot tears that blurred my vision. I couldn't wipe the tears away, since my hands and my tunic were covered in Martens' blood.

"This was not your fault, love," Ash said.

"I should have figured it out," I said. "I saw how he was living out of the Guild's hearse, and I didn't say anything. Maybe if I'd told somebody, or tried to get him some help..."

"Don't do this to yourself," he said. "He dug his own bloody grave, Jenna. He sold us out to the monsters. It's not your fault."

Then why was it so hard to breathe?

Chapter 50

"Hunters don't hide from ugly truths any more than we hide from our enemies."

-Jenna Lehane, Hunter

Zarkhov found Celeste beside a dumpster down a nearby alley. Amazingly enough she was alive.

Martens had talked Celeste into taking a few hits of Mandragora just before the eclipse began, "to calm her nerves." The witch hadn't needed much convincing. Once she was high on the drug, it also hadn't been difficult to keep her using until she passed out. Martens then dragged Celeste into an alley where she wouldn't be seen. He'd tossed her away like trash, but at least he hadn't taken her life—though some may argue that point.

Once Celeste regained consciousness, I found out that the doctor had been the one supplying her Mandragora addiction right along, using her grief and guilt over Ash's death to keep her docile and distracted. He couldn't risk Celeste using her magic to detect his role in Philip's scheme, so he skillfully eliminated the threat she posed.

Martens' hand in Celeste's addiction helped to allay some of my own guilt, but not all. I'd killed a man, a Hunter, and no matter how hard I scrubbed, I could still feel the warmth of his blood on my hands. I wanted to go hide in the shower, where I could kid myself that my tears were only drops of bath water, and then I wanted to sleep for a month.

But that wasn't an option. Hunters don't hide from ugly truths any more than we hide from our enemies. We face our problems head on, no matter the odds.

That doesn't mean it was easy.

The one thing that kept me going was the knowledge that Martens' daughter Clara was alive. Darryl, through a series of phone calls to Clara's boarding school, had ascertained that the girl was safe. Except for one pit stop to swap the real phial for the forgery before the procession reentered the basilica, I spent the rest of the day calling in favors and

breaking rules by sending every available Hunter to guard that
boarding school. I had promised to keep Martens' daughter
safe, and I never break my promises.

After a few hours of phone tag, I even managed to reach
Master Peeters, the master of the Bruges Hunters' Guild. He
wasn't happy when he learned of Martens' death or Chadwick's
temporary incapacitation, but once I explained the events of
the past week, he stopped threatening to have me stripped of
my rank.

Unfortunately, demotion wasn't the only thing Peeters
could do to make my life miserable. Now it was just a matter of
time until the Guild master's weighty boot dropped. I was
pretty sure his boot was going to land squarely in my ass.

It wouldn't be the first time I'd ended up on the
receiving end of a Guild master's punishment. Somehow that
didn't make it any easier to accept. You'd think I'd learn, but
no matter how loyal I was to the Guild, I could never stand by
and follow the rules when doing so cost the lives of innocents.

I let out a heavy sigh and wondered if this was how
Achilles felt when Paris shot that poisoned arrow into his heel.
It sucks having a weak spot.

I closed my eyes and tilted my head back against the
couch that Darryl had let me sprawl out and bleed on in the
archives. I'd have to get Darryl a thank you card. Did they
make Braille thank you cards? I'd have to find out.

My head spun and my side burned, so I remained still
except for the rise and fall of my chest. Right now, even that
hurt. Some of my stitches had opened, and I was dehydrated
from running around in fifty pounds of armor, but I hadn't let
them bring me to the infirmary. I wasn't ready to face the
doctor's empty desk chair, not yet.

Plus, if Chad woke up right now, I was likely to bash his
face in. I was tired and cranky and in no mood for insults and
lectures. Getting dressed-down by Master Peeters was bad
enough.

"You should get some sleep, love," Ash said.

The couch shifted as he sat next to me. I wasn't sure
how that worked. Sometimes Ash could float through walls,
and other times he was as solid as the books in this archive.

I'd lived with ghosts my whole life. I thought I'd known
the rules that governed them, but Ash changed all that, and
my head hurt too much to figure it out.

What I did know was that Ash hadn't left my side all day and long into the night.

"I can't," I said, forcing a grin and opening my eyes. "I have one more call to make."

"Just one?" he asked. "Somehow I doubt that, love."

I'd been making calls all day, so he had every right to be suspicious. But this time I meant it. I was nearly done for the night. Sleep was calling like a mermaid ready to pull me under the waves, and I was ready to let it.

"Just the one, I promise," I said, stifling a yawn.

Ash winked.

"I'll hold you to that," he said.

CHAPTER 51

"It's just us Hunters against the monsters, as it always has been, as it always will be."
-Niall Janus, Master Hunter

It was only one phone call, but it was over an hour before I was free to get any sleep. Master Janus was in another time zone, not that it would have mattered if he was as exhausted as I was. We had a lot to discuss, all of it important.

Master Janus was a powerful Guild master, but more importantly, I trusted him. I also respected his opinion. If he believed that my actions warranted punishment, then I would bow before Master Peeters and request an inquiry by the council of elders.

I'm sure Chadwick would love to see that. He'd probably sell tickets and save a front row seat for himself. I swallowed hard and pushed on, keeping my voice steady.

"Martens died of the wound I knowingly inflicted with my own blade," I said, finishing my report.

"And the wee bairn, Clara Martens?" he asked.

"I sent men to guard her, not that I had the authority," I said. "Master Peeters wasn't too happy about that. He's pretty angry about a lot of things I've done. But the girl is safe, for now."

"And why did you not go through the proper channels to assign guards to the girl?" he asked.

I stifled a yawn. I probably should come up with some flowery excuse, but I was too tired to make something up, and I've never been good at lying. Plus, Master Janus had a knack for seeing the truth of a thing. It was part of what made him such an effective Guild master.

"There was no time to file paperwork and wait for a hearing," I said. "I believed that the girl was in imminent danger. The Hunters I sent to guard her can confirm that a strike team of vampires bearing the mark of House Capet tried to enter the boarding school at nineteen hundred hours local time. But that doesn't excuse what I did. I broke the rules, and I did so knowingly and of my own volition."

It was true. A dozen vamps with fleur-de-lis tattoos had made their move on Clara's school just after dusk. The Hunters had staked and killed every one of Philip's vampires, preventing injury to the children and the school's staff. I didn't regret my decision to send those Hunters to Clara's boarding school, but I'd broken the rules to do so. I would live with the repercussions.

"You did a risk assessment and made a decision," he said. "In the heat of battle and with the blood of a fallen Hunter on your hands, I might add."

I stared at my free hand, wondering if I'd ever feel clean.

"Yes, his blood is on my hands," I said. "I accept whatever punishment you, Master Peeters, and the council see fit."

"Don't be daft, Lehane," he said, voice gruff.

I sat up, his voice pulling me up straight.

"Sir?" I asked.

"There will be no punishment, so stop your havering," he said, his words becoming thick with his native Scottish brogue. He was definitely annoyed with me. "You've proven yourself, lass. What you've done wasn't easy, but you never shirked your duty. You saved the life of a child you felt was in your charge, and you saved countless more by taking down Dampierre and preventing Philip from stealing a relic of great power. I'm proud of you."

Sobs burst from me with a gasping breath and big, ugly tears ran down my cheeks in waves. I'd been holding so much inside while I made phone calls and met with Darryl, Ash, and Zarkhov. I'd stayed busy issuing orders and checking status reports. But those four words from Master Janus broke through my defenses, shattering the last shreds of my control.

I'm proud of you.

I couldn't see how my mentor could possibly be proud of me, but the words held value all the same. Master Janus was a skilled Hunter and a venerable leader, but he rarely gave praise. I hoarded his words, greedily drawing them inside myself for days like today when I needed a reminder of how winning can feel like failure.

I had a nagging suspicion that this was one lesson that would bear repeating. As Jonathan used to remind me, I have an incredibly thick skull for such a tiny human.

"Thank you, sir," I said, when the sobbing subsided. I kept my voice low, not trusting that my crying jag was over.

"Don't thank me yet, lass," he said, sighing heavily. "You might wish I'd stripped you of your rank and knocked you down to novice by the time this is over."

I scraped a hand through my hair and let out a shaky breath. I didn't like the sound of that.

"What do you need me to do?" I asked.

I would do whatever Master Janus asked of me, and he knew it. For the first time, I wondered if he regretted that kind of power. It couldn't be easy, sending young Hunters to their deaths. Did he stare at his hands wondering if they would ever feel clean again? If so, we now had something in common.

"This is in confidence," he said, voice going hard. A chill ran along my spine at his tone. "There's a time and a place for bending rules, Lehane, but this isn't one of them. What I am about to tell you cannot pass the walls of the Guild."

"For Hunter ears only," I said. "Got it."

"There is a war on the horizon, lass," he said.

I swallowed hard. That wasn't exactly news to me. Some of the Hunters here in Belgium knew of the coming war, and I'd overheard Master Janus and another man saying as much before I'd left Harborsmouth. Would it count that I'd passed that information along to my friend Ivy Granger before Master Janus told me not too? I didn't think I'd be that lucky. Hopefully, Ivy was careful with what I'd shared with her.

Of course, I hadn't had much choice but tell her about the coming war. From what I'd overheard, the opening battle would likely take place in Harborsmouth. With the Guild sending me off to Europe, there was no guarantee I'd be there for the coming fight. That meant someone needed to start preparations for the war, and the psychic detective had proven herself a hero.

Ivy Granger had defended Harborsmouth against an *each uisge* invasion. She would do whatever was necessary to protect her city in the coming war. Ivy might be half-fae, but I trusted her with this implicitly. But I didn't think Master

Janus would share my opinion of the wisp princess, so I kept my transgression to myself.

"Yes, sir," I said.

"The supernaturals, the fae and the undead, are amassing their troops," he said. He paused, and I held my breath. "Military might is not the only thing to fear from the supernaturals. Their magic is also formidable, and they have found a new way to amplify that strength."

"How?" I asked.

I knew that a handful of witches would stand with the fae and the undead, but I didn't think that was what Janus was getting at.

"They are gathering objects of power," he said.

My blood ran to ice in my veins.

"Like the Holy Blood," I said.

"Aye," he said.

"How many magic items have gone missing?" I asked.

"More than a dozen, so far," he said. "Probably more that we don't know about."

"Athena save us all," I said.

"We can't leave this to the gods, lass," he said. "It's just us Hunters against the monsters, as it always has been, as it always will be."

I didn't completely agree with Janus. There have always been those, human or supernatural, who would stand with us. But I didn't correct him. Now was not the time for debate.

"What do you need me to do?" I asked.

"Assemble your team," he said. "Choose from the Hunters you've worked with in Bruges, the ones you trust."

"What about Master Peeters?" I asked. "These Hunters are under his leadership."

"Leave Peeters to me," he said. "You worry about your team, and your mission."

"And what is the mission?" I asked.

"Chase down those relics," he said. "Get them back, and keep more from going missing. We can't have those relics in the hands of the enemy. And don't forget, lass, that this is war. You're authorized to use all necessary force."

I bit my lip, considering what Master Janus proposed. The Guild was giving me a whole lot of latitude for this mission, and one hell of a lot of responsibility. I was pretty sure that I'd just received a promotion.

Janus was right, I'd rather they dish out a punishment.

"So you want me to lead a team to protect and retrieve objects of power that the rogue supes have targeted," I said.

"Aye," he said. "I'll text you a current list. So far, they are focusing their efforts on Europe, but it won't be long before we have a similar crisis over here, and in Asia, Africa, and South America."

"They're starting where there's the highest concentration of magical objects, aren't they?" I asked.

"It would appear so," he said. "Though our relations with the Asian branch of the Guild have been strained over recent decades. They may not be jumping at the chance to admit to what they'd see as a sign of weakness. They may already be missing such relics as well."

"You want me to stay in Europe, and focus on the locations on your list?" I asked.

"Aye," he said. "Asia and Africa will likely assemble their own teams. Your job is to stick to Europe, for now. Though we may see you back on American soil, before this is over."

The Hunters' Guild needed me in Europe. My lips lifted in a grin. Philip and I had unfinished business. If I could take the vampire master down while completing my mission for the Guild, I'd be one happy Hunter.

"Have any relics gone missing in or around Paris?" I asked.

I crossed my fingers and held my breath.

"Aye, as a matter of fact, one went missing from the Louvre this morning," he said. "I just got the report."

I nodded. Master Janus may not have faith in the gods, but that didn't mean they didn't award favors every once in awhile.

"Good," I said. "I'm going after Philip, the vampire master of House Capet. While I'm in Paris, I'll look into your missing relic."

"Philip is not your primary mission, Lehane, not unless he's the one behind the heist," he said. "You'd do well to remember that."

"Yes, sir," I said.

I smiled. He didn't say I couldn't go after the bloodsucking bastard, just that I had to find the missing relic. I was a Hunter, which meant that I was good at multitasking. I would take care of both.

"Have your team ready to take the bullet train from Brussels to Paris day after tomorrow," he said. "That'll give you time to make preparations and read through what intel we've assembled."

It also meant I'd be able to attend Martens' funeral. A day and a half wasn't a lot of time, but it was good enough.

"We'll be there," I said.

"Good," he said. "I'm sending Jonathan Baldwin. He'll rendezvous with you in Brussels."

"You're sending Jonathan?" I squeaked.

I hadn't expected Master Janus to send Jonathan, not that anything should surprise me at this point. I was being put in charge of a team of Hunters to protect and retrieve magic relics that had the potential to become weapons—weapons that our enemies would use against us in the coming war. But sending my werewolf roommate, the one who still had a crush on me the size of Texas, was a complication. I wasn't sure how I felt about having him at my back.

"Don't worry, lass," he said. "Jonathan's coming as a member of your team, not to usurp control. You've demonstrated an ability to lead. I have faith in you."

"Yes, sir," I said. "Thank you, sir."

"Good hunting," he said. "Good luck."

Janus ended the call, and I took a deep, steadying breath. I was going to lead a blind archivist, a forgetful, drug addicted witch, a thrill seeking, one-armed demolitions expert, a lovesick werewolf, and a flirtatious ghost into the city of an ancient vampire, a former French king, whose plot I'd thwarted.

I was going to need all the luck I could get.

CHAPTER 52

"Those who lead other Hunters must have a confidence and strength of purpose to rival their Guild brothers and sisters."

-Jenna Lehane, Hunter

I dropped my phone onto the low table beside the couch and turned to Ash who was looking at me, head tilted to the side like a cat.

"We have Master Janus' approval to go after Philip, so long as we retrieve another relic the supes have snatched from the Louvre in Paris," I said. I fidgeted, focusing on Ash's scarf. It was suddenly easier than meeting his eyes. "He's sending Jonathan. He'll meet us in Brussels."

While talking to Master Janus, I'd started to fool myself that I had what it takes to be a leader, but now that the connection to my mentor was severed, my confidence had gone to dance in the back room with the paintings of old vampires. Fatigue and insecurity came flooding in to join the darkness that killing Martens had left behind. I wanted the oblivion of sleep and yet, I feared being alone with my own thoughts and all that I had done.

Ash looked at me as if he could read my mind, and perhaps he could. As a ghost, he'd walked this city unseen for two years. He knew what it meant to be alone.

"So, this Jonathan, is he your boyfriend?" Ash asked.

For the first time since we met, Ash took off his hat and set it on the table, placing it on top of my phone. I lifted an eyebrow and shook my head.

"No," I said. "He's just a friend."

"Good," he said.

Ash leaned in close and tucked a lock of hair behind my ear. I shivered as his cool fingers traced the edge of my ear and trailed along my jaw. He lifted my chin, forcing me to meet his steady gaze.

"I'm glad," he said. The raw desire in his hungry gaze made my breath quicken. "If he was your boyfriend, I wouldn't be able to do this."

His hand moved to cup my face as he leaned in and brushed his lips across mine. Ash's touch was soft, tentative, driving me wild with his restraint. I returned his kiss, gently at first, and then with increasing urgency.

When I parted my lips, he let out a sound that was part growl and part moan that rumbled deep in his chest. He tasted of cinnamon and elderberry wine, an intoxicating mix that I could not get enough of. As our tongues met, I may have let out a small growl of my own.

His fingers trailed along my spine to move in slow circles at the small of my back. I let my hands slide from his hair, down his neck, and along his arms. I could lose myself in the way his muscles rippled and bunched as he stroked my back and drove me wild with need.

I reveled in the coolness of his touch, as his probing fingers calmed my mind and awakened my scorching skin. A small part of my brain warned that the reason his arms and chest felt so cool beneath my hands was that he was dead, but I didn't care. I didn't worry about the fact that Ash was a ghost, or that most of the time I found him more annoying than charming. For just a moment, the darkness of the past week was pushed away, and everything felt right.

I wanted to stay this way forever, but eventually Ash pulled away with a groan. I reached up to close the distance between us, but he held steady, his face mere inches from mine.

"You're really here," he said.

His eyes traced every line of my face, as if committing each detail to memory.

"Yes," I said, running my hands through his hair.

"When we met, I thought you were an angel come to take me to Heaven," he said. "I would have gladly followed you to Heaven, or to Hell."

His lips quirked and I wanted to feel them on me again, but instead I focused on his eyes. If Ash could show restraint, so could I.

"Are you disappointed, that I didn't take you to Heaven?" I asked.

"Who says you haven't?" he asked. "It doesn't get much better than this, love."

I had to disagree. I could think of something that would make this better.

"No more talking," I said.

Ash's eyelids grew heavy, and a smile tugged at his lips. With a growl that would make a werewolf proud, I dug my fingers into his hair and pulled him closer.

CHAPTER 53

"Hunters make enemies. It is the nature of our job."
-Jenna Lehane, Hunter

I awoke the next morning with my head on Ash's chest. His chest didn't rise and fall since he no longer breathed, unless it was out of habit. He also didn't sleep.

"Good morning, love," he said.

"You stayed," I said, lifting my head to search his face for clues.

I'm not sure what I'd expected, but after last night, I'd started to wonder if this was all a dream. But Ash was here, solid beneath me, more solid than any ghost should be.

"You don't have to sound so surprised," he said.

He leaned down and brushed his lips across mine in the hint of a kiss. I shivered in anticipation, but soon my teeth were chattering which made kissing difficult. I sat up, pulling the blankets over my shoulders, and rubbed my arms.

After I'd fallen asleep on the archive couch, Ash had wrapped me in three blankets, but I was still freezing.

"It's d-d-drafty in here," I said, wracked with another shiver from head to toe. "How can Darryl work down here?"

Ash curled his hands in his lap and swore. I raised an eyebrow at him, but he winced and shook his head.

"Sorry, love," he said. "I don't think the building's the problem."

"Then wha...?" I started to ask. "Oh."

Ash was a ghost. Ghosts create cold spots and icy drafts. I'd always thought it was something they did intentionally to haunt a particular person or place. Apparently, that assumption, like so many I'd made about the dead, was wrong.

I reached for Ash, but my movements were still slow from sleep, and he managed to stand and turn away.

"I'll see if I can rouse Darryl or Celeste and fetch a pot of tea," he said. "You have a busy day ahead."

I intended to go after Ash to clear the sudden awkwardness between us, but his last statement rooted me to the spot. Waking up in Ash's arms, I'd nearly forgotten what today was. The last vestiges of sleep fled my body, and I stared at my hands as my vision blurred.

Today was Martens' funeral.

We'd pulled some strings to have the ceremony so soon, but I'd worried that the Guild might ship me away to a Siberian desk job, and this was something I needed to be here for. As it was, we'd be leaving tomorrow for Paris.

Ash was right—we had a busy day ahead.

A medical examiner from the Hunters' Guild in Brussels came to assist with the hasty burial preparations. As per Guild rules, Martens was staked and decapitated—like the vampires he'd joined forces with. I left the M.E. to his job.

I spent the morning explaining our upcoming mission to my team and making preparations. We were traveling light, but Master Peeters had sent a fax giving permission for us to take what we needed from the Guild's arsenal. Zarkhov was grinning from ear to ear like a kid in a candy store, so I gave Darryl the task of keeping inventory. He'd also keep the Russian in check.

We were only crossing one border, and that was within the EU, but I still didn't want unnecessary complications. We'd travel with weapons, but we'd need to be smart about what we carried with us and how we transported it. That also applied to Celeste's magic components. Even if she didn't try to smuggle Mandragora in her luggage, which was probably too much to hope for, many of the herbs she used for casting spells were controlled substances. Packing kept me busy right up until the funeral.

*****

I stood in my newly repaired hunting gear. My skirt and bodysuit were functional, not fancy, but it was a respectable black. My gear also ensured ease of movement, and the skirt gave me a place to stash my weapons in case we had any unwanted guests.

Hunters make enemies. It is the nature of our job. But if any monsters planned on crashing this party, they'd have to go through me. So far, it was a modest crowd, and all of the guests—except for Ash—were human.

Martens' funeral was small. He had no surviving family besides his daughter. For most of Martens' life, like so many of us, the Guild had been his only family. Benjamin Martens had been part of our family, and he'd betrayed us, and then I'd killed him.

I kept to myself during the graveside ceremony, glad that Ash was keeping his distance. This was something I had to do on my own. After what seemed like days, the priest was done and mourners started to disperse.

My eyes followed Clara as the teacher who'd accompanied her from her boarding school led her toward a car that sat idling on the street nearby. A social worker—I could identify one anywhere, no matter what country we were in—waited with a pinched expression, holding the car door open and briskly waving the girl to get inside.

I moved quickly, dodging headstones as I closed the space between me and Clara. I hadn't intended on saying anything to the girl, but now that the ceremony was over there were still words that needed to be said. Apparently, I was the only one who would say them.

"Excuse me," I said, pasting a smile on my face and nodding to the social worker. "May I have a moment with Clara before she leaves? I was a friend of her father's."

The woman let out a sigh and checked her watch with an exaggerated movement of her wrist, but when I didn't disappear, she nodded.

"I suppose we can spare a moment, Miss..." she said.

"Lehane," I said. "Jenna Lehane."

I turned to Clara and took a deep breath, blinking away unshed tears. She was small and pale, her eyes red-rimmed from crying, but she lifted her chin with hands fisted at her sides. Except for the dark, unruly hair, she reminded me of myself at her age.

"D-d-daddy never mentioned a Jenna," she said.

Her lip quivered, but she didn't cry when she mentioned her dad. Clara was one tough little cookie. I smiled, this time with genuine warmth and nodded.

"We haven't worked together long, but it was long enough to know something important about your dad," I said.

The official Guild cover for Martens was that he was an EMT. His death was ruled a vehicular homicide, an accident while transporting time sensitive organs to a donor hospital. It explained the closed casket funeral, but it wasn't much of a story for a young child.

"He was a good man," I said. I reached out and placed a hand on Clara's tiny shoulder. "Your father died a hero."

I turned and walked away. I'd said what needed to be said. The car's engine faded away, followed soon after by the handful of mourners from the Guild. I wandered through the rows of graves, waiting for everyone to leave. I could catch a cab back into the city, but for now, I wanted to be alone.

I found my way back to where Martens was buried under a simple headstone in the back of the city cemetery. The Guild refused to bury him next to our loyal brothers, but I made sure his daughter would have somewhere to visit him when she was old enough.

I hoped that this place would someday give her some comfort, but I knew all too well the folly in that logic. Life wasn't that easy. Clara would face a lot of challenges in the future, more than most.

I lingered at the fresh grave, intently watching every shadow as a breeze stirred the leaves on the trees, but Martens' ghost never made contact. I squeezed my eyes shut and pinched the bridge of my nose. I don't know what I was hoping for. Martens had died at my hand. His shade probably wouldn't have been interested in forgiveness.

I let my hands fall to my side and walked away, ignoring the other ghosts who gathered here. I made my way between the moss covered headstones and elaborate tombs, the eyes of marble angels seeming to follow every step.

I turned back once and nodded, acknowledging their weighty gaze.

"If you really are watching Lord, we could use your help in this fight," I said.

My words were answered only by the squawk of birds and the buzz of insects, but I heard the message loud and clear. I may be on an honorable mission with the noble intent to stop the monsters and save the innocent, but there would be no divine help in this fight.

I was on my own.

Chapter 54

"When it comes to fighting the fae, cold iron does the trick every time."
-Jenna Lehane, Hunter

Martens' body was in the ground and my team was packed and armed for bear. That left one more loose end to tie up before catching our train tomorrow morning.

I smiled, baring my teeth as I entered the fog shrouded park. I was dressed in a school uniform, and my short, red hair was pulled into two ridiculous pig tails. Celeste had been more than happy to let me borrow the costume, probably thinking I intended a bit of naughty schoolgirl role playing with Ash.

I frowned, the memory of this morning ruining the thrill of the hunt. Ever since waking up in Ash's arms with my teeth chattering out of my skull, things had been awkward between us. I tried to explain that I didn't blame him for wracking my body with the shakes, or turning my lips blue, but it was a busy day and he'd made himself scarce.

It gave a whole new meaning to giving someone the cold shoulder.

I turned my attention to the approaching canal, pushing away thoughts of Ash. I skipped to the water's edge, nodding to the ghost boy sitting on the nearby bench.

"This is for you, kiddo," I whispered.

The ghost didn't look up, but I hadn't expected him to. Something splashed in the murky water of the canal, and I palmed my silver and iron KABAR knife. Unlike my battle skirt, the short plaid skirt I was wearing wasn't good at hiding weapons. But that was okay. I didn't need my wooden stakes tonight.

When it comes to fighting the fae, cold iron does the trick every time.

"Come, child," the grindylow crooned. "Come and play. The water is warm tonight, perfect for swimming."

I dug the fingernails of my free hand into the crusted scab on my palm, careful not to succumb to the faerie's voice.

The grindylow's voice may not be as musical as the rusalka's, but there was magic in it just the same. It wouldn't do to become ensnared by this creature's enchantment, not if I valued my internal organs.

"Ooh, I love to swim!" I squealed in my best girly voice.

"Then come closer," he said, waving a spindly arm.

His froglike head crested the water and I caught a glimpse of his needle-like teeth as he flashed a predatory grin. I stumbled to the water's edge, moving stiffly.

"Yes, I should...come closer," I said.

Faking a trance-like state was part of the job, but it was all I could do not to laugh. I'd promised the grindylow that if he touched one child while I was here in his city, I'd take him apart piece by piece. But seeing the ghost of the little boy on the bench had given me an even better idea.

"Come, youngling," he said. "Almost there..."

The grindylow lashed out, grabbing at my legs and preparing to drag me into the canal. Too bad I had other plans.

I spun, landing a kick to his throat and stifling his cries as soon as they'd begun. His hands flew to his neck, a predictable move given the circumstances. My blade was waiting, cutting his webbed hands off at the wrist. Grindylow arms are skinny, which made my job easy.

He wailed, a gurgling scream trying to push its way through his broken windpipe, and I shook my head.

"I warned you, Grindy," I said. "No eating children, not on my watch."

I grabbed him by the throat and lifted his bloated body out of the water. He tried to angle his head to chomp at me with his impressive teeth, but I'd neutralized that threat by grabbing his neck. He couldn't bite me, and his attempts to push me away with bloody stumps only made me shake him harder. Celeste was going to be pissed.

Blood stains are a bitch to get out.

"You should know by now not to judge a book by its cover," I said, gesturing at my schoolgirl costume.

With one last look at the ghost of the little boy on the bench, the one this faerie had disemboweled, I stabbed my knife into the grindylow's abdomen and dragged the blade in a long, jagged line.

The creature's bulbous eyes clouded over as bluish gray, ropey entrails fell from his abdominal cavity and onto the grassy embankment.

"It's what's on the inside that matters," I quipped.

I dropped the dead grindylow and kicked his body and his intestines into the murky waters of the canal. I rinsed off my hands and my blade, before turning back to face the park. I nodded, knowing that my job here was finally done.

"Safe travels, kiddo," I said as I made my way through the fog shrouded trees.

For the first time since arriving in Bruges, the park bench was empty.

CHAPTER 55

"Hugues repeated incessantly, 'Morte... morte... Bruges-la-Morte,' with a mechanical look, in a slack voice, trying to match 'Morte... morte... Bruges-la-Morte' to the cadence of the last bells: slow, small, exhausted old women who seemed languishingly—is it over the city, is it over a tomb?—to be shedding petals of flowers of iron!"
-Georges Rodenbach, *Bruges-la-Morte*

I'd entered the city of Bruges to the fanfare of bells, so it seemed only fitting that the bell tower chimed at my departure. But it's strange how one week can change one's perceptions. The bells that rang out over this medieval city once seemed quaint, but now they sounded ominous to my ears.

"Dead, dead, city of the dead," the city seemed to cry, the words whispering through dark alleys and along the canals. Everywhere I looked, ghosts flickered in and out of focus.

I'd helped hundreds of the restless dead find peace, but staking Guy Dampierre couldn't heal centuries of terror. The history of Bruges was so steeped in violent death it was surprising that the entire city didn't run red with blood.

The Count of Flanders was responsible for many of these deaths, but not every man and woman died by his hand, or his fangs. I shook my head, trying to dispel the image of blood running down the streets, red rivulets winding between the cobbles, into the canals, and eventually finding its way to the sea.

I thought of Benjamin "Doc" Martens. His broken body may be entombed in the city cemetery, but it was hard to imagine that his spirit could find rest. Not so long as his daughter lived.

I'd come to Bruges to protect the innocent, but I was leaving the city with one more orphan.

I swallowed hard and vowed to make sure that Clara found a good home. It would mean calling in favors, but I knew that the Guild could pull the kind of strings necessary to make that happen. That was the least I could do.

"You okay, love?" Ash asked, as if reading my thoughts.
"I'm fine," I said.

If I thought too hard about those we left behind, I'd never be able to move forward. So I ignored the heaviness of my limbs, fighting the paralysis that threatened with every weighty breath.

I kept my eyes on the street ahead, never once looking back. The bells continued to ring, matching the measured cadence of my stride as my boots hit the cobbles. Each tone of the bells zinged along my nerves and set my teeth on edge—like a mortician hammering the nails of a coffin.

Bruges had been a nightmare, but every fiber of my being knew that the horrors of the past few days were just the beginning. War was brewing. Holy relics and magical items were going missing around the globe, falling into the hands of monsters.

I was in a race against time and there was no way to know which side would win. I managed to keep one relic from the monsters, but even with the Holy Blood in our possession there was no guarantee that humans would survive this fight. There was only one thing that was certain.

I would protect the innocent, or die trying.

Did you enjoy Hunting in Bruges?

If you enjoyed this book and would like to read more from the Hunters' Guild series and the World of Ivy Granger, please write a review. Writing a review is one of the best ways that you can show your support for the book, series, and author.

Thank you.

Keep reading for a sneak peek of Burning Bright.

Burning Bright follows Ivy Granger's adventures back in Harborsmouth during the same time as Jenna Lehane's journey to Belgium in Hunting in Bruges.

Burning Bright

Ever play whack-a-mole with a jincan? No? Well, then aren't you the fortunate one. Not only do jincan look like overgrown caterpillars with pointy teeth, but they also breed like bunnies and have a knack for undermining integral weight-bearing structures, leaving piles of rubble in their wake. Oh, and they smell like rotten eggs when squished—just my luck.

I scanned the cratered parking lot and sighed. Ever since Jenna was shipped off to Europe on some top-secret Hunters' Guild mission, Harborsmouth's supernatural pest problem had grown out of control. Jenna was one of the youngest members in the Harborsmouth Guild office and, as such, was responsible for the less desirable hunting jobs—like taking care of a nest of jincan. Now that she was gone, that job fell to the private sector.

I tightened my grip on the iron hammer and scowled. With Jenna gone, and the Guild in no hurry to find a replacement, jobs had come rolling in. I guess I should have been happy for the work, but no amount of money would make this feel like a real case. These jobs were just trumped up pest control. I'd much rather be working a case that required more than whacking some creature over the head. Better yet, I wanted more time to focus on the search for my father.

I'd recently learned that I was half-fae and that my deadbeat dad was Will-o'-the-Wisp, or Willem as my human mom knew him, King of the Wisps. Most of my life I'd spent feeling abandoned by the guy, which pissed me off. My psychic abilities had labeled me as a freak and an outcast, relegating me to the sidelines where I watched other people live their safe, happy, normal lives. Even my mother and step-father had distanced themselves from their freak daughter. To say I had abandonment issues was an understatement.

Imagine my surprise when I discovered, in a search for answers about my awakening wisp abilities, that my dad had been a victim too. He'd been tricked by a demon, possibly Lucifer himself, to carry a cursed lantern that brought disasters wherever he walked the earth. In an attempt to keep me and my mom safe, Will-o'-the-Wisp had left Harborsmouth. Now I not only needed to find my father, I desperately wanted to.

But time was running out. As if my psychic gift and second sight weren't bad enough, I was growing into a whole new set of wisp abilities that I had no idea how to control. And fae who can't keep their supernatural side hidden from humans don't have a long lifespan—even for immortals. If I don't find my father soon, I'll be facing a fae firing squad. In fact, I could already feel the chill of fae assassins breathing down my neck.

Yeah, sorting out my family issues and finding a way to control my wisp powers should have been my one and only task, but information doesn't come cheap. It takes money to grease those kinds of gears, hence my jumping at the chance to fill the void that Jenna had left in her wake. Jobs like these paid in cash and favors, both of which were in short supply since beginning my search for answers.

As it was, I was accruing debt with the wrong people. Take, for example, my debt to the vampire master of Harborsmouth. I'd promised to work one case of that pompous, old dust bag's choosing. Yeah, that was bound to go well. As if that wasn't bad enough, I'd made not one, but two faerie bargains with The Green Lady. I just knew the glaistig would be calling in her favors soon. I'd caught her guards watching me more than once. I knew she was keeping tabs on her investment and that scared me worse than the threat of faerie assassins.

Unfortunately, the vamp and the glaistig weren't the only ones I'd made bargains with over the past few months. Their bargains were just the most likely to result in death or insanity. By comparison, my alliance with Sir Torn and the local cat sidhe was a walk in the park. And that was saying a whole lot about just how potentially deadly my bargains with The Green Lady and the vampire master of the city really were. Torn was a shadowy, feline, pain in my ass who obviously thought my roommate and business partner was catnip—like I didn't have enough to worry about.

One of the caterpillar creatures burst up through a pile of rubble to my left and, with a blur of writhing golden fur, ducked inside the ruins of a video store. Damn, these things were fast. I ran toward the alley at the back of the store, hoping to corner the jincan before it escaped back into the ground or into the multi-level parking garage. Chasing the jincan around in that warren of concrete and steel was something I'd like to avoid. There were fae who liked to inhabit those shadows and I'd rather not come toe to toe with any of them.

I gulped air as I came around the back of the building, scanning the area around the dumpster and metal exit door for signs of the jincan. No eight foot caterpillar here. Maybe I'd been wrong to think it would come this way. Heck, it could be tunneling through the shop floor this very moment. In fact, I could hear a rhythmic thud coming from inside. Crap, I wouldn't collect my fee if I let this critter slip away.

I spun on my heel, ready to sprint back down the alley when a furry steam-train came barreling through the cinderblock wall. The owner of the strip-mall wasn't going to be happy. There was hardly anything left of the place. Too bad I had more to worry about than pissing off my clients.

I needed to stay alive.

A chunk of concrete whizzed past my head and I ducked into a crouch. I blinked away the dust and debris that filled the air and honed in on the creature's location. There, it was halfway through the wall, its head already dipping into the parking garage.

"Oh no, you don't," I said. "Hey, Goldy, over here!"

The jincan raised its head and gnashed its large, brown teeth. Oh yeah, that's attractive. These critters could use some serious dental care.

With a bellowing cry it lunged toward me. I jinked to the right, avoiding those nasty teeth with a few feet to spare. As the creature's momentum carried it forward, I lifted the hammer, bringing it down at the base of its skull. Do caterpillars even have skulls? Whatever, the blow stopped the deafening chomp of its teeth—too bad it also squished the thing's head like a water balloon.

Smelly jincan goo hit me square in the face, on bare skin. I froze, hammer locked in unmoving gloved fingers, as a vision held me rigid in its icy grip. I tried to calm my breathing and ride it out. It wouldn't do me any good to fight it, and I needed to get this over with. If another jincan came along while I was imprisoned by the goo-induced vision, I'd be getting an up close and personal look at those rotting, pointy teeth.

I'd be caterpillar food for sure.

In fact, it looked like I'd be fed to this guy's queen if he had any say in the matter. Oh, goody.

Psychometry is a funny thing. If a strong psychic imprint is made on an object, then someone with my rare gift can read the information that's left behind. In this case, the caterpillar goo was giving me a vision whammy that made my stomach churn. This jincan had three images playing on a compulsive loop and the message of what drove the beast was clear. He wanted to kill, eat, and mate—not necessarily in that order.

And, oh boy, the gal he wanted to impress was a golden-skinned, furless grub the size of a semi truck. Protect the Queen, feed the Queen, and mate with the Queen. Oberon's eyes, I needed brain bleach.

Oh yeah, this vision was no joyride—they never were—but visions of jincan males lining up to hump their gelatinous queen? That was sure to give me nightmares. Damn that shit was nasty.

I gagged and shook off the last of the vision. Psychometry is a bitch of a psychic gift, but the thing is, sometimes it comes in handy. Now I knew how to stop these creatures from destroying another city block, even if it was out here in the suburbs. I just needed to squash their hive leader, and I knew right where to find her.

Aware of the gathering gloom, I sprinted into the parking garage. For the second time today, I wished that Jenna hadn't pissed off the Guild and got herself shipped off to Europe. This was one job where I could use some backup. The obese hive leader didn't seem like much of a threat—heck, she looked like a pulsating marshmallow—but I was pretty sure the masses of horny jincan males I'd seen in my vision weren't about to welcome me with open arms, even if they did have about twenty extra sets of the damn things.

I sighed and ducked into the parking garage as the first stars appeared in the darkening sky above the alley. It was going to be a long night.

The Ivy Granger Series

Shadow Sight

Welcome to Harborsmouth, where monsters walk the streets unseen by humans...except those with second sight, like Ivy Granger.

"I recommend this book to anyone who enjoys sarcastic wit, supernatural beings, a good mystery and one kick butt heroine."
-Paranormal Romance Guild

"Shadow Sight is well worth a 5 out of 5 rating...I enjoyed it even more than my beloved Hollows series by Kim Harrison."
-My Keeper Shelf

Blood and Mistletoe: An Ivy Granger Novella

Holidays are worse than a full moon for making people crazy. In Harborsmouth, where many of the residents are undead vampires or monstrous fae, the combination may prove deadly.

"As always Ivy was a fantastic main character who is always able to keep me chuckling and always kicking butt everywhere she goes. I love how much of a strong character she is. I also loved how creepy everything felt due to the fact that it was holiday themed...a very nice addition to the Ivy Granger series."
-Book Bite Reviews

Ghost Light

Ivy Granger, psychic detective, thought she'd seen it all...until now.

"Another brilliant installment of the Ivy Granger series."
-My Urban Fantasies

Club Nexus

A demon, an Unseelie faerie, and a vampire walk into a bar...

"I absolutely loved Club Nexus."
-Book Bite Reviews

Burning Bright

Burning down the house...

"Another amazing installment in the Ivy Granger series!"
-Twilight Sleep

Birthright

Being a faerie princess isn't all it's cracked up to be.

Winner of the BTS Red Carpet Award for Best Novel, PRG Reviewer's Choice Award finalist for Best Urban Fantasy series, and PRG Reviewer's Choice Award winner for Best Urban Fantasy Novel.

Hound's Bite

Ivy Granger thought she left the worst of Mab's creations behind when she escaped Faerie. She thought wrong.

"I devoured this novel."
-Sapphyria's Book Reviews

The Spirit Guide Series

She Smells the Dead

Yuki has a secret...she smells the dead.

"This series is like Nancy Drew meets the Winchester Brothers
from Supernatural."
-I'd So Rather Be Reading

Spirit Storm

Spirits of the Dead are coming...

"Part mystery, part adventure, part romance and all the things
a reader wants."
-Read For Your Future

Legend of Witchtrot Road

Surviving agitated ghosts, irritated witches, angry werewolves,
and the horrors of high school has never been so hard.

"I didn't think it possible to fall even more in love with this
series (and the characters, oh the amazingly swoon-worthy
male characters and the super snarky female characters), but
after having read this book, the third installment of this series,
I found that it is indeed possible."
-Avery's Book Nook

Brush with Death

Samhain was scary, but graduation is downright terrifying.

"Stevens has managed to once again create a wonderful
mystery filled with characters that are not only loveable but
completely realistic and unforgettable."
-My Guilty Obsession

The Pirate Curse

When Yuki starts smelling salt brine and seaweed, she finds her summer vacation hijacked by pirates...the DEAD kind. Will the ghost of Black Sam Bellamy, Prince of Pirates, lead Yuki and her friends to treasure or terror?

"What an excellent book! There's action, adventure, werewolves, witches and pirate ghosts."
-Eat Sleep Read

About the Author

E.J. Stevens is the bestselling, award-winning author of the IVY GRANGER, PSYCHIC DETECTIVE urban fantasy series, the SPIRIT GUIDE young adult series, the HUNTERS' GUILD urban fantasy series, and the WHITECHAPEL PARANORMAL SOCIETY Victorian Gothic horror series. She is known for filling pages with quirky characters, bloodsucking vampires, psychotic faeries, and snarky, kick-butt heroines. Her novels are available worldwide in multiple languages.

BTS Red Carpet Award winner for Best Novel, SYAE finalist for Best Paranormal Series, Best Novella, and Best Horror, winner of the PRG Reviewer's Choice Award for Best Paranormal Fantasy Novel, Best Young Adult Paranormal Series, Best Urban Fantasy Novel, and finalist for Best Young Adult Paranormal Novel and Best Urban Fantasy Series.

When E.J. isn't at her writing desk, she enjoys dancing along seaside cliffs, singing in graveyards, and sleeping in faerie circles. E.J. currently resides in a magical forest on the coast of Maine where she finds daily inspiration for her writing. Connect with E.J. on her website www.EJStevensAuthor.com.

Printed in Great Britain
by Amazon

21811151R00155